THE HAUNTING OF
THACKERY SCHOOL

SKYLAR FINN

CLASS OF '99

*T*he school grounds were pitch black. No one saw the five shadows who slipped across the green. They wore black hoodies, hoods up. The campus slumbered unaware.

On the front steps of the chapel, the tallest shadow reached into the pouch of her hoodie and produced a gleaming key. She grinned and held it aloft.

The others applauded, sardonic little golf claps. Their leader slipped the key into the lock on the front door, twisted it, and pushed open the chapel doors. She waited until the last girl had slipped past her, then closed the doors behind them with a resounding thud.

Frances was the last one in. She reached into the pouch of her hood and produced a book of matches. Her roommate, Elizabeth, reached into her backpack. She pulled out a series of five fat, round black candles from Pottery Barn. Frances lit them one after the other with her matches, and Elizabeth handed them to each girl.

Jane, the ringleader, held the candle under her chin

and grinned ghoulishly. Her mischievous face was lit from below. She had taken the key from the headmistress's office that afternoon. It was Jane's idea to sneak into the chapel. She wanted to perform the ritual at the back of the old black book they'd discovered in the library. She acted like it was a gag, but Frances knew that Jane was deadly serious about it.

Bethany's round, worried face was lit up by her candle, hovering below her chin. Bethany hated being out of bounds at school; hated the prospect of doing anything wrong and getting into trouble. She was a pleaser, one who was often conflicted between pleasing her parents and teachers and pleasing Jane. Ultimately, Jane offered more protection for her at school than any adult could. She was like the mob that way: sometimes you had to do bad things to remain in her good graces.

Haley was worried about getting into trouble for a different reason. The candle illuminated the stubborn set of her jaw but failed to give away her inner tension. Haley had an athletic scholarship and stood to lose much more than the other girls if they were caught. But there was nothing worse to Haley than losing face.

Frances knew that Elizabeth regarded the spectacle in a similar fashion to Frances. The light revealed only her bored expression, the same she always wore whether they were eating lunch (Diet Coke and celery sticks for Elizabeth) or breaking into the chapel. She was just along for the ride.

Frances pretended to be the same. For the most part, she was. But something in her thrilled at the wrongness of this and all their other miscreant activities. Part of her wanted to see what it would look like if they actually succeeded in causing something larger than themselves to happen.

Jane led the way up the center aisle between the pews. They stopped at the front of the room and lined the candles up on the floor.

"They shouldn't even have a chapel here, anyway," scoffed Jane. "Making all the Jewish and Hindu kids worship Jesus. There's a reason that public schools are secular." Jane had a way of making every wrong sound like a right. It wasn't them; it was the school.

"Maybe we shouldn't be doing this," said Bethany softly. She nervously toyed with the cross around her neck.

"We're not going to do anything bad," Haley reassured her. "Nothing's going to happen. You won't get into trouble." Frances knew she was really just reassuring herself. Haley lived in fear of getting caught doing something out of bounds and being relegated back to her New Jersey suburb to live out her glory days in public school.

"We'll see about that." Jane smirked in the candlelight. "Maybe the book is real."

"The book isn't real," said Elizabeth indifferently. "It's probably a prank left by the class before us, to see if five silly girls will think a spooky old book they found in the library actually has spells in it. They were probably just as bored as we are."

Jane ignored her. She reached into the pocket of her faded denim jacket and extracted a Xeroxed page, photocopied from the book in question. "I'm going to read the spell, and you'll all hold hands and chant," she instructed them. "You guys will repeat after me."

Elizabeth sighed and pushed up the sleeves of her hoodie. She took Frances and Haley's hands on either side of her. Haley, her teeth clenched, took Bethany's sweaty hand in her own. Jane remained outside of the circle, chanting what sounded to Frances like nonsense words, which they all obediently repeated.

Though Frances would replay the scene many times in her mind in the years to come, she was unable to say exactly what happened next. Something happened in the circle that caused Bethany to give an almighty shriek, but she never had the chance to ask her exactly what it was. The next thing she knew, the candles had fallen over. Fire raced down the center aisle of the chapel and ignited the pews on either side, as if someone had doused both them and the floors in gasoline. It seemed that Frances had barely blinked, and the entire chapel was wreathed in flames.

All of the girls were screaming now. Frances stumbled towards the side door that led out to the path that ran to the forest, Elizabeth right behind her. She glanced over her shoulder and could just make out Haley behind them in the thick plumes of smoke that filled the tiny chapel. She thought that Jane and Bethany were right behind them.

Frances threw her full weight into the door, bursting out into the cold, clean winter night air. She sprinted down the path towards the woods, their designated meeting spot in case anything went wrong.

In a clearing deep in the forest, there was a gnarled old

tree with a knothole that looked like a face. Frances stopped and leaned against it, hands on her knees. Her breath was ragged and there was a stitch in her side. Her breath billowed out into the frozen air in great white clouds. She straightened up as the sweat froze on her skin.

Elizabeth was wild-eyed, her face streaked with soot. Haley was flushed and frantic. Stray twigs had caught in their hair as they skidded to a stop beside her. Frances wondered if she looked as crazy as they did.

"Where are Jane and Bethany?" she demanded.

They looked at around in bewilderment. They looked at each other.

"I don't know," said Haley, frightened. "I thought they were right behind us."

"I could have sworn I saw them," said Elizabeth, almost to herself.

They looked above the tree line at the tower of smoke. Though they were a good bit into the woods, Frances felt sure she could hear the flames eating the building and feel the heat in the distance.

"What if they're still in the chapel?" asked Haley. Frances could hear the mounting hysteria building in her voice.

"They're not," Elizabeth said firmly. She had no idea where they were. "They probably just ran the other way."

"Yes, to the dorm," Frances quickly agreed. She was desperate to believe this. "They're probably already back in their room."

"What if they're not?" Haley stared at the smoke. In the distance, sirens approached.

"They *are*," said Elizabeth, with even more conviction. "We can't go back."

Frances imagined trying to make her way back into the burning building. Getting caught in the flames and the heat. Dying in the worst imaginable way, when they weren't even there. Were they?

"If we go back now, we'll get caught," she said.

The fear in Haley's face took on a whole other significance. "No," she said. "We can't get caught. We *cannot* get caught."

"Exactly," said Elizabeth. "You know what Jane's gonna say when we get back to the dorm." She looked at each of them in turn, staring deep into their eyes. "No matter what, we can't say anything about what happened tonight to anybody. We'll have our admissions to college revoked and we'll be kicked out of school. We'll probably get sent to juvie. Those of us under seventeen." She aimed a pointed look at Haley, who blanched. "The rest of us will get sent to a federal penitentiary for arson." Elizabeth's dad was a lawyer.

"We won't say anything," said Frances immediately. She and Elizabeth looked at Haley.

"Never," said Haley solemnly. They put their hands together in a circle, one on top of the other. Two hands were missing, but Frances tried not to think about that.

Just for now, she told herself. *Just for now.*

"Never," they all repeated, chanting in unison.

And for the next twenty years, none of them did.

2

THE SECRET LIFE OF FRANCES TELLER

*F*rances opened her mailbox. It was shaped like a rooster. The mail sat in its beak. It was filled with the usual cache of junk mail. She flipped through it absently as she made her careful way up the icy walk that led to her front door.

Technically, it wasn't her front door. It belonged to Velma, her landlady. Velma lived in the adjacent property flush with the backyard. She liked to drop in and chat. It was a small price to pay for the stately old Victorian, but Frances was already considering moving again. She'd moved frequently since finishing school, craving the feeling of starting over again and again. It was like a drug to her.

Her college friends—the few she kept in touch with—were mystified by the inclination. Why not just buy a house? Invest in property? But Frances knew they didn't get it. They had settled into their lives. They craved security and complacency; relished it, even. She liked the feeling that her life was insubstantial as smoke. At any moment, she could dissipate and simply disappear.

Frances glanced up and saw Velma hovering on the front porch near the door, clutching a casserole dish in her oven-mitted hands. Definitely time to move again. Then again, Velma knew that Frances didn't cook. She ate once a day and ordered take-out when Velma didn't show up with her home-cooked meals. It was a toss-up, Frances decided as she cautiously ascended the slick steps. Velma or take-out. Take-out or Velma.

"Tuna noodle," Velma declared as Frances reached the top step. "I know how much you like my tuna noodle casserole."

She did. It reminded her of something people ate on a Thursday night in their split-level Cape Cod growing up in the suburbs: a childhood Frances had never known, but often fantasized about.

"What's that?" Velma spied a creamy envelope in Frances's gloved hand. She noticed it before Frances did. "Is that from your gentleman caller?"

"Hm?" Frances glanced down, confused, and saw the letter. "Which one?" she added absently.

Velma laughed as if it was the best joke she heard all year. Velma thought Frances's roulette-style of dating was incredibly daring of Frances, interpreting her as "a thoroughly modern woman," as Velma put it. Whatever that meant. She supposed it was preferable to being married to the same person from nineteen to sixty-nine, as Velma had been.

She rarely entertained the notion of relationships. A relationship meant getting close to someone, sharing the past and one another's personal history. It would mean revealing the dark secret of her life that hovered menacingly in the background like a specter.

It wasn't that she thought no one could handle this particular baggage; she knew plenty of men who loved to play white knight and fantasized about rescuing a troubled woman. She couldn't stand the idea of either the judgement or pity that would accompany revealing her hidden life. How could anyone possibly understand?

All of her flings were superficial at best. They were defined by their fleeting and ephemeral nature. She had a number of excuses at hand: joining the Peace Corps, moving to Bulgaria, here on a temporary visa. She hadn't gone on any dates recently and was unsure who Velma was referring to. Probably the mailman.

"Tall, dark, and handsome?" Velma insisted. "Don't know how you could forget him."

"I don't know anyone like that," said Frances vaguely. Most people found her distant manner off-putting, but Velma didn't seem to notice.

"He seemed to know *you*," said Velma, with a chummy little wink. Velma liked to conspire with her, as if they were in cahoots. Frances tolerated this as the house was incredibly cheap for the space and it was preferable to being saddled to a mortgage.

"I see," said Frances, which was her all-purpose response when she wanted to appear like she was acknowledging the conversation while simultaneously avoiding it. "How interesting."

"He looked *very* well-kept," said Velma, which was her

way of saying "rich." "He looked like you shouldn't let him get away."

"I'll consider it." She was looking at the return address on the envelope. *Thackeray School.* A chill shot down her spine. What did they want? How had they even found her address? *The reunion.* That must be it.

"Thank you so much for the casserole," Frances said, finally looking up. "I've got to go in and draw a bath now, I'm chilled to the bone." She found bathing was an effective way of getting rid of Velma, who could hardly invite herself into the bathroom.

"Of course, of course," Velma blustered, pressing the casserole on Frances. "Come by later and warm up with a cup of tea, if you like." She beamed. Frances felt a twinge of pity. She knew Velma was lonely, in her big empty house without her lump of a husband to keep her company. (Frances had seen the pictures and she wasn't impressed.) Frances thought Velma should get a dog.

"That sounds lovely," Frances said warmly, without actually agreeing one way or the other. *Slippery as an eel,* she'd once overheard a jealous colleague describe her. Frances never attended faculty events. She always had a sick aunt or a sprained ankle. "Thank you again, Velma, really."

"Let me know what your love letter says," Velma called through the closing door. Frances smiled politely, as politely as one could as one shut the door in a persistent neighbor's face. She highly doubted it was any such thing. There was no love lost between her and Thackeray. She went over to the rolltop desk in the front hallway and used the thin blade of her silver letter opener to slit open the envelope.

DEAR MS. TELLER,

IT IS my great pleasure to inform you that a position at Thackeray has been recently vacated. It is one I think you may have considerable interest in.

We are looking for a teacher of psychology. More specifically: an introductory college preparatory course which we would have you design, based on your impeccable credentials. You would also fill the role of school guidance counselor.

You would, of course, be compensated adequately for performing dual roles, in addition to your room and board at the school. It is quite a generous package, as I'm sure you will agree.

I have fond memories of you during your time at Thackeray and would prefer to hire internally for the position. Loyalty to Thackeray is valued above all else save skill among our current faculty, and I would prefer to have a Thackeray alumna—acquainted with the virtue of discretion—among our number.

Best,
Margaret McBride

FRANCES FOLDED up the letter and placed it under a paper-weight. She was startled by the contents of the letter for several reasons, not the least of which being the revelation that Headmistress McBride was still alive. She seemed old when Frances went there, and that was twenty years ago. Maybe she was like the Queen and planned to live forever.

But return to Thackeray? The site of the private horror that hung over her life? Frances had graduated determined never to return. She planned to forget about Thackeray—and largely would have, had college not been a constant exchange of people wanting to know what pretentious private school she had attended so they could compare their own. But for the most part, since graduating and getting a job, she no longer had to answer such questions.

There was something odd about the offer. Why would the headmistress herself write directly to Frances? Surely an institution as prestigious as Thackeray had a fat file a mile thick filled with eager applicants for any potential vacancy. Why her? What was the school so interested in maintaining discretion about? The letter contained several very large blanks where information had obviously been left out, such as the reason the headmistress was so intent on finding someone who could keep quiet about whatever was happening at Thackeray.

And keeping quiet was in her nature, Frances thought grimly. She was an expert at it. It was odd, but the thought of returning to Thackeray didn't fill her with the revulsion she thought it would. She had been happy there, for the seven-and a-half semesters she attended before everything went so horribly wrong. It was really only half a term of panic attacks and night terrors, combined with a constant horror of being found out.

A relative blip in an overall happy education that had comprised much of her life there: the autumn leaves in fall, the lake in summer, the smell of chalk and disinfectant on a freshly cleaned board.

At Thackeray, they were all created equal by their uniforms and regimented schedules. She went where she was told at the regularly appointed times and had very little to think about. No one knew anything she didn't tell them. Instead of confiding the sorry state of her lack of a home life, she could pretend to be anything she wanted: a stalwart orphan, a beautiful waif being brought up by her glamorous aunt who'd retired from acting after a string of cinematic flops to a country house not so far from Thackeray.

In reality, her aunt couldn't stand the sight of her. She packed her away to various summer camps until she'd met Elizabeth at Thackeray their freshman year and spent every vacation after with her. Fresh lemonade on a wraparound porch, an endless dock out to the sparkling lake. Maybe it would be the good parts she remembered instead of the bad.

If it wasn't, she could always just move again.

FRANCES CLOSED the trunk of her sporty little roadster, locking her neat stack of suitcases inside. Her breath puffed out in icy white clouds. Velma, fortunately, was nowhere to be seen. That was the boon of making a convenient extra-early morning escape. In addition to giving a month's notice, she'd left a pleasant note inside on the table along with her key, promising to come back and visit—a promise she had no intention of honoring, but which still went far above and beyond the cry of a vacating tenant, as far as Frances was concerned.

She climbed behind the wheel of her car and drove slowly up the road towards the highway. Her car was a questionable choice for winter weather, but she discounted this for the sake of aesthetics. Whatever her inner state, from the outside she looked immaculately put together in her long, billowing coats and towering high heels. *Wear a red lip like you're wearing armor*, her austere aunt had imparted one of her few pieces of advice to Frances at the age of thirteen, and she'd taken the rarely doled out wisdom to heart.

The impulse to return to Thackeray was difficult to define, Frances mused. She guessed it was the unexpected feeling of excitement produced in her by the letter, one that mirrored her feeling at the start of every term: *Time to go back. Back to Thackeray.*

She would have thought the feeling would be one of dread, but there wasn't the slightest trace of it, which seemed odd. Shouldn't she feel anxious or guilty, or even afraid? But the fire had never once been traced back to them in the last two decades, so why would it come back to haunt them now? Even the headmistress remembered Frances's time there well, which indicated to Frances she hadn't remembered it at all.

Secretly, if Frances really admitted the truth to herself,

as devastated and guilty as she'd felt as a teenager, there had been a small unpleasant part of her that resented both Jane and Bethany for ruining Thackeray for her (mostly Jane). Why hadn't they gotten out when the others did? The door was right there. She could see clumsy Bethany becoming disoriented in the thick smoke and panicking, probably running straight into the fire, but Jane was clever and calculating. She was the last person who ever should have accidentally gotten themselves burnt to a crisp. It was her dumb idea to have the stupid séance or whatever it was in the first place. Jane who pressured them all into doing it. Bethany hadn't even wanted to be there.

Frances shook herself when she caught herself entertaining such thoughts. Who thought that way about departed friends? She was obviously a cold and remorseless person, to think such thoughts. That was what her aunt always said. *Such a cold child. Didn't even cry at her parents' funeral.*

"Different people mourn in different ways," her uncle responded, puffing on his pipe with a thoughtful little frown. "You shouldn't say such things in front of children. They're impressionable."

"You mean burdensome," her aunt would murmur passive-aggressively.

Passive aggressive. It was one of the first terms Frances learned in the many heavy leather-bound psychology tomes in her uncle's library. He was a psychologist with a thriving practice, and it was through her interest in his books that Frances had decided to pursue the same field— much to his delight. He'd paid for her education in spite of the trust her parents left her, a fact which enraged her aunt to no end.

She's just being passive aggressive, Frances would tell herself. It thrilled her to be able to define the odd habits and tendencies of the people around her, including her own.

Was there a term for wanting to return to the site of one's worst tragedy? Probably. What about a bizarre and inexplicable feeling of anticipation in association with it? That might be a new condition. Frances had considered getting a PhD but had no topic in mind for a dissertation. Maybe this experience would provide her with one.

It was also telling, she thought as she entered the small town of Westinghouse, Vermont. Telling that for all her moves, she had landed such a short distance away from the school: scarcely an hour's drive. Shouldn't she have wanted to go all the way across the country?

Then again, neither had Elizabeth or Haley. They'd gone to Bennington and the Vermont College of Fine Arts, respectively. After the fire, Haley's interest in sports had waned, and she'd taken to sculpting increasingly bizarre installations out of found materials. Frances found them distasteful, but the art world seemed to love them.

Perhaps they shared a similar state of mind. *What made you stay? What kept you tethered to this place, all these years?* Frances imagined asking them. She had no doubt she would receive only lies in response. Why not; it was the way she herself moved through the world undetected.

Frances was startled from her dark thoughts by the appearance of the wrought iron gates with two stately lions mounted on pillars at either end. She'd driven here as if on auto pilot, scarcely noticing the passing country-side around her.

The gates were open to the breaking day. On top of the steep hill, at the end of the winding drive, sat the imposing gothic stone silhouette of Thackeray. She hesi-tated a moment just outside the gates, engine idling. Then she shifted gears and made her way up the drive, unable to shake the mingling sensation of trepidation cut curi-ously with the feeling of returning home.

3

THE NEW GIRLS

*F*rances stared out of the backseat window at the imposing gates as her uncle's driver navigated the long, winding drive. The school was a gothic monstrosity, like something out of a VC Andrews book. Frances liked VC Andrews; a secret, guilty pleasure. She liked the dramatics of the put-upon, fraught orphans, relating her own life to theirs. Maybe this would be like that. She would just pretend she was in a VC Andrews novel.

She knew her aunt just wanted her out of the way: out of sight, out of mind. She'd always gotten rid of Frances at every possible opportunity—expensive and horribly boring tennis camps every summer, a myriad of activities and classes to attend on top of school during the rest of the year (ballet, painting, gymnastics). Anything not to be reminded of the sister she'd resented who had left her saddled with her only child.

Frances knew her aunt secretly wished to return to Hollywood. She never would but still harbored a fantasy she'd get a call to star in a movie, jump on a plane, and resume her previous life. Frances would be a huge obstacle, in that case. She could feel the relief radiating off her aunt in waves as her uncle's driver loaded her suitcases at the house. It was the only time she'd ever seen her happy. Frances didn't know what she'd find at Thackeray, but she hoped it would be better than life at her aunt's house. Trying to make herself invisible.

After the driver deposited her on the front steps along with her bags, Frances shouldered her backpack and carried her two suitcases up the winding staircase towards the dorm. She vaguely remembered where it was from the tour they'd gone on at the beginning of the summer. Her room was at the end of a dark and narrow hallway: the east wing. Music was already coming out the open door. Her roommate, she thought regretfully.

Frances had no siblings and had never shared a home with another child. Her aunt and uncle's house was filled with empty rooms and long, echoing corridors. She couldn't fathom being in a small space with another person. She hoped it wouldn't be terrible.

The girl lying on the narrow twin bed to the left of the window barely glanced up from her magazine when Frances entered the room, let alone took off her headphones. Her Discman sat on the bed next to her. Frances tried to make herself as unobtrusive as possible as she slid her suitcases under the bed. She'd unpack later. She didn't want to do it in front of the girl, for some reason. What was her name again? Frances glanced over at her side of the room and quickly glanced away. There was a large gold embossed cutout of an E over her bed. Elizabeth, that was it. They'd exchanged brief, cordial letters over the summer—one each—as suggested in the letter from the headmistress, neither of which revealed anything more pertinent than what sports they participated in and how much they were looking forward to school. Routine pleasantries, most of them false.

The girl—Elizabeth—got up, swinging her skinny legs to the floor. Her feet were encased in heavy Doc Martens. She threw her magazine on the bed and left the room without a word to Frances, headphones still on, Discman in hand. Would it be like this the whole year? Frances couldn't imagine having to tiptoe around a silent person who slept three feet from her.

The door opened. Elizabeth came back in just as silently as she'd left and wordlessly threw a Snickers bar on Frances's bed as she passed. Frances looked up with grateful surprise as Elizabeth sprawled across her bed again and popped the tab on her Diet Coke, eyes closed, her headphones still on.

Frances smiled. Maybe this place wouldn't be so bad, after all.

FRANCES'S first class at Thackeray was art. While this had been one of the many activities foisted upon her by her aunt, she had no particular affinity to it and had borrowed Elizabeth's Discman to keep her occupied while she used a series of q-tips to create a questionable pointillism painting of a tree near the lake.

"Oh! I'm sorry!" Frances jumped as a small plastic tray bounced off her shoulder. She glanced down to see a wide blue splotch of paint spreading across her "smock"—a men's shirt worn backwards, taken from a cardboard box in the corner. Frances looked up to see the round, worried face of a girl with shiny black hair pulled tightly back in a ponytail/headband combination. Her bright button eyes anxiously searched Frances's own. "Want me to get you some paper towels? I'm the worst, honestly."

"It's okay, it's just a smock." Frances glanced down at her shoulder and went back to her painting. When she realized the girl was still awkwardly hovering nearby, she put Elizabeth's headphones around her shoulders. "Really, it's fine."

"Well…okay then." The girl smiled tentatively. Frances had only thought she felt nervous and new in this place until she'd encountered this poor soul. She seemed so uncertain of herself. It made something in Frances want to reach out to her and reassure her.

"Do you want sit here?" She pushed out the stool next to hers with her foot.

The girl's face lit up. It was as if Frances was the first person who'd spoken to her. Maybe she was, she thought regretfully.

"Thanks. I'm Haley," the girl said. "I don't know anyone here—I mean, you might not either, but I definitely don't—and it's like they're all friends already, and it's like, how did that even happen?"

"I think they all went to Thackeray Day together." Frances turned back to her canvas and studied it disapprovingly.

"Thackeray Day?" Haley's face fell. "No wonder, then. I heard somebody mention it in the line for breakfast this morning, and it was like they were talking about the mother country. Like it was the only place to be from that mattered."

Frances shrugged. "Well, I didn't go there, and I'm doing okay."

Haley laughed. Frances offered her the headphones. "I'm Frances. Do you want to listen? They're my room-mate's, but she won't mind." She probably would mind, for all Frances knew, but what Elizabeth didn't know couldn't hurt her.

"Sure," said Haley, accepting the Discman. "Who is it?"

"PJ Harvey," said Frances. Elizabeth's tastes ran toward the angry women gamut, and Frances liked it. It was as if it touched on a previously repressed misery she'd never been able to fully articulate.

"This is good," said Haley with obvious surprise. "My parents are like, deeply religious and really touchy about what music we listen to. So I can't listen to the radio or make, like, a tape mix, you know? But I really like this."

Frances smiled at her. "Me, too."

They spent the remainder of class working on their respective projects in agreeable silence. And though they never made any formal arrangement or plan, from that day forward, it was understood by both that they were friends.

BY THE END of the week, they were all eating lunch together: Frances, Haley, and Elizabeth. They found an unobtrusive table in the corner unclaimed by any under-classman, with a full view of the rest of the dining hall/Thackeray ecosystem. Elizabeth narrated like a field guide on the Discovery Channel.

"So here's the four-one-one," said Elizabeth, cracking the tab on her Diet Coke. "Those are the field hockey girls. They're bitches, so don't bother with them."

"I'm a field hockey girl," said Haley in an injured tone. She nibbled apprehensively at her granola bar. Haley had already confided to Frances that Elizabeth made her nervous; she reminded Haley of the type of popular girl at her middle school back home who would never have given her the time of day. Frances assured her it was just a façade, that Elizabeth was actually quite warm at heart— though so far, the Snickers was her only evidence of the fact.

"Oh, sorry," said Elizabeth carelessly. "I didn't mean you." She glanced at Haley and narrowed her eyes as if re-assessing her, then apparently considered her on the side of good. "The soccer girls are even more closed-ranks and elitist, if you can imagine that," she continued. "If you're not on the team, don't even bother trying to speak to them, and if you're JV, you might as well be the varsity girls' handmaidens. That group of weirdos studying while they don't eat are the academic grinds. They don't care what you're like or how much money your family has as long as you're really, really into school. Then it's like, 'cool, join the party.' Or the study group, as it were." Her eyes landed on a table in the corner and she paused, as if puzzling something out in her mind. "I can't get a read on those two. The chubby one is like, the tall one's servant, as near as I can figure. She's always working while the tall one just looks around, hating on everybody. You can just tell she's a hater by that expression on her face while she looks at us and hates. Then occasionally she'll like, issue instructions to her little assistant and she goes and does whatever she wants her to do. Look, she's doing it right now! She's getting her food."

Frances watched as the serious, dark-haired girl scurried across the dining hall to the fruit basket near the coffee, tea, and hot chocolate station. She picked through all the apples in search of the perfect one.

"Maybe it's for herself," offered Haley. She was a champion of the underdog. Frances suspected she secretly considered herself one.

"I think that's her roommate," said Frances.

"You don't see me asking you to bring me a fruit basket, do you?" asked Elizabeth.

"Well…no," she admitted.

They watched as the girl scurried back to the table to her boss, who examined the apple imperiously before taking a bite.

"I *told* you," hissed Elizabeth. "God, that shit is so weird."

THEY GOT ready for bed in the shared bathroom of the east wing that night, then prepared to part ways with Haley at her room. "Bye, guys," she said wistfully. Haley's roommate, a Thackeray Day soccer player, barely acknowledged her existence and made her deeply anxious.

Frances and Elizabeth walked to the end of the hall to their room. As they arrived at the threshold, the door across the hall opened. The two girls Elizabeth pointed out at lunch exited their room, shower buckets filled with toiletries in hand.

They paused when they saw Elizabeth and Frances walking towards them. Elizabeth pretended not to see them, throwing open the door to their room. Frances smiled politely and a little apologetically on Elizabeth's behalf. The tall girl merely tossed her hair and strolled away, but the shorter one smiled shyly back at Frances before scuttling after her.

"That was strange," commented Frances once they were safely in their room. "Like looking into a funhouse mirror."

"Yeah, they're like our evil doppelgangers." Elizabeth threw herself onto her bed. "I can't believe we live across the hall from those weirdos."

"Maybe we'll become friends," ventured Frances.

Elizabeth snorted. "Oh, Frances," she said. "I highly doubt that."

4

THE OTHER TEACHER

*T*he school grounds were as beautiful as ever, even beneath a thick blanket of snow. The bare tree limbs of the surrounding forest at the edge of campus stretched into an empty, open sky. Frances could see the frozen lake in the distance that separated them from the boys' school. Thackeray itself towered like a looming, gothic monstrosity. The main building was a lumbering old Victorian, the dorms built in wings shooting off on either side. Frances left her car in the faculty lot in a spot marked GUEST as she had been instructed. She went up the stone steps to the imposing wooden front door, heels clicking on the cold flagstone.

The foyer was empty, and Frances climbed the steep and winding staircase to the headmistress's office, passing a line of portrait photographs of headmistresses past. All of them seemed to harbor the same severe brow, stern expression, and imposing demeanor, as if these traits had been criteria for the job.

Frances reached the top of the stairs and paused at the

end of a long hallway. At the end of it was McBride's office. Predictably, it was closed, necessitating that Frances approach the frosted glass door, knock, and wait to be admitted. Heaven forbid that Margaret McBride make anything about the process easy.

Frances slowly made her way down the hallway, expecting to be hit with a wave of memories that never came. The place felt oddly empty and devoid of any emotion. She thought this was strange. But then, she'd never spent much time in the administrative wing. For as much trouble as she and her friends had gotten into during school, they'd never actually gotten into trouble *officially*. Jane was a mastermind at getting away with things. Frances assumed this lack of a record was why the headmistress remembered her so favorably.

She knocked. Waited. Knocked again.

"Enter," the clipped, cold voice issued from behind the heavy door.

Frances cautiously pushed the door open and entered. The headmistress's office was just as she remembered it: heavy wood, brass fixtures, and a fireplace in the corner. The walls were lined with shelves and the shelves were lined with books. Margaret McBride, the headmistress herself, sat in a wide wingback leather chair behind her massive old oak desk.

"Miss Teller," she greeted her. Not exactly warmly, but with familiarity. The headmistress was not a warm individual. "Thank you so much for making the journey, and for accepting the position here."

"Thank you for the opportunity, Headmistress," said Frances politely. This she did remember. The constant ingratiating air conferred back and forth between everyone at the school at all times. At Thackeray, they were ladies first, above all else. Haley used to make fun of it, calling it a charm school, but secretly Frances loved it. It was the complete opposite of a world often callous and vulgar by comparison.

"I asked you to come on a Friday so you could take time over the weekend to get settled and become re-acquainted with the school," said McBride. "Your accommodations will be at the end of the east wing with the senior girls. The English teacher, Anna Raine, also resides there. Please feel free to tour the grounds and attend lunch and dinner. Do you have any questions for me?"

Frances's mind, as it always did when asked this, went predictably blank. "No, I don't think so," she said after a thoughtful pause. "Not at this time."

"Please feel free to address them if you do." McBride smiled thinly. "I think you will find Miss Raine a most helpful companion, as she also started recently herself." Frances could tell this was code for *so ask her if you have any questions rather than troubling me with them.*

"All right, I will. Thank you, Headmistress." Frances smiled, wanting desperately to be free of the imposing woman's presence. She'd always felt ill at ease around the headmistress. She rarely interacted with the adults in her own family, so outside figures of authority had always seemed even more daunting and unfamiliar. She never knew quite how to deal with them or how to act.

"Certainly." Just as Frances thought the headmistress was about to dismiss her, she fixed her with a beady and intense gaze. Frances immediately stood at attention. "I would suggest," McBride added delicately, "that you refrain from mentioning the tragedy that occurred during your matriculation here. It might draw a lot of unwanted questions that bring up painful memories for you, ones I assume you wish to avoid."

"Of course," said Frances, startled. "I appreciate your concern." Why would she want to talk about the fire? Jane and Bethany died. It was a dark moment not only for her, but for the entire school. Who would *want* to talk about it? Even if she hadn't been there—and no one, to the best of her knowledge, knew that she and the other girls had been at the chapel that night instead of their rooms—she would never want to bring it up again.

"There might be curiosity," McBride continued. "If anyone were to discern that you attended the school when that terrible night occurred. Let alone that you knew the girls who died."

"Why would anyone be curious about it?" Frances forgot her eagerness to flee the office, her curiosity piqued.

"You know how these things go," said McBride, as if she found it tasteless to even delve into the topic. "They become part of a certain kind of…folklore, surrounding the place. Stories get told and blown out of proportion. People become ghoulish about wanting to learn the details. It's like a…*podcast* to them." Frances could tell the word was as foreign and distasteful to her as a Big Mac or an obscenity. Something that had no place in the mouth of Margaret McBride.

"People still talk about it?" asked Frances, concerned. "Do they know who I am?"

"I doubt that," said McBride dismissively. "They talk about the fire; they barely know the names of the girls who perished that night. It's more the silly little rumors that you may wish to prepare yourself for."

"Rumors?" Frances felt a cold sweat form on the back of her neck. "What kind of rumors?"

The headmistress frowned. She seemed reluctant to even utter it. "Some of the girls like to pretend," she said slowly, "that the school is haunted."

Frances let out a short, shocked laugh. "Haunted?"

"Stories about ghosts in the corridor and the new chapel. Sounds coming from the hallways and the dorms. Things of that nature. The usual teenaged hijinks to amuse and distract themselves from their studies. It's all quite silly, of course. But I imagine in your case, it might strike a nerve."

"Yes, of course, Headmistress," Frances said, her mind racing. "I'll be mindful of that."

"We have always appreciated that you never chose to disseminate the details of that night publicly," the Head-mistress said. "I assumed you didn't care to bring it up or re-live it in any way." She was obviously referring to Haley, whose family had convinced her to mine the tragedy for all it was worth.

Frances hadn't read the book, but heard it was histri-onic and maudlin, ghost written in the imagined simplistic voice of a teenager—which wasn't the way Haley wrote at all. Haley wrote like a middle-aged man on his second divorce: cynical and wry. She'd also talked to Diane Sawyer and a couple of others in the imme-diate aftermath of the fire, the summer they'd all gone home—Barbara Walters, Oprah. Elizabeth had been livid.

"She broke our pact," she fumed over the phone to Frances, late at night as Elizabeth's parents and Frances's aunt slept in their respective homes. "She's attracting attention to us."

"Yeah, now everyone thinks we're victims of a terrible tragedy," said Frances, shrugging. She felt oddly blasé about the situation. Her uncle had prescribed her antidepressants after the fire and now she felt oddly blasé about everything. "Imagine if she'd gone on TV and said that we killed them," Frances added, almost as an afterthought.

"We didn't kill them!" Elizabeth shrieked before remembering what time it was/how late it was in addition to the secretive nature of the conversation. She lowered her voice accordingly. "We didn't *kill* anyone. It was a terrible accident. That's all."

"Then we have nothing to worry about," said Frances.

Secretly, she did worry. Not about Haley, whom she felt happy for: she no longer had to worry about money anymore. But about other things.

Haunted, the headmistress said. There was no such thing as ghosts, of course. But sometimes, Frances wasn't so sure.

THE HEADMISTRESS HAD GIVEN Frances a key. She brought her bags and suitcase to the east wing. She felt a surge of trepidation as she wheeled her suitcase down the corridor. This was where she, Elizabeth, Haley, Bethany, and Jane had lived before the fire.

Bethany and Jane seemed an unlikely combination of roommates, until you took into account how often Bethany did Jane's homework for her. Haley lived at the opposite end of the hall next to the stairs with a detestable girl named Angela Franklin. She constantly lamented this as she felt it separated her from the others: on top of the difference in their upbringing, another thing that made her insecure.

Haley and Bethany seemed to be in an unspoken contest about which of them fit into the group the least. They were always trying to make up for it. It was just one subtle underlying dynamic among many that orbited their friendships. Sometimes Frances suspected their friendships were borne more of proximity than anything else.

The old hallway looked and smelled the same. The mingling combination of perfumes dueling for dominance might have been different, but the dust and the wood and the closed doors lined up with their white markerboards affixed to them, covered in snide or coded messages, were all the same. That is, until Frances got to the end of the hallway. Then it hit her: the smell of Davidoff Cool Water.

Jane's signature scent.

Frances stopped in the middle of the hallway, swaying on the spot. Jane loved to shoplift. Every birthday and Christmas, she got all the girls perfume. The girls would fight over them whenever they got back from a weekend trip to the mall, when Jane would dole out fragrances like a drug dealer. The dorm would be doused in Bath and Body Works sprays for hours. Country Apple and Japanese Cherry Blossom. Bags of glittery lotion and hair scrunchies dumped on a bed and swapped among them. But no one was allowed to wear Jane's signature scent.

It was telling, Frances thought, which ones they picked. Frances liked Happy by Clinique, as if simply wearing the scent could imbue her with the emotion. (It didn't.) Haley avoided Vanilla Fields because it was the cheapest, even though she liked vanilla. She picked out Sunflowers because it sounded fancy and Elizabeth made fun of her because it was what her mother wore, which deflated Haley visibly. Bethany liked Tommy Girl and Candies, because Bethany was basic that way. She wanted to smell like everyone else when they went to formals at the boys' school. Elizabeth, whose walls were papered with cut-outs of Kate Moss, took both cK One and cK Be for herself. But no one touched the Davidoff. That was Jane's thing. She didn't care about smelling expensive or sweet, she just wanted to be distinctive.

Frances heard a door open at the end of the hall and shook herself from her stupor. Of course girls still wore Davidoff; it was a drug store cologne, so it was cheap and affordable. Some of them might have hefty allowances from generous families, but they were still teenagers with highly regulated disposable incomes.

It did not mean there were ghosts.

It didn't prevent her from wondering, as she opened the door, if anyone could smell it besides her.

Frances's accommodations were spartan but quaint: wood floors, a window seat overlooking the grounds, an antique wardrobe, a private bathroom with checkerboard floor and a clawfoot bathtub. The big brass bed in the corner had a thick and fluffy down mattress, white as the freshly fallen snow outside. There was a bookcase tucked into the corner, and all Frances wanted to do was curl up with a book and a cup of tea as if she'd never left. But she was curious about the rest of the school and how it would feel when she recognized no one in it. On top of that, she was getting hungry.

Frances parked her bags next to the wardrobe and her suitcase on the bed. She removed her hat, gloves, and overcoat, but kept her scarf and heavy sweater on. The dorms were often overheated and dry, but the rest of the school was cool and drafty—from the corridors and classrooms to the dining hall. She remembered there was a section towards the front of the dining hall with a full-length window that transmitted just enough weak winter sunlight to make it quite warm in the afternoon and hoped it wouldn't be dominated by the most powerful clique of girls as it was when she'd gone there (hers). Or should she eat in the faculty lounge? Did she remember where it was?

Lost in thought, Frances didn't see the other woman as she left her room and locked it until she turned and bumped right into her. "Oh!" Frances said. "I'm so sorry."

The other woman, tall and dark-haired with unusual hazel eyes and a ruler-straight nose, smiled politely. A Thackeray woman through and through.

"Not to worry," she said brightly. "The headmistress told me you were coming. Frances Teller? I'm Anna Raine, the new English teacher."

"Nice to meet you," said Frances with a cordial nod. Thackeray girls didn't shake hands.

"Would you like to walk with me to lunch?" asked

Anna. "I could fill you in on what I've learned so far."

"That would be wonderful, thank you," said Frances gratefully. "I'm famished."

"Me, too. They just got this paleo vegan gluten-free cook, so not everything is edible. But it's nice to see their tuition dollars are going towards something, I guess."

Frances laughed. "I actually went here, for high school," she admitted, then immediately thought back to the headmistress's words. I don't have to say when, she thought. "But I'm sure it's very different now."

"I doubt it," said Anna. "I mean, I went to public school down the hill myself, but this place seems pretty hung up on its rituals, if you know what I mean. Not that there's anything wrong with that," she added quickly, as if concerned about offending Frances.

"I know what you mean," said Frances with a quick smile to put the other woman at ease. She was startled her initial impression had been incorrect. She'd always thought she could spot a Thackeray girl from a mile away.

Frances marveled at how quickly Thackeray had already permeated this poor soul. *Down the hill* was how the girls referred to the town, the townies, and public school students. As in, *we're going down the hill this weekend* or *you can't take him to formal, he's from down the hill,* which were standard declarations.

Frances remembered their casually-patronizing banter as she and Anna walked down the drafty hallway and inwardly sighed. She wrapped her oversized thick wool cardigan more tightly around her body. They had nearly reached the cafeteria when an ungodly shriek erupted from just behind the doors.

5

LIGHTS OUT

*F*rances and Anna rushed over to the double doors as they burst open. Two girls tumbled out, clawing at each other and pulling one another's long hair as they screamed bloody murder.

"I'm going to kill you!" The tall, stately dark-haired girl who seemed like she was winning had a face contorted with rage. The prim set of pearls encircling her neck belied the violence of her words.

"Try it, bitch," sneered the peroxide blonde whose hem was well above the requisite length. "See what happens."

"Girls!" Anna rushed over and put herself between the two. "Stop this, immediately!"

She held them apart at arm's length. "Who started this?"

"She did," they both said sulkily at the same time.

Anna's expression was frustrated. She glanced over her shoulder back at Frances. Frances could see her inward debate: trouble the headmistress, and potentially raise questions about her own competence as a new teacher, or handle it herself?

"Frances, will you walk Rowan back to her room in the east wing while I take Brandy to her next class?" asked Anna. "That way, we can get both sides of the story."

Frances thought wistfully of the food just beyond the doors. "Of course," she said reluctantly, thinking *you are a teacher, teachers put children ahead of themselves, the student's well-being is more important than your hunger.* Anna had only been here for a few weeks and already knew the girls' schedules.

"Come on." Frances turned briskly on her heel without turning to make sure Rowan followed her. She had no intention of revealing any trace of uncertainty in front of the girl, knowing all too well how she would have viewed such a show of weakness during her time at Thackeray. She could only imagine what the girls made of Anna-from-down-the-hill. They would probably eat her alive.

She heard Rowan's little black ballet flats slapping obediently on the floor, another deviation from the dress code. Some of the girls would never sacrifice their identity and whatever small indication of individuality they could squeeze in, no matter what the repercussions. It took a certain level of skill to contrive the invisibility required to get away from it. She supposed having a screaming fight with a classmate was an effective means of distraction from her choice of footwear.

"Do you want to tell me what happened?" she asked Rowan as they walked down the hallway. Rowan was silent, and for a moment Frances thought she might not answer.

"Brandy thought she could flirt with my boyfriend and I wasn't going to find out about it," Rowan said. "She was mistaken."

"Does he go to the boys' school?" asked Frances.

"Obviously," said Rowan. "Like *I* would ever date a public-school boy."

Frances shrugged. "I would have never dated a high school boy when I was at Thackeray," she said. "I assumed he was in college."

She could feel Rowan eye her, assessing. "They don't really let us get away with stuff like that anymore," she said, feeling her out. "Maybe in your time, but it's a little stricter now. In case we decide to shoot each other, I guess."

They reached the east wing. Frances held the door open for her. "They didn't let us get away with it then, either," she said. "Maybe you're just not that motivated, nowadays." Rowan stared at her as she passed through the door. "Do you think you can manage to find your way back to your room without pulling anybody's hair?" asked Frances sweetly.

"Aren't you going to get my side of the story?" asked Rowan, her brow furrowed. "And lecture me?"

"I think you've embarrassed yourself enough for one day, don't you?" said Frances.

Frances turned and left the younger girl in the hallway, staring at her. With her back turned, she couldn't see the satisfied smile on her face. *Once an alpha, always an alpha.*

FRANCES LEARNED MORE about the argument and the

parties involved when Anna came to her door later that afternoon. She opened it to find her standing there with a pot of tea, two mugs, and a slightly abashed expression.

"I'm so sorry I had you intervene," said Anna as Frances ushered her in. Space was at a premium, so Frances pulled out the chair at her desk for Anna while Frances sat on the foot of the bed. "You've been here all of five minutes."

"Just part of the job, right?" Frances shrugged as she accepted the cup of tea Anna handed her. Secretly, she had reservations. She had once been a troublemaker at Thackeray and had never considered what it was like to be on the receiving end. She'd been there all of two hours and the girls she'd encountered so far were waking nightmares. What if they were all this way? Hadn't any of them been good, when Frances went here? Bethany was good, Frances remembered with a surge of guilt.

"Normally, it's not," Anna was saying. "It's usually just the typical problems we all have as teenagers—everything seems so important, like any problem could be the end of the world. Brandy is a tad difficult, but Rowan is a different story. Rowan is…volatile."

"In what way?" asked Frances.

"She's hot-headed and mercurial," Anna explained. "A brilliant mind, but impatient. She's the best student in my upper-school class. Her papers are easily college level, if not post-grad. So much intelligence confined by such a small place…" Anna trailed off and shook her head.

"Do you mean small spatially, or small-minded?" asked Frances.

"Both, I suppose." Anna still seemed reluctant to offend Frances's alma mater.

"I know what it's like here," said Frances. "You're not going to offend me."

"I know you know," said Anna. "I was never a fan of Thackeray growing up, and it seems hypocritical of me to work here now. But as a teacher, I love it; I really do. I just always try to check myself for those negative little references I used to be so fond of making."

"The headmistress seemed particularly on edge these days," said Frances. Maybe Anna knew why McBride was so concerned about any negative publicity regarding the school.

"It's social media," said Anna knowingly. "She knows the moment something negative happens on school grounds, there are hundreds of voices with multiple accounts who could instantly publicize it, and it chills her to the bone. 'It should be against the law,' she's always saying. Like you can put the lightning back in the bottle. If everyone were perfectly well-behaved, it wouldn't be such a problem, but the girls have become extremely unruly and difficult recently."

"Why is that?" asked Frances.

"All it takes is a ringleader," Anna explained. "As I mentioned, a girl like Rowan Makepeace has a beautiful mind, but it's like she doesn't know what to do with it yet. I believe she's bored here, and boredom breeds destruction. She has two sidekicks who are willing to do her bidding, regardless of what it is. Most of the girls in school are afraid of them, except for Brandy. I believe she tries to provoke her deliberately, just to prove how unafraid of her she is."

All of this was starting to sound familiar. "What have they been doing?" Frances asked apprehensively.

"Nothing new or novel," said Anna dismissively. "They sneak out after curfew, but no one can ever seem to catch them out of bed. Food goes missing from the kitchen, sometimes things disappear from rooms. Small items, nothing major, but often enough to garner serious complaints. Aside from breaking curfew and stealing, which are serious enough offenses to warrant expulsion or even suspension—assuming they were caught—they're not suspected of anything else but the pranks. And I think that's what bothers the headmistress the most, truth be told."

"Pranks?" asked Frances. "What kind of pranks?"

"Well, I don't know when you went here, or if you've heard about this," said Anna, lowering her voice confidentially and glancing at the door. "But twenty-one years ago, the chapel burned down. It was a horrible accident, and two of the students died."

Frances remained expressionless. "I know," she said, making an on-the-spot decision. "It happened the year after I graduated. I heard about it at college. It was terrible."

Anna nodded. "It was unspeakably tragic," she said. "Of course, it all became the stuff of legend. The girls love to scare each other with stories about the haunted chapel, or the ghosts of the east wing where the two girls lived before the fire. Children's stories, really. But some of the girls…" She paused and seemed to be contemplating how to best explain it. "Some of the girls are more…malevolent about it."

"In what way?" asked Frances, concerned. She thought again of the headmistress's words. *Silly little rumors. You might wish to prepare yourself.*

"Rowan and her group, for example," said Anna, "are particularly fond of tormenting the freshmen. Not only do they tell them there are ghosts, but they do things to make them believe it. They record their reactions and share them. Not publicly: then we could find them and punish them accordingly. But they message each other and various others, humiliating the girls in addition to frightening them. We can't even be entirely certain it's them, but they're my most likely suspects. I haven't been here long, but I have eyes. They're influential and they know it. They're bored to the point of cruelty."

Anna could have been describing Frances and her friends. She wondered briefly if this was her karma for what happened in the chapel. But she'd chosen to come here, hadn't she? Maybe she knew she deserved to be punished.

Shaking herself from these dark thoughts, she asked, "What kind of things do they do?"

Anna rolled her eyes. "It's really so pedestrian," she said. "Ridiculous. If you weren't fourteen years old and away from home for the first time, you'd never fall for it. They had to get a cage for the breaker box, because they kept switching the power off and running through the west wing, moaning like ghosts. They were back in bed by the time we turned the lights on. Or they'll hide in girls' closets, wearing sheets, and come out after they're in bed.

They don't do anything, just waltz around until the poor girls have screamed themselves half to death and woken the dead, by which point they're safely back in their rooms."

"No one has ever caught them doing any of this?" asked Frances dubiously.

"They're just too quick," said Anna, sounding a little embarrassed. "They have it coordinated somehow, probably via their phones. By the time we get to the west wing, they're back in the east wing. I reassure the girls who are frightened, while the headmistress looks for the culprit. But they're long gone by then."

"Are there no faculty members in the east wing?" asked Frances.

"There were," said Anna. "Patricia Cress, the biology teacher, who just got married and moved into town. And Jennifer James, the former guidance counselor, who quit."

"Why did she quit?" asked Frances.

Anna looked troubled. "No one knows."

THAT EVENING BEFORE BED, Frances filled the clawfoot tub with steaming hot water, lit a candle, placed it in the windowsill, and sank into the deliciously hot water. She thought this could be a pretty cushy gig, if Rowan and her little hellraisers didn't make too much trouble. The ghost stories disturbed her, but they were just stories. She expected to feel more guilt, more shame at the mere sight of these hallways. If anything, it was her lack of it that troubled her.

Why didn't Bethany weigh more heavily on her

conscience? Or Jane? She had been so young; she should have been scarred for life. She was sad when she thought about them. She often wondered if what they would be doing today, what they would be like, who they would be. But she didn't feel directly responsible the way she thought she should. At the same time, she knew that it was Jane. Jane was the reason they did anything out of bounds. If it hadn't been for Jane, they would have never so much as left their rooms at night.

But then, she wasn't unaffected. Frances slipped beneath the hot water and thought, watching the candle-light flicker on the white wall. She had carefully isolated herself ever since then, wary to let anyone else in. Because she was afraid of losing them? Like her parents, like Bethany? Or because she was afraid of letting in anyone like Jane?

She and Elizabeth had remained roommates through their freshman year at Bennington until Elizabeth had a nervous breakdown the summer before sophomore year and transferred to NYU. Frances would have assumed the memory of the fire had driven her insane, but she knew that Elizabeth had a diet pill addiction and subsisted largely off ephedrine and Diet Coke. Her body dysmor-phia and substance abuse landed her in a rehab upstate, and Elizabeth's parents thought NYU would be a "fresh start."

She could have been starving herself out of guilt, Frances supposed, but she doubted it. She'd asked Eliza-beth once if she ever thought about Bethany and Jane. Elizabeth had given her a look. They had a tacit agreement never to mention the pair. Then she went back to brushing her hair, her gaze level in the mirror.

"Better them than us," she said.

It gave Frances a chill. She knew Elizabeth didn't particularly care for Bethany, finding her social and physical clumsiness as irritating as Frances found it endearing. Elizabeth hated Jane and concealed it admirably in order to keep the peace. But Frances had never realized the extent of Elizabeth's combined irritation and loathing until that night. She'd never heard Elizabeth sound so cold. And Elizabeth was known pretty widely (and infamously) at both the girls' school and the boys' as The Ice Queen.

Frances didn't really know how to make new friends after Elizabeth left, which was why she had boyfriends instead of friends. Boys were easy; they never wanted to know anything about you or your inner life. They just wanted to talk about themselves and wanted you to either listen while they talked or pretend to. All she had to do was sit there and nod, and they were happy.

"You're so easy to deal with," they said. "So laid-back." Frances was so laid-back she was barely there. And they never even noticed.

It was depressing, really. Maybe she should have headed west to forget her past and joined some kind of commune. People did that, didn't they? She had gone to a therapist who had concluded that her grieving process for Bethany was normal—which relieved her. The therapist had no idea she'd been in the chapel that night as Frances was certain being present at the time of Bethany's death hardly constituted doctor-patient privilege.

So maybe she wasn't entirely right about grieving her correctly, which probably would have involved confessing to being there and having her life ruined. And for what? Bethany, who would never return? So her parents could have someone to hate? Jane, who had terrorized them all four years of high school?

It was Jane that concerned the therapist. Jane's power over them, the control she exerted. The therapist described her as "narcissistic, sociopathic, megalomaniacal." She said that escaping such a person could stay with someone for a long time.

"There are many different kinds of abuse," the therapist said. "It's not limited to romantic relationships or within families. Anyone in a position of authority or power is capable of abuse. Even your friends."

"But she was a kid," said Frances. "She was my age."

"That does not normalize her behavior," the therapist said.

There was a popping sound as the light above Frances's head went out. The only light that remained in the bathroom was the flickering of the candle.

Was it the weather? Or was it the girls? But Anna said they'd put a cage over the breaker box. So it must be the weather.

There was another darker, more frightening possibility that Frances refused to acknowledge, pushing it to the back of her brain. It arose, nonetheless. Maybe there was someone who agreed with Frances, that she should feel guilty. Maybe they weren't alive anymore.

But maybe they were still here.

6

THE WRITING ON THE WALL

*F*rances got out of the tub and wrapped herself in her white fluffy hotel robe. The eerie candlelight cast strange shadows on the wall. She picked up the candle and made her way to the hallway, shoving her feet into fleece-lined slippers on the way out of her room.

Anna's door opened seconds after Frances opened hers. "Is it the girls again?" Frances asked, curious to see the stories in action.

"I can only assume," said Anna grimly. "This time, I'm determined to catch them. Come on."

They hurried down the darkened hallway, stopping in front of a wire mesh cage affixed to the wall. Anna examined it in the light from Frances's candle. Her expression was puzzled. "It's still locked," she said.

"Could it be the weather?" asked Frances. "Maybe not a prank?"

"Maybe." Anna frowned, as if she doubted it. A long,

drawn-out shriek penetrated the otherwise silent halls. Anna sighed. "Maybe not."

Anna rushed around the corner to the adjoining hallway towards the sound, Frances following closely at her heels. She charged through the double doors that led to the landing of the sweeping staircase that went downstairs to the common room. A small, scared girl stood shaking on the landing. She covered her face with her hands. Anna put an arm around the girl.

"What is it, Maribel?" she asked. "What did you see?"

"I tried to use the bathroom, but I couldn't get the door open," she said in a small, shaking voice. "I thought maybe it was closed for cleaning or someone had locked it. I was going to use the one in the common room, but then I saw—" She glanced fearfully up at the wall over the landing. Frances's gaze slowly followed hers. She held her candle up higher.

Burned into the wall was the charred outline of a young woman in profile. Frances squinted. There was no way anyone could have done such a thing without waking up the entire dorm. It looked positively unnatural.

"As soon as I saw it, the lights went out," said Maribel, quaking. "I heard this long, high-pitched screech in the darkness, downstairs. I thought it was coming for me."

"You thought what was coming for you?" Frances asked.

"The ghost," said Maribel in a shivery little voice.

"That screaming wasn't you?" asked Anna.

"No, it came from downstairs," said Maribel. "I was so afraid I couldn't move or talk."

"I'll go check," said Anna decisively. "Frances, can you walk Maribel back to her room?"

Frances didn't move. She didn't look at the burn on the wall, either. "I don't think you should go downstairs alone."

Anna exhaled, thinking. "Frances, I'm sure it's just one of them. If I get down there now, I can catch them in the act. Maribel is the one who shouldn't be alone."

Frances clutched Anna's arm and leaned over, whispering in her ear. "I don't think a student did this, Anna. And if whoever did is still in this building, I don't think you should confront them."

A flicker of fear stole across Anna's expression. Frances glanced over at Maribel, staring at the wall as if entranced. "I think we should both walk Maribel back," she continued. "And if you're still feeling hellbent on catching the culprit, we'll go downstairs together." Frances was surprised to hear herself sounding so calm and reasonable, concerned for the welfare of others. Yet at the back of her mind, she couldn't help but think that if the culprit were very much not a teenaged girl and still downstairs, she would have a fifty-fifty chance of getting away if they went after Anna first.

She shook herself of this thought. Still the same Frances, she thought grimly. Anna, oblivious, responded with a reluctant "Okay." Frances could see she'd scared a little bit of sense into her. She eyed the burn on the wall as they passed. How could Anna possibly imagine that a child had done this?

Doors had started to open as they went down the hall,

revealing sleepy-faced girls rubbing their eyes. "Go back to your rooms," Anna said briskly. "Just a power outage."

"Again?" One of the girls whined as they passed her room. Frances recognized her as Brandy, the girl from the cafeteria dust-up that afternoon. "When are you going to suspend them, Miss Raine?"

"Quiet. Get back to bed." Anna marched on without answering. Maribel quivered between them. Midway down the hall, they paused. Maribel pushed the door open. She lingered at the threshold. Frances saw she was afraid to go into the dark room.

"Here." She held out her candle to the frightened girl. The flame just illuminated her scared face and the outline of her roommate, slumbering on the bed closest to the door. "I have my phone." She reached into the pocket of her robe and withdrew her phone, clicking on the flash light app.

"Thank you," said Maribel in a voice barely above a whisper. Anna shut the door behind her, then took out her own phone.

"Are you ready?" Anna turned to her as she turned on the light on her phone.

"Are you sure this is a good idea?" Frances whispered. The doors up and down the hallway were closed again, but she knew all too well how easily sound carried in these halls. "What if it's someone dangerous?"

"You don't know these girls yet, Frances." Frances could just make out the stubborn set of her jaw. "I haven't been here long, but they're capable of things you would never imagine a teenage girl could do." Frances remembered the chapel on fire all those years ago and shuddered. Maybe it *had* been one of the girls. But then she remembered the outline on the wall. There was something odd about it. Something almost…otherworldly.

"All right," Frances said reluctantly. "Let's go." She could see that if she didn't follow Anna downstairs, the other woman would simply go by herself. She followed her down the sweeping carpeted steps, their lights held aloft in front of them.

"I'll check the bathrooms and the parlor. You check the kitchen and the study room," Anna instructed Frances when they reached the bottom.

"Great idea," said Frances sarcastically. "Let's split up."

Anna gave her a look. "I'm telling you, it's them."

"I'm telling you, if you're wrong, we're dead," said Frances.

"What kind of murderer breaks into a girls' school and vandalizes it before going on a killing spree?" demanded Anna.

"A creative one?" suggested Frances.

"Check the kitchen and the study." Anna turned away, her light bobbing off into the darkness before she vanished entirely, swallowed by the shadows. Gone were any traces of the polite, deferential teacher Frances had met that afternoon. Midnight Anna was a different person altogether.

This other persona of hers was probably key to her surviving in an environment as cutthroat as Thackeray, Frances mused as she headed towards the kitchen. She couldn't see the girls pushing this controlling individual around the way they might some uncertain adult from down the hill.

The kitchen was still and silent. The room was empty. Moonlight through the window provided some extra illumination on top of the light in Frances's hand. There was nothing here. Frances moved on, walking down the hallway towards the study room. She could feel the draft as she approached. It was ice cold, as if the winter weather outside had been transferred here indoors.

She paused. Wasn't there something about ghosts and the temperature changing? She imagined what this new Anna would say if she went back and told her she hadn't checked the study room because she thought there might be ghosts. She sighed and pushed herself forward. *No such thing. No such thing. No such thing as ghosts,* she chanted to herself.

The blinds were down in the study room, rendering it pitch black until Frances aimed her light in all the corners. It looked like there was someone at the carrel in the corner. Frances bit back a scream as she looked closer and realized someone had left their hoodie draped across the back of the chair. She took a step into the room.

It was even colder in here, the temperature frigid. Frances shivered and clutched her robe more tightly around her body. Why was it so cold? She was on the verge of bolting when she saw it: on the far side of the room, opposite the one she stood on, the window had been left open. She went over and closed it, cutting off the icy draft.

Satisfied she'd solved the mystery of the cold room, she went back to the hallway and promptly ran smack into someone in the dark. Frances screamed.

Anna screamed back. "It's just me," she hissed. "What are you doing?"

"The window was open," Frances hissed back. "Still think it was one of the girls?"

"They might be outside," said Anna, whirling around in the dark. "Maybe hiding, just outside the building."

"Anna, do you hear yourself?" Frances argued. "It's twenty below outside and there's three feet of snow on the ground." Winter had come early to Thackeray; even earlier than it usually did. "They are not *outside*. Someone from the outside came in."

Anna was shaking her head. "They're so crafty, that must be how they're doing it," she said. "We'll have to check their rooms tomorrow. They must be climbing out of the window in the study and climbing back up to their rooms."

"You think they're scaling the side of the building?" asked Frances incredulously. "How? Repelling up the walls with grappling hooks?"

"You don't know them," said Anna darkly. "Rowan Makepeace is capable of anything."

Frances thought of the arrogant, beautiful girl fighting in front of the dining hall. "I don't doubt that," she said gently. "I just think it's really unlikely, Anna. I know you want to bring a solution to this to the headmistress, but it will keep till morning. We should get back to bed."

Frances could see she'd reached the root of Anna's rabid insistence on catching the culprit that night: her fear of displeasing Margaret McBride. It flickered across her face as Frances spoke, reconciling itself into a resigned expression by the time she had finished.

"Okay," Anna sighed. "Fine. We'll wait till morning."

Frances was thoroughly relieved she wouldn't be obligated to go traipsing through the snow in freezing temperatures in a bathrobe, which she would have point blank refused to do. It would have left the option of physically restraining Anna from chasing the vandal or whoever (whatever?) it was through the snow. She led the way up the stairs.

Back in her room, Frances found herself regretting her decision to give Maribel her candle. Without the light of her phone, the room was unbearably dark, save for what little moonlight shone through the window on Frances's side of the building. She'd just pulled the covers up to her chin when she looked at the foot of her bed. It was then that she saw it.

There, in the dark, was the outline of a girl. The silhouette stood stock still at the footboard. Frances couldn't see it clearly, but felt that it was staring at her. She was instantly paralyzed, unable to move. Frances opened her mouth to scream. The power came back on. She glanced up, startled, as light flooded the room.

There was nothing at the foot of the bed.

HEADMISTRESS MCBRIDE STOOD POISED at the podium, back ramrod straight. She surveyed the collected auditorium of students with a look of profound disapproval. The chattering and giggling that rippled across the auditorium in soft waves quickly fell silent.

"I am highly dismayed to report there has been another act of vandalism," said McBride with a severe expression. "I cannot begin to convey to you my disappointment, especially so soon after our last assembly regarding this unacceptable behavior. I was assured then that it would not happen again, and I see now that was a lie. I know this does not represent the student body as a whole, but the actions of a select few individuals determined to upset our otherwise peaceful ecosystem. And it must cease. I have discussed this with the headmaster, and we have determined that if this continues, we will relocate you to the boys' school temporarily while we conduct a thorough investigation."

A general outcry spread across the auditorium like wildfire, and the headmistress continued to talk over it. "It is there you will matriculate until the culprit is caught. I hope that encourages the person or persons responsible to cease these antics entirely. Failing that, I hope that someone will come forward to shed light on this nonsense."

Headmistress McBride stepped away from the podium as a wave of horrified chatter broke out over the collected students. It was as if she'd threatened to close the school. The girls' school was extremely competitive with the boys' school, and this rivalry had gone on for decades. Threatening to send them to the other side of the lake —*their* side—was on par with relegating them to the status of refugees at their own school, vulnerable to the opposition on their home turf.

The boys' school had, unsurprisingly, been established a hundred years before the girls' school was. The girls' school was in reality merely the old dorms from the Thackeray School before it became co-educational. The boys' school on the other side of the lake was the school itself, with several wings of classrooms converted to dorms.

The boys were perpetually bitter that the main house from the original Thackeray had gone to the girls, and the girls were perpetually angry at the injustice that the main facilities remained with the boys, as if their education was somehow more valid or important than theirs. They had to cross the lake in order to use the gym or the soccer field and had never in the history of co-educational Thackeray ceased to complain about it.

This rivalry had been going on long before Frances's time and would likely continue for the foreseeable future. If anything shook the mischief out of the culprit (or culprits), it would be this.

Row by row, the girls stood and filed up the aisles in orderly lines, each row waiting their turn to leave. As they exited the room, the girls whispered frantically, looking angry and unnerved.

"…isn't fair…"

"If the stupid upper-school girls would just stop…"

"…find out who it is and turn them in…"

"I wouldn't mind living on top of John Brady, would you?"

This last statement among the otherwise mutinous students was declared by Brandy-from-the-east-wing. Frances watched from the side as she strolled by amid the otherwise disgruntled remarks of the worried students. She wondered if John Brady was the boy she'd gotten into a fight with Rowan about.

One row in the auditorium seemed unruffled by the

headmistress's words. Frances watched the very back corner where Rowan Makepeace sat with her friends: her "sidekicks," Anna had called them. One was a slight, mousy girl with dark hair and thick glasses; the other a stone-cold blonde who could have given Elizabeth a run for her money. The blonde filed her nails and looked bored. The bespectacled girl was hunched over a notebook, scribbling frantically.

Rowan was watchful and silent, staring at the stage where the headmistress stood. As if aware she was being watched, she turned her head slowly to where Frances stood.

She smiled.

7

HAUNTED

*F*rances had her first class after the assembly. She pretended to organize the papers on her desk while secretly observing the girls as they filed in. She wanted to see their real resting faces and not who they pretended to be when they were aware that they were being observed.

Most of them looked sleepy and indifferent, though some were still clearly outraged from the events of that morning. They spoke in hushed tones, mindful not to let their voices carry up to Frances's desk. Rowan Makepeace was the last to enter the room, her two maids-in-waiting following closely behind her.

Frances glanced down at the seating chart. Assigned seating alphabetically by last names was still the rule of the day. In this way, she was able to discover the names of Rowan's two lackeys: the girl in the glasses was Tibbets Carlton. She huddled over her desk, her nose in a book. The icy blonde Elizabeth incarnate was Blair Vanderbilt.

Frances thought it best that the three were separated by their names, scattered across the classroom and unable to form a triumvirate against her. Though Rowan, counter to her previous encounters with her, hardly seemed combative this morning. She didn't look like the intimidating young woman Frances had encountered the day before, just an ordinary teenager: wide-eyed and inquisitive, her hair still damp from showering that morning, hastily put up in a scrunchie.

It was a kind of optical illusion, Frances thought. The way these girls could vacillate between apex predators and naïve young women on the turn of a dime.

Frances rose from her desk and walked to the front of the room. Rather than calling them to attention, she waited for them to fall silent. New teachers (outsiders) always made the mistake of trying to rein them in. The more established teachers at Thackeray merely waited for the respect they were due. She was not an established teacher, but she knew the drill. Though it was strange now to be on the other side of it.

She surveyed them austerely, as the headmistress had, and waited until they fell silent. She felt them examining her curiously and felt a brief surge of power and authority. The authority Jane had used to influence them, the feeling she had constantly abused. Frances vowed in that moment never to do the same.

"We might as well discuss what's on your minds," said Frances with no introduction. "Seeing as how it will only distract you during class, anyway. As this is a rudimentary intro to psych class, I imagine you're all under considerable psychological distress." She turned and wrote her name on the markerboard. "I'm also the new guidance counselor, by the way," she added over her shoulder.

"Miss Teller, you went here," said Rowan without raising her hand. Frances turned to survey her, expressionless. "You know how we feel. Imagine if they'd made you live at the boys' school. Do you know what they'll do? What they'll say? We'll never hear the end of it."

"It doesn't have to be that way," said Frances reasonably. "Either the person responsible might stop, or one of you might turn her—or them—in. There are a number of possible outcomes."

"Three," Rowan corrected her. "They might stop, they might get caught, or they might get turned in. But what if it's something else? What if it's someone from the boys' school, framing us to look bad?"

"Do you think it is?" asked Frances.

"None of those boys is remotely clever enough for that," scoffed Brandy at the back.

Tibbets looked up from her notebook. "What if the school really is haunted?" she said, her brown eyes intense behind her glasses. "What if it isn't any of us?"

Blair laughed. Tibbets turned on her angrily. "I'm serious," she said.

"I know," said Blair consolingly. "That's what's so sad about it."

"Do any of you believe the school might actually be haunted?" asked Frances in a neutral tone.

"Don't you?" countered Tibbets. "You were here when it happened."

Frances was startled, though she realized immediately that she shouldn't have been. She didn't use any social media except LinkedIn, but there were any number of other ways they could have found out.

"We looked you up, in the yearbooks at the library," said Rowan. "Did you know them? The girls that died?"

"We were acquainted, in passing," said Frances reluctantly. They would know if she lied and she would lose their respect on the first day of teaching. "As you are with the girls in your year with whom you're not directly friends."

"Was it horrible?" asked Tibbets in a hushed voice. "When they died?"

Blair shot her a withering glance. "Obviously it was horrible, Tibbets. Her friends got burnt to a crisp her senior year. Kind of puts a damper on spring break."

Frances winced. They didn't pull any punches. "It was a terrible tragedy," she said in a monotone voice, as if reading from a press release. "Obviously, it's troubling to find that they've been remembered in such a macabre way. I can assure you that there was no mention whatsoever of ghosts in the immediate aftermath. It's disappointing to find it's been trivialized after all these years."

Tibbets looked abashed. The other students, who had been watching her solemnly, glanced down at their desks, as if out of respect. Rowan, however, eyed her levelly.

"But what if it *is* real?" she challenged her. "What if the stories are true? You don't know what it's been like, since you left. You don't know about the things that have happened."

"She's a teacher; of course she knows," said Blair dismissively with a roll of her eyes.

"No, I don't, actually," said Frances. "What exactly is happening at the school now?""You really don't know?" asked Blair, arching an eyebrow.

"I just returned," said Frances dryly. "Humor me."

"Didn't the headmistress tell you?" asked Rowan skeptically.

"*Would* the headmistress tell me?" asked Frances. "What do you think?"

"Of course she wouldn't tell her," Tibbets said, looking down at her notebook. "She doesn't want it to get out."

Rowan considered this. "That's true," she said. "Well, we'll tell you, then. They think it's us, that we're playing these pranks or whatever just to torment the freshmen, but it's not. The school is haunted."

"It's like, a known fact," added Brandy.

"Weird sounds at night, the power going out," Tibbets said. "Whatever appeared on the wall last night. We're not *doing* it, Miss Teller. The headmistress is blaming us because she refuses to believe in ghosts."

"Which we get," said Blair. "Clearly it sounds ridiculous. But she doesn't live here. She goes back to her little manor on the hill at night and she doesn't hear or see anything. Of course she doesn't believe us."

"We live with it every night," said Rowan. "We *know*. There's something here. Something that shouldn't be. Something...angry."

Frances felt a chill at these words. "I see," she said carefully. "Listen, I'm not discounting what you're telling me.

As Shakespeare once said, there are more things on heaven and earth than were ever dreamt in your philosophy. I don't know what happens when we die, or where we go or do not go. I don't know if I believe in an immortal soul and an afterlife, after what I witnessed during my time as a student here: both those girls, their entire futures, snuffed out. But I'm willing to listen. I know what it's like to be afraid." Her eyes landed on Tibbets, who immediately looked down at her desk. "My door is always open to you. For the time being, however, let us suspend our discussion of the paranormal and turn our attention to psychology."

Frances went to each desk in the front row, distributing their texts for their term. The girls accepted them silently. Frances was relieved they didn't push the issue of the alleged haunting. She felt she had won their respect—for the time being, at least—through her honesty. She'd always resented being kept in the dark and lied to by figures of authority when she went to Thackeray. It felt easy to be sincere in defiance of that without making herself entirely vulnerable.

All the girls obediently cracked the spines of their books and inhaled the new book smell. Only Rowan Makepeace, in the middle of the center row, continued to gaze at Frances. As if she was a puzzle that Rowan intended to solve.

"How was your first class?" Frances found herself behind Anna in the lunch line. No trace of the brisk and obsessive Anna of the night before remained. She seemed just as friendly and open as she had when they'd first met. Frances wondered if she'd imagined Anna's behavior the previous evening but knew that she hadn't.

"It went well," Frances said cordially. "The girls seemed fine."

"They're always on their best behavior the first day of the term," said Anna knowingly. Frances felt a flash of irritation. What did Anna know about the first day of the term at Thackeray? Frances felt her old elitism rising and made a conscious effort to put it on the shelf. "Indeed," she said politely. "Do you eat in the dining hall, or the lounge?"

"The lounge," said Anna promptly. "I overheard one of them say on my first day that there was nothing sadder than seeing a teacher eating in the dining hall."

Frances smiled. It sounded like something Elizabeth would have said. Some of the teachers—typically the art and music teachers—preferred the well-lit dining hall to the dark cave of the lounge, but she could see where such an assessment would frighten Anna into sticking to the lounge.

She followed her down the hallway to the wooden door and was pleased to see that it had been redone. Gone was the hunting lodge-like ambiance of old wooden furniture and tufted leather, replaced by modern modular furniture and a wide array of plants.

"Apparently this was a dedicated project on the part of the faculty to modernize the old lounge," Anna explained as Frances gazed around appreciatively. They took a seat at a table near the Keurig. "The headmistress didn't even want Wi-Fi in here."

Frances stifled a laugh. McBride's loathing of technology had clearly increased exponentially in the ensuing years since technology had merely been a menacing shadow, hovering at the gates.

"Did you meet the girls?" asked Anna, busily drizzling olive oil over her pasta salad.

"The students seemed nice," said Frances absently, watching Anna prepare her alarming array of carbs. She buttered her roll—one of two—with rabid enthusiasm.

"No, I meant The Girls," explained Anna. "Capital T, capital G. Rowan and her crew."

"They didn't seem so bad," said Frances. "They seem convinced that the haunting, as they put it, is real. That there are no pranks being pulled."

"Oh, I forgot," said Anna. "You're the resident psychoanalyst. Do you think it's mass hysteria?"

"Mass hysteria?" Frances contemplated this momentarily before shaking her head. "No, I don't think it's anything like that. I think they were being sincere."

"Either that or they were covering for someone," said Anna knowingly. Frances studied her as she tore vociferously into a roll, like a lion taking down its prey. She seemed set on the idea that one of the girls was responsible.

"One suggested that maybe it was one of the boys," said Frances. "Or several."

"If it was anyone from the boys' school, it would have to be John Brady," Anna mused. "And if it's John Brady, rest assured that he's doing it at the command of his queen, Rowan Makepeace."

"Is that the boy they were fighting over yesterday?" asked Frances. "Rowan and Brandy?"

"I don't know about 'fighting over,' exactly," said Anna. "I'm sure Rowan has claimed her territory and has her hooks in deep already. Brandy probably flirted with him at a home game just to irritate her and bait her into a confrontation, which Brandy has been known to do. She knows how to get a rise out of Rowan."

"Why does she dislike her so much?" Frances asked. There was definitely something odd about the girl, odd and a little unsettling. But there was also something about her inquisitive nature, her intelligence, that Frances found relatable.

Anna shrugged. "Sport and spite," she said. "It's easy to resent a girl like Rowan, who seems to have everything on the surface: money, looks, brains. Most of them are a little afraid of her, but some of them outright loathe her. Brandy is the only one brave enough—or stupid enough— to say it to her face."

"Do you think Rowan is behind the incidents at the school?" asked Frances.

"She's the only one both intelligent and dedicated enough to do it," said Anna. "I really think she's just bored and acting out. Try to get close to her. See if you can get her to admit it. Otherwise, I'm afraid this will continue, and they'll all be uprooted and sent to the boys' side. It's the last thing they want and the last thing I want for them. You as well, I'm sure."

Frances didn't want to move to the boys' school any

more than the students did. She'd felt the same rivalry with the other side of the lake just as intensely in her time and wouldn't wish that on any of them.

"One thing is for sure," said Anna as she polished off the remains of her pasta. She eyed Frances's plate of arugula and tempeh with open disdain. "If these pranks continue and the headmistress makes good on her threat, we're going to have an out-and-out mutiny on our hands."

8

BOYS ON THE SIDE

*I*t was fall. Frances buried her mittened hands in the pockets of her peacoat. Haley had a home game against their number one rival, Hyde. She later discovered that he came to the girls' field hockey games for the exclusive purpose of picking up Thackeray girls, but at the time she just thought he was there to see his cousin play against Hyde because that's what he told her.

His name was Rutherford Hayes. He had perfect, even white teeth and perfectly windswept hair. Everything about him seemed perfect, in the way that only a young girl can idealize others. He wore a peacoat as well. His was black, hers was navy. He had a long crimson scarf—"Cashmere," he later told her when he looped it around her neck as the temperature dropped and a strong gusty breeze blew the colorful autumn leaves across the lake.

Frances had noticed him out of the corner of her eye when she'd first arrived at the field, but she quickly looked away. Something about the Thackeray boys bothered her, the way the Thackeray Day girls frightened Haley. She wasn't frightened, just…annoyed. They were all confident to the point of arrogance, brimming with stories about their vacations at their parents' compound in the Bahamas, how their brother was a Harvard man and they would be, too. France found them insufferable. If any of them had ever known hardship a day in their lives, they didn't show it.

Not that she thought suffering made you a better person, she thought, watching as Haley drove—dribbled? sticked? —the ball upfield for a clean shot past the goalie into Hyde's net. A round of groans went up from the visitors; a round of cheers on Thackeray's side.

"Hot chocolate?" Rutherford appeared at her side, clutching a Styrofoam cup. Frances was startled.

"What?" she said, and immediately cursed herself for her lack of cool.

"I'm not going to drink it," he said. "Too sweet." Frances thought later that he must have gotten it before he left the boys' side, then decided who he would give it to at the game. It was his opening. Girls liked chocolate.

"Thank you." Frances took it, more for something to warm her hands than anything else.

"You don't play field hockey?" he asked her. She shrugged.

"I'm not really a sports person," she said. She sighed. She couldn't seem to stop saying the wrong thing. Everybody at Thackeray was a jock on both sides of the lake, except for the hardcore academic grinds. And even they were still required to take a sport in the fall and spring.

Admitting her indifference to sports at Thackeray probably made her sound lazy and indifferent.

"Neither am I," he said confidentially. "I mean, I'm playing lacrosse and also baseball because it's basically like, required in my family. But I don't actually *like* either of them. You know?"

"Then why do it?" Frances asked. Her aunt and uncle's parenting style was so hands-off she barely saw them. Sometimes Frances wandered the empty rooms of their oversized house, pretending to be a ghost.

"Are you kidding me?" He snorted. "And let down Cliff Rutherford, who once said that sports were a sign of character? Not an option."

"Is that your dad?" she asked, for lack of anything better to say.

"Yes, but I refer to him as Cliff so I can pretend that he's more like a neighbor," he explained. "An annoying neighbor I have to put up with until I can move across the country and never see him again."

Frances wasn't yet used to the dark ways the other students casually referred to their parents. She wondered if she would have this same offhand bitterness to her own, had they lived. In her memory, they would always be perfect. They would always be missed.

"What's your favorite class so far?" he asked. She wasn't used to anyone being so interested in her and her life; what she did, what she thought about it. She searched her mind for something sufficiently charming and witty to say. She came up short.

"English," she said. "I like Dickens."

"Dickens?" He feigned an elaborate double take.

"Nobody *likes* Dickens. You know he got paid by the word?"

"No wonder he's so verbose," she said, pretending to fix her attention on the game.

He chuckled. Maybe that had been the witty remark she was going for. Either that or he was just pretending to find her witty so she'd let her guard down.

"I'm Rutherford," he said, sticking out a gloved hand. "What's your name?"

"Frances," she said, taking it. It seemed to her that he held her hand just a second longer than he needed to, releasing it only after he gave it a firm squeeze.

"Frances," he repeated. "Frances, Frances," he chanted. She looked at him strangely.

"I'm just committing it to memory," he said, smiling.

"Why?" She wanted to play it cool, but her curiosity got the better of her.

"I feel like we're going to be seeing a lot of each other," he said with a little wink.

ELIZABETH DIDN'T LIKE RUTHERFORD. It annoyed Frances. She felt like Elizabeth didn't like anyone—anyone besides her and Haley.

"I just heard that he has a terrible reputation," she said while they got ready for class one morning. "That's why he goes after freshmen, because we don't know about him yet."

"Where did you hear this from?" Frances pulled on her navy tights, carefully masking the annoyance she felt from her voice. She was long practiced at this from life with her aunt. She didn't want Elizabeth to know she was perturbed. She got along with her better than anyone in her life, and she couldn't stand the idea of something coming between them, or even arguing with her.

"Everyone. Upper school, sophomores—a lot of people have crushes on him, so they talk about him from that perspective; he's one of those old-money families where like every single male has gone to Harvard. But then some of the other girls—like in the bathroom or whatever—just talk about how he plays people, how he uses them and then moves onto the next."

It was too late for Frances. Her mind was already clouded by pheromones and Polo Sport. All she heard was *a lot of people have crushes on him.* But he liked her. Frances. Not them. He chose her.

"I'll keep that in mind." She slid her feet into her regulation Oxfords and went for the door. "You coming?"

Elizabeth glanced at her. She could tell that Frances was unhappy but chose not to push the issue.

"Yeah, just let me grab my bag," she said.

On their way out, they ran into the girls across the hall again. As before, they stared at each other before briskly—and awkwardly—walking down the hall together, but not together, to the dining hall for breakfast.

FRANCES OFFICIALLY MET Jane in the bathroom in the science wing, smoking a cigarette and blowing the smoke out of the window. Bethany, her roommate/servant, was nowhere to be seen. Frances exited the stall and glanced at her briefly as she went to the sink.

"Going to narc on me?" Jane had said conversationally.

Frances said nothing. She went over to Jane, took the cigarette from her, and took a drag. She exhaled straight into the bathroom, then gave it back and walked out. Jane smiled.

The next day, Jane sat next to her at assembly and spent the entire time writing crude but pithy observations of McBride on the back of Frances's notebook, making her laugh. Elizabeth always skipped assembly because they didn't take attendance and Haley got out of it for morning practice, so Frances was alone. She found that she kind of liked Jane. It was like with Rutherford: Elizabeth just liked to hate on everyone.

Truthfully, she found her a little cliched: like a caricature of a bad girl from some high school indie coming-of-age drama. Who actually sat on the windowsill of the girls' room and smoked cigarettes? Her performance—from the cigarette to the leather jacket to the windowsill—seemed heavily cribbed from Angelina Jolie in *Foxfire*. But didn't they all imitate other girls in places far away from here, trying to pretend they had identities when they didn't? They were all poured into the same mold: a plaid kilted doll with a bright future and no life.

That morning might have been the end of Frances and Jane, but Jane had a way of insinuating herself into a person's life. When Frances partnered with Haley for gym, Jane joined their group once it was established they had an uneven number in class. She was exceptionally gifted at sports, almost as much as Haley, and Frances could see that this impressed her. Frances couldn't keep up with them and eventually gave up, flopping down onto the grass to lie on her back and gaze at the sky, until Ms. Haven yelled at her. But it was a point over which the other two bonded, that much Frances knew. (They later became co-captains of the freshman field hockey team.)

When Elizabeth entered the dining hall after that particular gym class and saw Jane sitting at their table with Frances and Haley, she stopped and stared. Bethany had come in at roughly the same time and almost ran into her. She looked worriedly around for Jane, absent from their usual spot, and when she spied her sitting with Frances and Haley, she immediately darted over. No questions asked.

Elizabeth issued a deep sigh that Frances could see all the way across the cafeteria. She got a Diet Coke and a piece of fruit before she headed over to their table. She didn't say anything negative. Then again, she didn't say much of anything. Jane spent all of lunch regaling them with tales about spending the summer shoplifting and getting high with her brother on the roof of her house.

Elizabeth plainly didn't like her. That much was clear. She bit her tongue, for Frances's and Haley's sake, but whenever Frances and Elizabeth were apart from the rest of the group, she never mentioned her by name. It was as if she didn't exist.

But Elizabeth didn't like anyone. If Frances went along with everything Elizabeth thought and felt, disliked the same people she did and isolated herself accordingly, she'd never make new friends. She wouldn't have a boyfriend. Was Rutherford her boyfriend? She was supposed to sneak out after curfew and meet him at the boathouse on the boys' side of the lake, so she guessed that made him her boyfriend. Didn't it?

She debated whether or not to tell Elizabeth. She didn't want to keep anything from her, but she didn't want the judgement, either. She would tell her. Eventually. Maybe just not that night.

Elizabeth was a sound sleeper. Every night before bed, she took one of the pills her mother had given her to fall asleep and was dead to the world until dawn. Frances got up as quietly as possible and put on her coat, hat, and gloves without turning on the light. She had her hand on the door and was halfway out of it when Elizabeth's sleepy voice issued from the darkness.

"Be careful," was all she said.

FRANCES TRIED NOT to be afraid when she cut through the woods to get to the boathouse. Rutherford had slipped her a flashlight at the last field hockey game for this very purpose. The beam bobbed ahead in the dark.

Through the trees, she saw an identical beam and froze. Someone else was here. Someone knew she had snuck out, and she was about to be caught. What if it was the groundskeeper? Or the headmistress? She'd be kicked out of school. Her aunt would be livid. She'd never see her new friends—or Rutherford—ever again. No Thackeray student would want to hang out with a loser who got expelled the first term of freshman year.

"Frances." She heard his whisper in the dark before she saw him. "It's me."

It was only Rutherford. She breathed a sigh of relief.

She wasn't caught; she wouldn't be expelled. She shined her light in his direction, and the two beams of light bobbed towards each other in the dark to meet.

So Frances was the one who found the clearing. Or accidentally discovered it, on her way to meet Rutherford. She never told the others how they found it, but when Jane was looking for a place to smoke during free period where they wouldn't get caught, Frances mentioned it to her and after that, it was like it became theirs.

Oddly enough, it was the only thing that brought Elizabeth and Jane together. The two had brokered an uneasy peace over the fact they both smoked. They would sometimes stand silently in the clearing, passing a cigarette back and forth while the others shivered and waited for them to be done. Jock Haley thought that cigarettes were the devil. Bethany, who had an uncle with lung cancer, was terrified of them. Frances just didn't feel like smoking. Other times she did. She could go either way.

"I swear, Frances," Jane complained one day as she clutched the butt in her fingerless gloves. "It's like you don't have a personality. You don't care about anything."

It was an exceptionally cruel thing to say to a young girl still forming her identity, but Elizabeth swiftly corrected Jane before the sting could set in. "Frances has ten times the personality you do, Wilcox," she snapped. They were in the habit of referring to each other by their last names, like rival greasers at a fifties high school. "And she cares. She just keeps it on the inside. Unlike you."

"Yeah, yeah. Whatever." Jane rolled her eyes but didn't

comment any further. Frances shot Elizabeth a smile. Elizabeth smiled, but her eyes were fierce as she regarded Jane.

"Just remember," she told Frances later on in their room. "No matter what happens, you have my back, and I have yours. I know you like her, Frances, but Jane? She doesn't have anybody's back but her own."

9

THE BOOK OF LOST SOULS

*F*rances couldn't get the image of the shadow standing at the foot of her bed out of her head. The sight combined with the utter seriousness with which the girls had declared they truly believed the school was haunted was giving Frances serious pause about what might really be happening at Thackeray. Both the head-mistress and Anna were certain it was the girls. Frances wasn't so sure.

It wasn't the first time she'd seen something, only to turn on the light and see that there was nothing there. When she was young, shortly after the plane crash, she'd awakened in the middle of the night in the unfamiliar bed at her aunt's house. She woke up suddenly, for no apparent reason, to see the shadowy outline of two people in the bedroom doorway, watching her.

Frances lay perfectly still and unmoving. She didn't feel afraid, exactly. She felt sure it was her parents. She couldn't tell if she was dreaming, or if her life the last month had been a nightmare and she'd just woken up to find that they were here to pick her up from her aunt's after their trip. She hovered in this state, not wanting to move and disrupt the possibility that this might have all been a terrible dream and her parents were here after all. Then the second-floor landing light clicked on in the hallway and her aunt's footsteps ascended the stairs. Frances saw then that there was no one in the doorway.

As an adult, Frances didn't like to go into dark rooms alone at night. She felt certain that the darkness concealed things normally invisible in the light of day. It wasn't her parents she feared; the idea they might be watching over her from some other place was one that reassured her. It was more the idea that if her parents could come back, maybe anyone could. And maybe the others weren't good.

What if Bethany and Jane *were* haunting the school? She couldn't imagine Bethany wanting to do anything more than sneak into the kitchen and steal food from the dessert tray. But Jane, as a ghost? With the ability to pass through walls, to appear and dissipate at will? The thought of this chilled Frances to the bone. She had no doubt in her mind that Jane would use it for evil. Like burning sinister silhouettes into the walls, for example.

Frances had an idea. After she finished lunch with Anna, she decided to go to the library. There was one particular book she wanted to look for, and she was curious to know if it was still there.

THEY FOUND the book in the library senior year. Unlabeled and handbound, it clearly didn't belong with the other books, as if it had been shoved hastily on the end of a shelf in the very back. The girls were looking for an obscure reference book for their World Cultures group project, one that Ms. Harkins insisted was in the library, in spite of the librarian's insistence that it wasn't.

Jane was now their unofficial ringleader; the one who orchestrated their every scheme. They agreed, by unspoken consent, to follow everything Jane did without question. They had nothing and no one else to follow. They didn't trust the adults in their lives—either their parents or teachers—and Jane always seemed so certain of everything. She was persuasive and it was hard—impossible—to tell her no.

To deny Jane would be to fall from her good graces, and only regain their place at her side through constant groveling. Which only worked some of the time. Just ask Liddy Cook, who still ate alone in the cafeteria. No one was sure exactly what had transpired between her and Jane, but whatever it was had made her untouchable.

Frances wasn't the type to grovel. She went along with Jane's plans in a bored and careless sort of way, like a cat flicking its tail. As if it made no difference to her one way or the other. But she knew better than to contest Jane's iron rule over their clique and the rest of the school. It was social suicide to contradict Jane Wilcox. So she acted like she didn't care. Anything was better than Bethany's tireless, fearful sucking up. She followed Jane around like a dog waiting to be kicked. She even carried her books for her in the hallway. Frances would never stoop that low.

Elizabeth was from one of the old-money families who'd been going to Thackeray for generations: so rich they were eccentric, and influential enough that no one commented on their eccentricities. She treated Jane in a similar fashion that Frances did. She pretended to go along with Jane in order to rebel against her well-bred, upper crust family. But Frances knew that secretly, Elizabeth was under intense pressure to perform, much like a thoroughbred horse. She studied constantly and slept little, determined to get into the Ivy League college of her parents' dreams.

Haley had become the class clown and the school's premiere athlete. But Haley followed Jane so no one would judge her for being a scholarship student. Frances told Haley no one cared; they were too caught up in their own insecurities and dramas playing out within their respective minds. But Haley constantly conspired to conceal her middle-class background: a perfectly pleasant upbringing in Ocean City, New Jersey. It was ironic that Haley looked to Jane to protect her from this when Jane was the one who made her insecure about it in the first place, innocently asking if Haley was really born in a place where public school kids went on spring break.

Frances never talked about her family. She knew it made her seem mysterious and enigmatic. Combined with her air of indifference, it made her appear untouchable. She resented Haley's constant attempts to conceal a life that Frances would have gladly killed for: family dinners and a golden retriever. Haley had no idea what she took for granted. But Frances would never tell her that. She didn't tell anyone about her family.

In the library that day, the girls had taken over their usual table in the back. Jane, procrastinating their World Cultures project, was the one who discovered the book.

"Hey, check it out, guys," she said, pulling it off the shelf and blowing off the dust on the cover. Frances watched her, rather than the book. Jane was someone you had to keep an eye on at all times, lest you fall victim to some sleight of hand she was performing. Frances had the thought that Jane hadn't really discovered the book but had planted it there and pretended to find it.

"What *is* that?" asked Elizabeth in a bored tone. It was the tone she used for everything, whether they were studying for exams or planning a raid on the kitchen. The only time Frances heard Elizabeth get worked up about anything was the time she dropped her hot curling iron on her foot.

"A book, obviously," said Haley with a roll of her eyes. There was perpetually tension between her and Elizabeth, their friendship based solely on their friendships with the others.

"This isn't just any book," said Jane, studying the table of contents. "This clearly doesn't belong here."

"What is it?" asked Bethany tentatively, peering over Jane's shoulder. They had been roommates since freshman year and were the oddest of couples but were probably the closest of anyone in the group—closer than Frances and Elizabeth, who'd also roomed together since ninth grade. They were like yin and yang.

"Some kind of occult thing," said Jane, flipping rapidly through the pages. "This definitely does not belong here."

"Wait, what?" Haley crowded in next to Bethany and Jane. "Let me see it."

"Do you think someone put it here?" Frances asked, watching Jane. She didn't react.

"Like who?" Jane asked without looking up.

"Like some seniors in the class before us, hoping to trick stupid people into thinking they found an old magic book in the library and then make idiots of themselves trying to perform spells," said Elizabeth. She had her notebook open to her heavily highlighted notes and hadn't given the book a second glance.

"Do you think it's real?" asked Bethany anxiously.

"Oh, please," Haley scoffed. "Of course it's not real."

"Maybe it is." Jane closed the book and regarded them, her eyes aglow. "Only one way to find out."

FAMOUS LAST WORDS *if there ever were any,* Frances thought darkly as she made her way to the library on the second floor. Jane had smuggled the book back to her and Bethany's room that afternoon. She became obsessed with it. She insisted she'd discovered something—a ritual, she said—that could make them all eternally successful.

Elizabeth thought Jane was insane. She thought the fact that Jane was unmedicated, as she put it, was becoming a real problem. Elizabeth herself subsided on a cocktail of Adderall and Zoloft, claiming that it was perfectly fine to admit when you needed a crutch—or two. She thought that Jane needed several.

Frances wasn't so sure. What if the book was like the shadows she saw? What if there was an explanation for them? Frances wanted to look it up in the book just to see. But Jane guarded the book like a jealous lover, keeping it closer to her than a diary.

It was the book, Frances determined in the ensuing

years, that had sent Jane off the deep end. Maybe not the book itself; but it had become a conduit for her madness, giving Jane a dangerous focal point on which to fixate. It became a sort of McGuffin for her delusions, causing her to believe they could empower themselves with it at a time when they all felt powerless. Frances could see the appeal, but she knew it took more than a simple set of words to restore someone's sense of autonomy.

Jane had photocopied a page before she returned the book to the library, hiding it in the back behind several old obscure tomes that no one ever had reason to access. She didn't want the book to be traced back to her and the others, discovered in her room after the ritual was performed.

It had been so long since then. It had been twenty years. Frances knew it was highly unlikely the book was still there, that it had sat undetected for all these years. But maybe there was something to Jane's madness. Maybe the book was only discoverable if it wanted to be found.

Frances was unsurprised to see the same set of dusty leather-bound reference books in the same place they'd been two decades before. So little changed at Thackeray, at least in terms of the physical environment. And there was no reason for the students there now to even resort to using such an outdated means of research.

She paused in front of the shelf. She didn't really think the book was still there, did she? And even if it was, did she want to know what was in it? Frances had pushed all thoughts of the book to the back of her mind after the fire. She wouldn't go near the library for the rest of the year, and neither would Haley or Elizabeth. It seemed too much like the cause of their troubles.

What was she so curious about? What did she think she might find? Answers? Even if she did, did she really want to know what they were? Before she could over-think the matter any further, Frances quickly pushed the books aside and checked behind them. There was nothing there.

She gave a sigh of relief. She had to at least check, she told herself. She had to know. But now that she knew, she was glad it was gone, ideally forever. If they had been so easily led astray by the suggestions of an old book in the library, any impressionable student could be.

Just as Frances pushed the final reference book back into place, she heard voices on the other side of the shelf. She peered through a small gap between books and watched as Rowan came in, Blair and Tibbets following closely behind her. Frances wondered if she'd been mistaken in thinking that students no longer used the library the same way.

Then she saw by the way they arranged themselves around the back table in the corner—the same table where Jane had shown them the book—that this was merely a stealth meeting spot where they wouldn't be overheard. Frances moved closer, staying low and keeping behind the books.

"What if they find out?" Tibbets was saying. "What then?"

"What nothing," said Rowan. "They're not going to *find out*, Tibbets, because they're never going to catch us."

Frances's eyebrows shot up towards her hairline. Were

Anna and the headmistress right? Were Rowan and her sidekicks the ones responsible? But how had they done it?

"What is even the point of this?" said Blair. "You can't possibly imagine that it's worth it, Rowan."

"How do you know what I think is worth it?" Rowan challenged her. "You and I have very different ideas about worthiness, Blair. I would think that you'd know that by now."

"I think we should stop," said Tibbets in a small voice. "I think this is getting out of control."

"One more time," Rowan insisted. "That's all the book says we need. We'll just do it once more, and then if nothing happens, we'll stop. I promise."

Frances went cold at the girl's words. *That's all the book says we need.* She could have been watching her own memories play out from the shadows. Rowan could have meant any number of books; she could have been talking about any number of things.

But Frances felt, with an unmistakable certainty—without knowing exactly how she knew—that the book they were discussing was the same as the one she'd gone looking for that day. It had found a new group of girls to influence and corrupt, and Frances might be the only one who could stop it.

10

THE COTTAGE

*F*rances decided to keep a close eye on the three to see just what it was they planned on doing a final time. It would have been easy to assume that they planned on staging another act of "vandalism," if that's truly what it had been, or another game of lights out. But if they were following instructions they found in the book, it was possible they were up to something else altogether. Something even more dangerous than staging a power outage and defacing school property.

Frances knew that if she confronted them, she'd only be met with flat-out denial. They'd become more paranoid and go to greater lengths to conceal their plans, making it harder for her to discern what they were up to and catch them in the act. So she decided to keep quiet about what she heard and simply watch them. She could only stop them if she could catch them in the act. And she was determined to do exactly that.

Frances debated only briefly whether or not to include Anna in her plan. She knew that Anna wanted to catch the girls to ingratiate herself to the headmistress, and that wasn't Frances's agenda. She wanted to protect them from the mass psychosis caused by the book. She wanted to stop them from making the same mistake that she had, all those years ago.

It was doubly important to do so now in the days preceding Parents' Weekend. The headmistress was on high alert for any trouble which might reflect poorly on the school before the people paying tuition arrived to witness any mischief. Teachers were asked to patrol the corridors when not instructing a class and keep an extra close eye on the students. Students complained the school felt even more like a prison than usual. Teachers complained they were being asked to perform the role of both teachers and security guards. All said and done, everyone was unhappy and paranoid.

Frances ran into Headmistress McBride in the faculty lounge during breakfast. Frances, who was starving, had just made short work of a stack of gluten-free pancakes. She was on her way to get more coffee when McBride appeared seemingly out of nowhere, startling her at the Keurig.

"Frances, I'm so glad I've found you," said McBride, as if Frances had been stranded atop a mountain during a blizzard rather than adding nondairy creamer to her hazelnut coffee. "I know this is hardly your job description, but we're all a bit up to our ears ensuring that everything goes smoothly this weekend when the parents arrive. Could you by any chance pass along a message to Tom, the gardener?"

There was no sense in asking the headmistress why

she didn't just call, email, or text Tom herself. Not only did McBride not own a cell phone, she also refused to have a landline in her office, interrupting her all day with calls from overbearing parents. She had a receptionist, but Frances guessed she was busy. Which obviously left Frances to do her bidding. She was probably the first person McBride saw.

"Certainly, Headmistress. What's the message?" asked Frances. It clearly wasn't a request she had the option of refusing.

"Please request that he see to it that the driveways are cleared and freshly salted," said the headmistress. "The last thing I need on Parents' Weekend is a slew of twisted ankles and potential litigation."

"Of course," said Frances. "Where exactly is the gardener's cottage again?"

"At the edge of the grounds, halfway between the girls' side and the boys," said McBride. "The path around the lake should be freshly shoveled and passable for you to circumnavigate. Thank you in advance for your trouble."

"It's no trouble at all, Headmistress." Frances snapped the lid in place on her coffee and addressed this last statement to the headmistress's back as she bustled from the room. She thought that no amount of rock salt could deter an angry ghost but thought it better not to mention in the presence of the obviously frazzled and disbelieving headmistress.

The walkway around the lake was freshly shoveled, but it was still freezing cold out. Frances buried her gloved hands deep in the pocket of her overcoat and nestled her face inside her scarf to protect it from the stinging wind that whipped off the surface of the lake as she cursed herself for accepting this thankless errand. She was sure the gardener was well aware that the driveways needed salting before the parents arrived and would probably be insulted by the implication of having to be told.

In the distance, she could make out a plume of chimney smoke billowing up over the quaint and charming gardener's cottage at the edge of the lake. The sight unpleasantly invoked a similar, much larger column of smoke in Frances's memory, and she swiftly repressed it.

The gardener's cottage had been the one place that even her perpetually out of bounds group had never breached. The gardener back then had been a thoroughly unpleasant woman by the name of Gretel Hildebrand who would have impaled them with her rake without a second glance if they so much as looked at her cottage askance. There was nothing of any interest about the cottage to Jane, anyway, nor to any of the students. There was a vague understanding that the presence of the gardener directly correlated with the immaculate state of the grounds they inhabited, but it was all very much background landscape to the more pressing dramas of their daily lives at the school.

Now Frances found herself feeling curious about the cottage and the gardener. Perhaps he'd caught a glimpse of out-of-bound students from his vantage point on the grounds. Frances resolved to ask him.

The man who answered the door was a far cry from Gretel Hildebrand. His cheerful, ruddy face defied any attempt at guessing at his age, and he immediately opened the door wide for her with a bright "Hello, I'm Tom. I'm assuming you're here on a mission from the headmistress?"

Frances smiled wryly. "I'm afraid so." She stepped inside. The cottage seemed to be all one room, save for a narrow hallway that led off to what was presumably a bedroom. A fire crackled merrily in the hearth and a tea kettle whistled on the stove.

"Tell her I'll have the drive cleared and thoroughly salted in time for the parents, if you will," said Tom. He went over to the stove and lifted the kettle off with a fat quilted oven mitt shaped like a hen. "Can I make you a to-go mug of my finest Lady Grey for your trip back? I feel badly about you coming all this way to pass on such an obvious message from her majesty just because she doesn't like phones."

"That would be wonderful, thank you." Frances smiled gratefully at the kindly gardener, to whom she had taken an immediate liking. He was so warm and friendly it was impossible not to. "I think the head-mistress is in a state of micro-management as the result of Parents' Weekend."

"She's just trying to control what she knows she can to make up for what she can't, which is the students," said Tom matter-of-factly, pouring hot water over a tea bag in a thick ceramic mug. He considerately left the lid off in case Frances wanted to add milk or sugar.

"Are they really so bad?" Frances asked as she accepted the mug and reached for the honey on the cottage's small table in front of the fire. She sat in the small squashy armchair in front of the fire, breathing a sigh of relief at the pleasant heat it radiated.

"More recently, yes," said Tom frankly, taking a seat across from her. "Not really sure why they're acting up all of a sudden. I can't count the number of times I've seen flashlights on the grounds headed straight for the woods, even in this weather. I can't wrap my head around it. Usually it's them sneaking around the lake late at night for their secret rendezvous. Not exactly in my job description to stop them."

"The woods?" Frances asked, concerned. "Why are they going into the woods?"

"Damned if I know," said Tom. "That I worry a bit more about, so I have on occasion attempted to go in and break it up, whatever it is. When they sneak around the lake to meet each other, they use the path. But the woods are a different story. It's easy to become disoriented out there if you don't know the woods well and get lost, let alone in this weather. I don't want anybody to freeze to death, if I could have done something to stop it. I'd never forgive myself. Funny thing is, I've never caught anybody in there. I see lights going in, and lights coming out, but I've never seen a trace of anyone in there myself when I go in after them."

Frances furrowed her brow as she blew on the surface of her piping hot tea. "Strange. Is there someplace in the woods they might be meeting? A place you might not know about?"

"There's not a place in these woods I don't know about," said Tom. "I've tended these grounds the last ten years. Inherited the job from my mother. I used to play in those woods as a kid. I can't imagine where they'd be going that even I don't know about."

"Gretel Hildebrand is your mother?" said Frances, startled. She'd never imagined imposing Gretel as having small children. Though she supposed even grizzly bears had cubs.

"Doesn't exactly seem like the maternal type, does she?" Tom laughed. "I can assure you, she's just as formidable a mother as she is a gardener."

"I don't doubt it." Frances took a pensive little sip of tea. "So you've never seen which girls have been going into the woods?"

"I can't even say for a fact that it is the girls," said Tom thoughtfully. "I've never gotten close enough to see who it is. It could be the headmistress herself, for all I know." He snorted. "Though I doubt it. Miss McBride's not much one for the outdoors, as I'm sure you well know yourself."

Frances couldn't help but smile. "No, she always has preferred to avoid the outside world in every sense," she said thoughtfully. "So it could be anyone going into the woods?"

"Anyone, or anything," said Tom darkly. Frances was startled, and he laughed at her expression. "I don't mean *anything* like supernatural or what have you. I don't give credence to the rumors that run wild up at the school. Too many people—especially young people—living on top of each other like that, ideas are bound to spread whether they make sense or not. It's why I avoid the school, truth be told. I just meant that it might not be students. It might be people who don't belong on school grounds at all."

"People from the town?" asked Frances puzzled.

"Maybe. Who knows?" Tom shook his head. "I'll tell you one thing my mother always told me: that fire that was set here, back in ninety-nine? She doesn't believe it was an accident. She thinks someone did it on purpose. Could be someone angry at the way all these rich people have sealed themselves off up here, lording over the town like some kinda feudal manor. You know they don't hire anybody from town to work at the school, right? Even if they're qualified? Only alumni and Ivy League folks, no disrespect to you at all, ma'am. Did I offend you? I didn't mean to." Tom regarded her with chagrin.

Frances felt the blood drain from her face the second the words left his lips about the fire. Someone knew that it hadn't been an accident. Someone outside of their little group who had sworn themselves to secrecy. It might have been only a retired gardener and her son, but if they knew, that meant other people could, too. And Frances knew it wasn't angry townies who had set the blaze. She wondered how friendly he'd be if he knew he was looking at one of the people responsible.

Frances got to her feet a little unsteadily. "Thank you so much for the tea," she said in a rush, wanting to flee before she broke down and lost her composure completely. "I really appreciate it. I'll be sure to tell the headmistress about the salt, and the drive."

"I really am sorry," said Tom, looking abashed. "I see that I've upset you. That wasn't my intention. Sometimes I just get to talking and I can't seem to stop."

"No, no, it wasn't that, truly." Frances felt oddly obligated to assure him after his kindness and hospitality. "It's just such a bad memory for the school, the fire. I can't stand the thought that someone might have done it on purpose." Inside her head, her conscience chanted: *hypocrite liar hypocrite.*

"Oh, that's just me talking out of turn," said Tom, shaking his head. "Please don't listen to me. I don't mean anything by it. I'm sure it was an accident, really."

"Of course," said Frances, forcing a smile. "I really must get back up to the school before the headmistress has my, uh, head. Thank you so much again for the tea."

"Any time." Tom opened the door for her. "Let me know if there's anything else I can do." He patted her on the back as she left.

The guilt Frances had always expected to feel but never did was finally hitting her in full. All she could think about was Bethany, trapped in the chapel. How had she compartmentalized it for all these years? The evil of what they'd done. They could have gone back. Maybe they could have done something. Maybe they could have saved her.

As badly as she felt, however, she still couldn't seem to summon the same feelings regarding Jane. Bethany had always been under her control. They all had. Maybe they hadn't done everything in their power to save her, but Jane had certainly done everything in her power to endanger them in the first place. It was Jane's idea to go to the chapel, Jane's idea to perform the stupid so-called ritual in the first place. They could have said no, could have rebelled against her, but what teenager ever rebelled against her own friends?

Maybe she was just rationalizing, thought Frances as she made her way up the winding path back to the school.

Of course she was. No matter how many times she attempted to psychoanalyze herself—her actions, her thought process—regarding the night of the fire, she always drew the same conclusions: that she had been weak and wrong, and two girls lost their lives because of it. She could have stood up to Jane, and then she wouldn't have been in the chapel that night, either. None of them would have.

Frances could no more turn back the hands of time than she could stop the planet from spinning on its axis. She couldn't change the past and bring both Bethany and Jane back to life. But maybe she could stop it from happening again.

THE BIRDS

*H*er aunt and uncle never attended Parents' Weekend, and she was excused to remain in the dorm. The others said they envied her, playing Solitaire on her laptop and eating Smart Food. Frances smiled slightly as if acknowledging her good fortune over them, but inwardly she couldn't believe they could be so callous and dense.

Of course she would rather be going downstairs with the rest of them in order to see her parents. What ungrateful brats they were, she silently fumed. Only Jane said nothing, studying her from the back of the group as they chattered, fixed hair bows, applied make-up, and let down their hemlines.

That was the thing about Jane: she always saw more about all of them than they normally let on. Usually, Frances considered it one of the ways she controlled them; one of the things about Jane she found so unsettling. But if she was really honest with herself, it was the reason she was friends with Jane in the first place. She got it. She understood, in a way the others didn't. She made Frances feel seen.

Elizabeth still secretly hated her, of course. But that was Elizabeth for you. She secretly hated everyone.

After an hour in her dorm room, Frances felt claustrophobic. But where could she go and still avoid the legions of happy families crowding the campus? They were reading *Anna Karenina,* and Tolstoy said that happy families were all alike. Frances didn't know about that. All she knew was that all happy families were all equally capable of causing her pain compared to her own sad and isolated life.

She decided to sign out and take a bus into town. They were so cloistered on campus that aside from their trips to the mall to visit the outside world, she often forgot there even was a world outside of Thackeray. It was probably psychologically unhealthy, she thought, to imagine Thackeray as the center of existence.

Westinghouse had a quaint main street full of small shops and eateries. Frances wandered down the street until she arrived at the end. She planned to turn back and walk to the bookstore she'd passed at the beginning of Main when a small alley off behind the bakery caught her eye. It had a sign, Crawley Avenue, and it looked like there were more stores in it.

Frances saw immediately why they were tucked away on this narrow side street. The boutiques and cafes on Main Street were upscale and seemed to cater to the boarders at Thackeray and their visiting parents. There was even one with nothing but Thackeray paraphernalia —sweatshirts, t-shirts, mugs, snow globes. Here, the stores were different. She passed a shop with handmade scarves and incense displayed in the window, next to a seedy-looking little thrift store.

Frances was debating going into the thrift store when another sign caught her eye: a silver moon and three gold stars painted onto a purple wooden background, swinging slightly in the chilly wind that swept down the alley. A tumbleweed of trash blew past Frances as she contemplated the sign. The store didn't even have a name. It was like something out of one of the books she'd read as a kid, holed up in her aunt's mansion: about kids who discovered magic after wandering off the beaten path. She went in.

The door swung shut behind her with a creak. The store was dim and lit with candles. The dusty shelves were lined with crystals and old books. It looked like a New Age shop, or a fortune teller's. Frances had always wanted to have her fortune told. She imagined it would be like in the movies, when a wise old seer at a carnival imparts the wisdom of the ages on a curious young girl.

"Looking for something?"

Frances jumped. She turned to see not a knowing old crone, but a pleasant-looking young woman behind the counter. She'd been concealed by a towering stack of books which she now peered out from behind.

"Um, are you…are you a fortune teller?" Frances felt a little silly even asking. What if the woman laughed right in her face?

She only smiled. "Palmistry, you mean?"

"Yeah, that. I guess," Frances said uncertainly.

"I dabble." She tucked her long black hair behind her ear, revealing the six silver rings she wore on her right hand. "Would you like me to read yours?"

"Okay." Frances stepped forward and hesitantly held out her hand. The woman reached out and took it in her own. Her hand was warm, and as she touched Frances, a strange jolt shot up her arm.

"Oh!" Frances flinched and looked up into the woman's eyes. They were unusual, a deep midnight blue that seemed to shift in the strange light to violet.

"You seem highly sensitive to auras," the woman murmured. "I'm Cassandra, by the way." Frances could tell she introduced herself just to put her at ease, though she couldn't say how she knew.

"I'm Bethany," said Frances. "Bethany Jones."

"Well, Bethany," said Cassandra. "Let's have a look at that palm of yours, shall we?"

Frances turned her hand over. Cassandra studied it with utmost seriousness, as if studying microbes on a slide in biology class. Her eyes flicked up to Frances's. "You've experienced great tragedy at a young age," she said, her eyes filled with sorrow.

"Yeah, I guess so," said Frances, uncomfortable. She was already regretting doing this.

Cassandra gave her hand a reassuring little squeeze. Frances, unaccustomed to physical affection, squirmed. There was something radiating off the woman in waves, something she couldn't quite pinpoint. Something she didn't understand, and it made her afraid.

Cassandra continued to study the topography of lines on Frances's hand. "Your great tragedy was the first of your young life," she said. "But it won't be the last. However, your lifeline is strong and unbroken. You will survive, no matter what storms you must weather. It's important that you know that."

Frances stared at Cassandra. She wanted to snatch her hand away but didn't want to appear rude. Was she seriously telling her that something even worse might happen to her? What kind of fortune teller was she? She was supposed to impart wisdom, predict untold riches and handsome men. That was how it played out in the movies of her mind. Frances wanted to leave.

"I should get back to school," she said softly.

Cassandra gently folded Frances's fingers, closing her hand into a fist. "I can see that I've upset you," she said. "That wasn't my intention. Occasionally, a girl from up the hill wanders in, and I always try to be honest. I just had another girl come in recently, and she was so curious, wanting to know everything. I forgot not everyone wants to know. I didn't mean to scare you."

"You didn't." Frances backed away, eager to break eye contact and get away from this strange woman and this horrible store.

"Take a look around," said Cassandra, even as Frances turned to hurry away. "Let me know if you see anything you're interested in."

Frances made a show of glancing around just to be polite, but she couldn't wait to get out of the weird old shop with its thick, choking smell of sandalwood and something else she couldn't quite pinpoint—something ancient and mysterious, something burnt.

As she left, her eyes wandered over the spines of the old books on the shelves. Some of them didn't have names. Frances loved to read more than anyone she knew, but something about the books gave her the creeps. They reminded her of the book Jane said she found in the library. Or so she claimed. What had the fortune teller said? *I just had another girl come in recently.*

Turning away, she hurried as quickly as she could from the store.

WHEN THE OTHERS got back from visiting with their parents, talking loudly in the hallway as they filed into Jane and Bethany's room, Frances remained in her room. She didn't want to see them and have to hear about their happy families, so unlike her own.

Frances heard the door across the hall open and close, their voices fading, and then her own door immediately opened. Elizabeth came in. She walked over and put a Snickers on Frances's desk where she sat reading the book she got in town. (From the normal bookstore, well-lit with plenty of cheery, unassuming store clerks.) Frances smiled without looking up. Elizabeth squeezed her shoulder, then picked up her bucket of toiletries and left to take a shower.

Frances opened the Snickers and thought that maybe it wasn't the worst thing, to be an orphan on Parents' Weekend. Not when you had true friends.

. . .

FRANCES'S first day as guidance counselor saw an incredibly high turnover of girls who were anxious and worried about their parents showing up for Parents' Weekend. They were always able to harass them regarding their extracurricular and academic performances via phone, text, email, or social media, but it would be impossible to ignore and avoid them in person. Many of the girls were worried that their parents would be disappointed in them, and Frances soothed their frayed nerves to the best of her ability.

"What are you worried your parents will take issue with?" Frances asked Laney Randall, a borderline hysterical girl who scheduled an appointment with her first thing in the morning."Everything." Laney wrung her hands in her lap, her foot twitching frantically under the table. "That I'm a junior still playing JV, for one. My dad thinks it's disgusting. I know he does. He doesn't say it, he just rolls his eyes about it and never comes to home games, but I *know* that's what he's thinking. And my mother will get on my case about my diet. She thinks I'm overeating, but I'm not! My dad thinks it's because I play JV."

"Thinks *what* is because you're overeating and playing JV?" asked Frances, perplexed.

"The fact that I need to lose like, five pounds. Like I'm not aware of it."

Frances surveyed Laney over her legal pad. She looked like a perfectly ordinary, healthy teenager. She sighed.

"Laney. You do not need to lose five pounds." She set the legal pad to the side. "Do you ever think that maybe your parents are projecting their own shortcomings onto you? Living their lives vicariously through yours? Maybe your mother feels she could stand to lose five pounds. Maybe your father never made varsity and hated himself for it a little bit. Could it be that?"

Laney looked at her, wide-eyed. "Yeah, actually. He always played JV. Second-string. And my mother is obsessed with her weight. *Obsessed.*"

"Don't let them in your head," said Frances. "I'm going to level with you: as soon as you graduate and go to college, *no one* is going to care that you played junior varsity field hockey. Literally no one. I can't imagine anything less important. Seriously. Just trust me on this."

She opened the door for a relieved-looking Laney. She checked her ledger. The next student scheduled was Tibbets Carlton.

She was curious to talk to Tibbets for a number of reasons. Tibbets obviously knew what Rowan's plan was and was probably involved in it. If the girls were behind the recent vandalism and after-hours activity, Tibbets knew about it. She was likely an active participant. And if there was something much darker going on with Rowan and her friends, then Tibbets knew about that, too.

Frances didn't expect her to disclose any of this, of course. Teenaged girls were like spies holding state secrets when it came to safeguarding their illicit lives. But maybe in talking to her, she could get a better idea of what she was up against.

Tibbets entered the room quietly, without any greeting. She seemed subdued as she sat in the chair across from Frances. "You're probably wondering why I'm here," she said.

"Not really," said Frances. "Maybe you just needed to decompress and get away from the rest of the school. We don't even have to talk, if you don't want."

Tibbets studied her. "You remember what it's like here, don't you." It wasn't a question.

"Unfortunately." Frances put her legal pad face down on the desk. She could tell that someone like Tibbets would be uncomfortable having someone take notes on her while they spoke. Most people were. *What are you writing*, they always wanted to know, paranoid. Frances theorized it was more of a protective barrier between analysts and their patients than an actual necessity.

"Why 'unfortunately'?" Tibbets asked. "Didn't you like it here?"

"Oh no, I liked the school just fine. I liked it better than my own home. It was more like…social pressures." Now Frances was the one who studied Tibbets, to see if these words had any particular resonance. Aside from a slight twitch in her right eye, Tibbets didn't react, remaining expressionless. "With my friends, you know? A lot of the girls here are worried about impressing their parents. I was always more preoccupied with impressing my friends."

"What did you think would happen if you didn't?" Tibbets asked.

"I'm not sure." Frances mulled this over. "Being exiled, maybe? Being alone? Being shunned, an outsider. Having no escape, in a space this small. All I knew was that I couldn't allow that to happen, no matter what."

Tibbets regarded her gravely. Frances could see that her words had hit home. Often, she liked to describe seemingly revealing information to those who were particularly reticent to talk. It allowed them to remain feeling concealed, especially if they were shy or hesitant. Often Frances found they revealed more through the questions they asked her than they would answering any question Frances had for them.

"What would you have done to avoid it?" Tibbets asked.

"Almost anything, I'd imagine." Frances looked at Tibbets. "Is there someone who's pressuring you at school?"

"What would happen to the people responsible for what's been happening lately?" asked Tibbets instead of answering. "Would they be expelled?"

"It depends," said Frances carefully. "It depends on whether they came forward, or whether they were caught."

Tibbets considered this. "I'm not saying I know who did it," she said slowly. "I'm just saying I have concerns. For people that I know. For me."

"Do you want to talk about those concerns?" asked Frances.

Tibbets bit her lip. Frances could see the inner war being waged in her mind. "Not yet," she said finally. "When I'm ready. I'll tell you then." Tibbets looked at her seriously. "You're not going to tell the headmistress, are you? What I said just now?"

"I would consider that unethical," said Frances. "I should tell her. But I won't. For the time being. Unless I suspect that you or the other students are in danger. Is that the case?

Tibbets frowned. "I'm not sure…not yet. No, I don't think so."

"But maybe in the future?" Frances pressed.

"Maybe. But maybe not." Tibbets shrugged. She glanced up at Frances. "I'll tell you if that happens."

"All right, Tibbets. Is there anything else I can do for you today?" Frances watched her as she pushed her glasses up her nose and shook her head.

"Not today, Ms. Teller. Thank you." She got up and headed for the door.

"You're welcome," Frances said to her retreating back. She disappeared around the corner and vanished from sight. Frances felt an unexpected tug of sadness. She'd forgotten what it felt like to feel so helpless and closed-off. Now she was merely closed-off.

It felt like a relief, by comparison.

THE FACULTY STOOD in a line at the front entrance, waiting to greet the parents as they arrived at the school. Frances stood at the end, bored. It was one of those pomp-and-circumstance formalities she despised. She'd never had to stand on the assembly line, or even attend the meet-and-greet section of the weekend.

Frances felt a sense of déjà vu in her room before she'd gone downstairs. Now she was the one getting ready for Parents' Weekend, even though there was still no one showing up for her. At least today it was a given.

The first parents were arriving, clicking up the front

steps and through the double doors in their high heels and polished Oxfords. The early birds, who disregarded the official time and showed up half an hour early, because the world should be on their schedule, not the other way around. This was what necessitated that the faculty be there so far ahead of time and remain an hour later for the lazier but equally entitled parents, who also felt that whatever time they arrived was the acceptable time to be there.

The first couple came in issuing a cloud of mixed perfume and cologne that made Frances gag all the way at the end of the receiving line. They were an ordinary-looking pair distinguished by their matching expressions of superiority, whatever nest egg they sat on elevating them above the rest of the plebeians. They went down the line, cordially greeting their daughter's current teachers, and Frances felt relieved when she realized she wasn't one of them. The prospect of making small talk with these people was unpleasant, to say the least. Based on some of the conversations she'd had with their daughters in the preceding days, she found their presence invasive and unwelcome, an opportunity for them to criticize rather than offer love and support. Many of them felt their financial support should be enough.

It was then that Frances heard a noise behind her, somewhere in the back of the building. She glanced around. No one else appeared to have noticed it besides her. The other teachers remained in a line, shifting from foot to foot, quietly talking or conversing with the early parents and the headmistress.

Frances stealthily broke away from the receiving line

and slipped into the hallway behind her. It wouldn't do for some kind of incident to occur when the parents were first coming into the school, she reasoned. Best to investigate the situation now.

The noise seemed to resonate from the study room she'd checked the previous night when the power went out. Frances felt the same draft she had when she had looked into the room the night before. She gazed around, puzzled. Her eyes landed on the window at the opposite end of the room: it was the same window that had been left open last night.

Slowly, Frances approached the window and reached up to close it. The sash was stuck, and it took several tries to get it closed. Finally, she applied her full weight against the counter-resistance and the window slid down with an unholy creak.

Just as Frances got the window closed, a great and almighty shriek echoed in the foyer. Frances rushed out of the study room back to the main entrance of the school. Six black birds fluttered madly overhead. Ravens, or maybe crows. Frances was never much one for ornithology.

The early arrivals looked up fearfully, one of the women covering her head with her Louis Vuitton bag as if afraid of being pecked to death at any moment. The whole scene reminded Frances of something out of *The Birds.*

Anna appeared at her side, seemingly out of nowhere. "Rowan's room," Anna whispered in her ear. "Go check it. Right now."

Frances highly doubted the girls had caught and

released a murder of crows without anyone noticing, but preferred leaving to disagreeing with Anna in order to stick around and deal with angry parents. Frances hurried off towards the stairs, passing the parents, huddled in confused and irritated clumps. Snatches of their disgruntled conversations drifted after her.

"…not paying to have my child…"

"…what the meaning of this is…"

"…will be hearing about this, rest assured…"

The east wing was bustling and noisy for a Saturday. Usually students left campus and went into town or took a bus to the nearby mall. On this particular weekend, they were all in their rooms getting ready for Parents' Weekend.

Frances saw that the door to Rowan's room stood open, revealing that it had been converted into a suite. A daybed was pushed against the window seat with two twin beds on either end of the room. Rowan, Tibbets, and Blair all popped their heads up simultaneously like prairie dogs as Frances paused at the doorway.

"Everyone almost ready?" she asked.

"Yes, Ms. Teller," said Rowan as she ran a brush through her thick, dark hair. Tibbets resumed scribbling in her notebook and Blair turned back to her vanity to apply mascara. "We're just finishing up."

"All right. I'll see you downstairs." Frances turned away as her phone buzzed in her pocket. It was Anna.

Were they there? Frances read the text and shook her head with disbelief.

They were there, she wrote back. *Maybe someone left the flue in the common room fireplace open.*

I doubt it, wrote Anna. Frances rolled her eyes. For whatever reason, both Anna and the headmistress were determined to hang Rowan and the others for the odd happenings occurring at the school. She wondered if this would be grounds for relegating them to the other side of the lake.

Frances decided to stop in her room and grab an extra sweater to layer over her thin cardigan before heading down to the cafeteria. It was especially chilly in the east wing and the dining hall would likely be even colder.

Frances inserted the key to her room and the door swung inward with a long, drawn-out creak. She stepped through the doorway and stopped. Sitting on her pillow, like a little gift, was a hardback book.

Frances approached the book and stared at it. It was her high school yearbook. Or a copy of her high school yearbook, seeing as she knew hers was in a storage space, stashed at the bottom of an oversized hat box. It was bound in the black leather of every Thackeray yearbook. But instead of the current year embossed in gold script, this one read *1999*.

Frances felt a chill wash over her before she even opened the book. The pages flipped by themselves as if turned by an unseen hand. The window was closed in her room and there was no breeze.

The pages stopped moving towards the middle of the book, on a series of candid shots of various students taken around campus. In the middle was their group: Jane, Bethany, Frances, Haley, and Elizabeth. She knew it was them because she had the same picture—also in the hatbox—tacked to her bulletin board the entirety of senior year. Otherwise, she might not have been able to tell.

Jane and Bethany's faces were clear enough, but the faces of the other three—hers, Haley's, and Elizabeth's—had been scratched out with a pen, as if someone had pressed so hard they had torn right through the page.

PARENTS' WEEKEND

$\mathcal{F}$rances stared at the yearbook. Then she seized it and threw it into the open wardrobe, slamming the door shut and turning the key. Her mind raced. Was Anna right about the girls? Were they playing a cruel prank? What about the pages, then? How had they turned by themselves? Frances looked wildly around the room. Heat gushed from the radiator. That must have been it. Yes.

Frances hurried down to the cafeteria. Better to be early for brunch than return to the receiving line, which had no doubt only grown more annoying in the brief time since she'd gone upstairs. She wondered if they'd gotten rid of the birds.

The birds. How could the girls have herded six birds into the foyer at the exact moment the parents arrived? It seemed unlikely. Maybe the birds and the appearance of the yearbook were not connected. Maybe there was both something supernatural going on, and something simultaneously considerably more mundane.

Something supernatural. Frances crossed her arms across her chest, wrapping her sweater more tightly around her body. But she couldn't fight the deep shiver that seemed to emanate from within her very core. Were Bethany and Jane still here? Were they angry that Frances had never paid for what had happened to them?

The girls began to file into the cafeteria. Most of the older girls looked glum, but the underclassmen—particularly the freshmen—looked excited. They were not as likely to be interrogated about SATs, college applications, or making varsity. They were just happy to see their parents for the first time since leaving home.

The parents showed up next. They converged on their daughters, making excited remarks about how much weight they had lost and how good they looked. The daughters beamed. The parents fussed. After the requisite greetings, the diehard caffeine addicts made beelines for the coffee station.

The headmistress came in last. Even beneath her frozen smile conveying utter ease and a certain good nature that Frances knew she in no way felt, Frances could tell that beneath her calm exterior, she was livid. This was sure to have repercussions. She would wait until the parents were gone, dismissing the birds as an unfortunate and strange accident of nature colliding with the indoors in the meantime, but Frances knew she thought one—or more than one—of the students were responsible.

After greeting their children and filling their coffee mugs, the parents began to drift towards the teachers, either to make small talk or to commence with interrogating them about their lesson plans and little so-and-so's preparation for the college of their dreams. Frances felt unable to stomach such inane discourse this early in the morning, and though she knew it would be frowned upon if anyone noticed, she slipped out the side door and into the hallway. She breathed a sigh of relief. Once a truant, always a truant, she supposed.

Frances wandered down the dark hallway with no particular destination in mind. She realized she was in the old music wing. At the very moment her revelation occurred, she heard a piano being played at the end of the hallway in the rehearsal room. A single note, over and over. Frances assumed one of the girls must have ditched the parents' brunch and snuck into the music room. Now she would have to confront them, talk them down, and herd them back to the brunch.

Frances sighed. She had gotten a master's degree specifically for the reason that she wanted to teach college and never deal with anyone under the age of eighteen, ever again. She was starting to have second thoughts about the perks of working at Thackeray outweighing the considerable drawbacks.

The door to the rehearsal room was closed. Frances pushed it open and the music ceased at once. She approached the piano, the bench obscured by the piano's open lid. She expected to find a guilty-looking girl, caught, ready with some excuse. Claiming she was practicing to impress her parents, no doubt.

The bench was empty. There was no one there.

Frances looked around the room, spooked. She went straight to the drum closet and threw the door open. It was just as empty as the bench, as empty as the room. There was no one in the room but her.

Frances practically ran from the room. Maybe she was losing her mind. Maybe she had repressed the events of Thackeray all those years ago, and now that she was here, all the sights and smells were triggering the traumatic event. Maybe she was in denial about how strongly she felt and was slowly starting to unravel to the point of auditory hallucinations. Yes, it was possible. Certainly, it was more likely than ghosts.

Frances slowed her footsteps as she reached the cafeteria. She suddenly needed to be surrounded by people. Even nosy parents were a preferable alternative to auditory hallucinations. Or ghosts in the music room.

Could ghosts possess people? Was that just the stuff of movies? Frances felt certain that if Jane could possess anyone, she most certainly would. Maybe she had died that night. Maybe it was her dark presence she felt in every corner and corridor. Frances remembered the one repetitive note being played in the music room. But it wasn't Jane who played the piano.

It was Bethany.

BETHANY EKED out Heart and Soul on the piano in the music room while Elizabeth smoked out the window. The music wing was always abandoned on weekends and the girls liked to sneak down there after dinner. It was fall and night came early. Frances looked out the window at the cool fall night, imagining the bright stars in the sky outside. Out of the five of them, it was she who romanticized Thackeray the most. She was the one with the least outside these walls.

Jane was rolling a joint in the drum closet. Haley was pacing nervously. Frances could tell she wanted to leave. "Do you want to go back upstairs?" she said to her kindly. "I'm kind of tired."

Haley stopped pacing. Relief flooded her round, innocent features. "Yes, I do," she admitted."

"I do, too." Elizabeth flicked her cigarette butt out of the window. "I'm bored. The last thing I need is a demerit before break for being out of bounds." She glanced at the joint in Jane's hand as she exited the closet. "Or an expulsion for possession and being under the influence on school grounds. I'd never hear the end of it."

"You were already smoking, Elizabeth," said Jane testily. Frances could see that Jane immediately attributed this minor mutiny to Elizabeth, even though it had been Frances's suggestion. "Besides, this is a lot better for you. You might actually eat something for a change."

"I'm going to go," said Haley decisively, a first for her. Jane's eyes flicked over to her.

"Me, too," said Frances. "I'm tired. We're all tired. Maybe later. We have the whole weekend, you know."

Jane surveyed them incredulously, as if she couldn't believe what she was hearing. "Are you seriously all going to bed right now? That's the lamest thing I've ever heard."

"I'll stay," volunteered Bethany from the piano.

Jane sighed with disgust. "Never mind," she said. "We might as well all go."

They exited the music room in a stealthy single file, splitting off into separate groups of two and three in case anyone should see them or stop them. They had a number of alibis worked out in advance—Bethany was tutoring Jane in AP Chemistry, Elizabeth and Frances edited the literary magazine, and Haley was helping with the layout —should they be questioned.

On this night in particular, they ran into no one—not suspicious faculty, nor any other students. "Thanks," said Haley gratefully and a little awkwardly to Frances as she broke off from them at her room.

"Don't worry about it." Frances smiled at her. Elizabeth remained silent until they were safely in their room.

"It shouldn't be that hard," she said as she pulled on her pajamas.

"What shouldn't be that hard?" asked Frances. She'd already taken up a similar position on her bed as the one she had in the music room on the window ledge, and was now staring out the window again, not really paying attention.

"Getting away from her," said Elizabeth. "Doing something other than what she wants to do."

Frances glanced over at her. She was already under the covers, contacts out, glasses on, paging through Peterman's Guide to Colleges. She knew that Elizabeth didn't like Jane; they all did. The enmity was mutual. But Frances often neglected to think about why, and she did so as she looked out onto the grounds. Why did they always follow Jane and do whatever she wanted them to do? Were they just sheep? Were they that badly in need of a leader? What if there was no Jane? What if it was always as easy as it had been tonight, to just come to a conclusion and agree, with little to no pushback?

As Frances looked out the window, she saw a solitary figure traipsing across the green into the night alone, towards the woods. She felt certain without looking more closely that she knew exactly who it was.

THE NOISE of the dining hall swelled as she pushed the door open. She quickly wove her way through the chattering crowd, straight towards the coffee station. She poured herself a large mug from the spout, her hand trembling. Frances jumped, the coffee sloshing, when she felt a hand fall lightly on her shoulder.

Frances turned to see a well put-together woman with dark hair tied tightly back in a chignon standing with a hand over her mouth, looking abashed. "Oh, I'm so sorry," she said. "I didn't mean to startle you. I'm Martina Makepeace, Rowan's mother. I just wanted to meet all her teachers this morning."

"So nice to meet you, Mrs. Makepeace," said Frances, forcing a polite smile in return. "It's my fault, really. Too much coffee." She forced herself to set the mug down even though she wanted to chug it. She forced a laugh that sounded false even to her own ears.

Mrs. Makepeace nodded knowingly. "I couldn't get out of bed without it," she said, as if confiding a deep secret. "My husband is over in the corner, grilling the calculus teacher." Mrs. Makepeace gave a slight nod towards the opposite end of the room. Frances looked over to see a tall, silver-haired man in a navy blazer talking at—rather than to—Harmony Carruthers, who had the expression of a mouse in a trap. "But I was much more interested to talk to you," Mrs. Makepeace continued.

"Rowan is a very engaged and inquisitive student," said Frances. It was true, but also exactly, Frances felt sure, what Mrs. Makepeace wanted to hear. "It's really such a pleasure to have her in class."

"Oh, she's always been that way," said Mrs. Makepeace idly. "We couldn't do anything without being given the third degree, once she learned to speak. 'Why' was her favorite word. Which is the case with most gifted children, but Rowan was especially relentless." This didn't surprise Frances. Rowan had her back against the wall the first day of class until she'd extracted every bit of information she'd desired. Frances could see now how easily she'd gotten the upper hand. She was probably used to it.

"Really a wonderful sense of curiosity," Frances repeated herself, already wondering what it would take to extract herself from this conversation.

"I was more curious what you thought of Rowan's mental state?" inquired Mrs. Makepeace. "As a teacher of psychology?"

"Her mental state?" Frances was startled. She was more than used to constant requests to ply her trade for free in casual conversation, but she hadn't expected it from a parent on Parents' Day. Frances remembered the parade of girls through her office during the preceding days and realized she should have. "She seems fine, Mrs. Makepeace. Is there anything in particular you're concerned about?"

"It's those friends of hers." Mrs. Makepeace lowered her voice confidentially. "Blair Vanderbilt and Tibbets

Carlton. They've been a horrible influence on Rowan, you know."

"Blair and Tibbets?"

"Well, Blair more so than Tibbets, obviously. That Tibbets is a little mouse who will go along with anything Blair says, but she's been encouraging Rowan to skirt boundaries and push the envelope ever since they started rooming together freshman year. We've encouraged her to find a different roommate, and different friends, but you know how girls that age can be. That only made it *worse*. We should have said we approved wholeheartedly of the friends she had, and maybe she would have gotten bored of them. Now they're thick as thieves."

"And you think they're having a negative effect on Rowan?"

"I absolutely do," said Mrs. Makepeace fervently. "Rowan is a very ethical child, with sound values. *Our* values. She's never once questioned our authority, and now we get nothing but questions."

Frances thought this ran rather contrary to what Mrs. Makepeace had just told her about Rowan's nature as a child but didn't care to point it out. Mrs. Makepeace clearly wasn't receptive to being contradicted or even having obvious truths pointed out to her.

"What are you concerned about, in terms of their influence?" asked Frances. "Do you think they'll get Rowan into trouble?"

"They absolutely will," said Mrs. Makepeace vehemently. "Especially that Blair. If you could just keep an eye on her for me, maybe even separate them somehow, I would appreciate it so much."

Frances rolled her eyes inwardly. Of course she had nothing better to do than appoint herself Rowan's personal keeper, as far as this woman was concerned. Aloud, she said only, "I'll do my best, Mrs. Makepeace."

"I *so* appreciate it. I really do." Mrs. Makepeace squeezed her hand and looked deeply into her eyes. Frances, who hated physical contact with strangers, resisted the impulse to shake her hand off like a dead rat. "Not all of the teachers here look out for the girls, and it's such a relief to find one that does."

Mrs. Makepeace excused herself to join her husband in his interrogation of Mrs. Carruthers, who was clearly making excuses to try and extract herself from the pushy pair. Frances shuddered and turned back to her coffee, busying herself with the sugar and cream.

"Ms. Teller?" Frances turned to find a small bespectacled woman surveying her with concern from behind her small, round glasses. *Mrs. Carlton*, Frances realized. "Do you have a moment?"

"Certainly," said Frances, suppressing a sigh. She gulped her coffee and steeled herself for whatever concerns Tibbets' mother was prepared to voice.

"I'm Liddy Carlton, Tibbets' mother," said Mrs. Carlton. She had a shy, soft voice like a Disney deer. She was much more unassuming than Martina Makepeace. Frances felt herself relax slightly. "Tibbets has spoken so highly of you. I just wanted to come by and say hello."

"That's so kind of her—and you—to say," said Frances, surprised. She was expecting another tidal wave of complaint and subtle accusation.

"It can be difficult, sometimes, for Tibbets to confide

in adults," said Mrs. Carlton. "It's been just the two of us for so long, we have our own little bubble we like to reside in." So, Mrs. Carlton was a single mom. Frances wasn't uncouth enough to ask what happened to Mr. Tibbets. Affair, acrimonious divorce, death. Roll the dice. "I'm so glad she has someone here at Thackeray to talk to."

"She's been a pleasure," said Frances. Sensing an opportunity to turn the tables, she added, "Has Tibbets vocalized any concerns to you, about her friendships here at school?"

"No, not lately." Mrs. Carlton looked concerned. "She was very anxious about making friends when she first started, but then she took up with Rowan and Blair, and the three have been inseparable ever since. Has she mentioned anything to you?"

"No, not as such," said Frances carefully. "Some speculation seems to follow Rowan wherever she goes. I just wondered if you had any specific concerns, or if it was merely the typical gossip such a competitive environment often fosters."

Mrs. Carlton nodded. "Oh yes, it's very competitive— and gossipy—here. I think that Rowan has been an exceptional influence on Tibbets. She's really come out of her shell. I couldn't be happier that the girls are friends. It's probably just petty jealousy, in my opinion."

"Thank you for your insight," said Frances. "It's hard to determine these things initially, as a new teacher."

"You're welcome." Mrs. Carlton smiled warmly, and Frances found herself wanting to continue talking to the woman in the hopes of keeping the less pleasant parents at bay. But it was too late. Mrs. Carlton had barely finished speaking when an icy blonde in stiletto heels and a black power suit appeared at her side, nudging her out of the way. Mrs. Carlton looked startled.

"Hello, Lydia," the blonde woman tossed over her shoulder with barely a glance in the smaller woman's direction. She stuck out her hand and Frances, after a confused pause, reciprocated. "Homily Vanderbilt. I'm the founder of Integra, the college comparison app?"

"Oh, I just started using that," said Mrs. Carlton brightly. "I didn't realize that was you, Homily."

"Obviously it's me," said Homily. "Everyone knows that, Liddy." She turned back to Frances, who was still reeling at her sudden appearance. Homily? What kind of parents named an innocent, unsuspecting baby Homily? Although it seemed more likely that this woman had sprung from her father's skull fully formed.

"Listen, I've got to talk to you about Blair," said Homily, zeroing in on Frances. "You must keep her away from that brat Rowan Makepeace, or I'll have to wring her neck myself."

"I like Rowan," said Mrs. Carlton meekly.

Homily ignored her. "All that girl cares about is sneaking out after hours to meet boys," she said. "Blair's got more important things on her plate. Blair is getting her MBA from Barnard, just like I did. Rowan's a society girl, but Blair is a worker. Do you see what I'm getting at?"

Frances didn't see either of the girls through this lens, disagreeing entirely with these assessments. But like Martina Makepeace, she could see that Homily Vanderbilt wasn't one to accept a counterpoint.

"Blair's very hard-working," Frances agreed. "I've seen

it. I've already got a close eye on her, Ms. Vanderbilt." She felt certain that if there was a Mr. Vanderbilt, he had changed his name, not the other way around. "I'll certainly continue to do so."

"Good." Homily gave a satisfied little nod. "That's all I wanted to hear." Her agenda fulfilled, she clicked away rapidly on her icepick heels.

"Well!" said Mrs. Carlton brightly. "Isn't she something!"

"That's one way of putting it," Frances accidently said out loud. Mrs. Carlton snorted with laughter, then quickly looked around to see if anyone had heard her.

FRANCES WAS RIGHT about the headmistress. She waited until the Monday morning assembly to make her announcement.

"I see none of you took my previous requests to heart," she said with no preamble after she'd approached the podium. "Yet another one of these ridiculous pranks! The morning of the recession on Parents' Weekend, no less. I'm sorry to see that someone here is so determined to cause a disruption, undermine the school, and flout authority that they would be so blatant. As I previously stipulated, we will be relocating all of you to the other side of the lake until we've apprehended the culprit. If you're averse to this scenario and have any information regarding the guilty party—or parties—it would obviously be in your best interest, and the best interest of everyone, to come forward."

The headmistress surveyed the audience imperiously

as the students erupted into cries of dismay and flurries of discussion, little fires all over the room. Frances found her eyes drawn to the back row, where Rowan and her ladies-in-waiting sat. She wanted to evaluate their reaction. Tibbets and Blair were whispering frantically.

Rowan, seated between them, looked positively serene.

13

THE OTHER SIDE OF THE LAKE

The girls marched around the lake in a grim single-file line, hunched beneath the weight of their backpacks like little turtles. They had the air of prisoners-of-war being marched into the enemy camp. They would be permitted to return to their side of the lake for meals, free periods, and at night, but all their classes would take place on the other side of the lake at the boys' school until the headmistress "got to the bottom of things," as she put it.

The relegation to the boys' school was not a punishment, she insisted. Frances thought that unlikely since she had essentially framed it as such. Now she claimed it was to have them out of the way while the faculty conducted room-by-room searches, until they found evidence of the culprit behind the recent rash of pranks.

Meanwhile, any of the girls were welcome to schedule a private meeting with either the headmistress or any teacher regarding information about "the suspects." They were encouraged to come forward during free periods and meals, but if their schedules didn't permit, they would be given an excused absence from any class for such a meeting—barring one that took place during a test. Frances could already anticipate the litany of false evidence this would yield from girls hoping to get out of class.

The headmistress seemed to think this was a sterling plan to catch the culprits, but Frances wasn't so sure. (Especially for someone who'd engaged in her own less-than-kosher extracurricular activities during her time at Thackeray.) First of all, why would anyone involved be foolish enough to keep evidence of their involvement in her room? Secondly, someone was very likely to be unfairly accused just so the girls could stop taking classes on the boys' side of the lake.

Not everyone was disgruntled about the move. Brandy was positively whistling as she walked around the lake. "At last, the convent goes co-ed," Frances overheard her say to her roommate.

Frances was walking at the back of the line with her hands buried deep in her fleece-lined pockets. She had no particular feelings about teaching at the boys' school, save a mild curiosity about how much better their facilities likely were. Had she been a student, she would no doubt feel equally as mutinous as the girls. As an adult, her feelings over the matter were far more neutral. She could sympathize but would hardly be affected as her peers—the other teachers—were far less likely to torment her regarding her presence at the school.

If anything, Frances thought as she surveyed the group from the back, the girls might be the likelier tormentors.

It would be too cruel an injustice, to their line of thought, to lose their school only to be harassed. They would ensure that they were the ones doing the harassing. They were no doubt up to something already. She watched them whisper conspiracies, likely a combination of resentment directed at the merry pranksters who relegated them to this cruel fate, plans to find and reveal them, and how they planned to deal with the boys once they arrived at the other campus.

"Is it really so bad?" Anna asked her doubtfully. She was also watching the girls whisper, her expression one of nervous concern. "For them to have classes together?"

"In theory, no," said Frances. "If they were used to it, they wouldn't think twice about it. But they inherit all the old rivalries when they come to Thackeray. The girls think the boys get everything good; the boys insist the same. They get along well enough at mixers and sporting events, where it's more like good-natured teasing. But for some of the legacies, it's a bitterness that runs very deep." She had no doubt in her mind that Homily Vanderbilt, for example, had probably loathed the boys' school in her day.

"But why?" Anna seemed genuinely bewildered. "Why aren't they all just grateful for what they have, this beautiful campus and the academics? How can they possibly have room for concern about who has more beautiful facilities and better academics?"

It was a perfectly reasonable question for someone from down the hill to ask. Frances shook herself of this elitist notion, as it was a rather reasonable remark for an objective outsider to make.

"It's relative," she said. "If they had anything normal to

compare their situation, they would probably be pleased with it—even, as you say, grateful. But this is all they've ever known. Most of them come straight here from Thackeray Day, which is quite similar an environment. They've grown accustomed to their outlandishly high expectations and are incapable of settling for anything less. They consider it a compromise—and a gross imposition— on what they consider themselves entitled to."

"Is that healthy?" said Anna dubiously.

"Probably not," admitted Frances. "The thinking goes that if they have these expectations of themselves, they will never *not* be successful because they cannot accept anything less. I suppose to some degree it's true: things that would be considered perfectly amenable or even highly accomplished for the average student are simply considered beneath them. They have to strive, aspire, and achieve in order to feel validated. They simply don't have a choice. So, it *works*, certainly; but I wouldn't say that it's necessarily good for them. Many of them will grow up without the ability to compromise. To have less is considered on par with failure. It's troubling, I suppose, from that perspective."

Anna shook her head. "I'm starting to think that my wish to go here all my life was a fallacious one," she said.

"It's not a fate I would necessarily wish on an innocent and unsuspecting teenager," Frances acknowledged. "Though for the most part, I found it agreeable."

They had reached the high and imposing gates of the boys' school, wrought iron curlicues elaborately ornamenting the cold black metal. Tom the gardener pulled them open one by one. The girls filed in, cold and exhausted. Classes hadn't even commenced for the day. Frances thought spitefully of the headmistress then, and how unnecessarily taxing this would be for both students and teachers alike.

Just inside the main entrance, everyone huddled together briefly in confused and angry clumps, buzzing like hornets over the crystal chandelier and winding staircase. It wasn't *that* much more elaborate or showy than the girls' own school—but it was noticeably older and more austere, certainly enough to annoy them.

The headmistress glided through the resentful throng and ascended the steps to regard them from above. "You have all received your schedules with your temporary classroom assignments," said McBride. "If you are not familiar with the boys' school, find your first period teacher or a buddy and walk with them to your first class. If you have any difficulty finding the second, feel free to ask anyone in the hallways. Everyone has been instructed to act with utmost respect, decorum, and chivalry."

There was a loud snort in front of Frances, and she glanced over to see Blair surveying the headmistress with raised eyebrows and a haughty expression. "Yeah, right," she uttered under her breath.

The headmistress ignored the rippling murmurs of dissent and descended the stairs. To Frances's surprise, she approached her immediately.

"Frances, you have a free period first thing, do you not?" McBride studied her so severely that for a moment, Frances forgot her own schedule.

"I'm overseeing a study hall in the library," Frances said, recovering her bearings.

"That's right. After the study hall, if you could join the task force in searching the east wing, I would much appreciate your assistance." *Task force?* That sounded a little extreme.

Frances felt herself deflate. She had just hiked all the way around the frozen lake and was now being asked to make the trip another three times—for the search, for her class, then back to the dorm in the evening. Clearly, the headmistress had not designed her "task force" with any regard to the teachers on it.

"Certainly, Headmistress." Thackeray girls were stalwart, first and foremost, and complaining of the cold or its ensuing discomfort would do her no good.

"Thank you," the headmistress said cordially, as if she had offered her a choice. "If you find anything…unsavory, please remember to bring it to me first before you mention it to anyone else."

"Yes, Headmistress." Frances watched her retreat into the crowd, feeling frustrated and resentful.

What was McBride so certain they were going to uncover? And why was she so desperate to cover it up?

THE STUDY HALL, which was shared in the library with a boys' study period, started off peacefully enough. The girls and boys congregated uncertainly on opposite sides of the room, not unlike a middle school dance. Frances remembered her conversation with Anna that morning and wondered how healthy this environment was for any of them. Even when integrating the school, the powers that be had determined it was best to keep the girls and boys separate so they wouldn't "distract" each other. Now they eyed each other warily, as if dreading having to one day share society with one another.

Frances sighed and settled into her hard, wooden chair towards the back of the library. She cracked an onerous tome profiling abnormal psychology, her principal interest since high school. Since the first abnormal personality she'd ever encountered: Jane.

Today Frances was reading about the damage incurred by narcissistic personalities, and the ease they exhibited in controlling and gaslighting those around them. She was curious to see how traits correlated with what she'd witnessed in Rowan Makepeace. Frances had scarcely glanced at the first paragraph of the chapter when a shadow fell over her from above. She glanced up and nearly dropped her book on the floor.

It was Rutherford Hayes, the love of Frances's sophomore year—until he'd tried to date Elizabeth at the same time and convince her not to tell Frances. To Elizabeth's credit, she'd told Frances immediately. For the remainder of school, he was her greatest enemy. Now he stood here, hovering over her as if they were dear old friends. Frances narrowed her eyes. What was he even doing here?

"You teach here?" she finally asked in lieu of a greeting.

"Since I finished grad school, actually." He drew up a chair next to her as if she'd invited him, rather than inwardly replaying every betrayal and humiliation he'd subjected her to on a loop inside her head.

"Weren't you supposed to become a hedge fund manager or something?" Frances asked. She determinedly fixed her gaze on her book, as if she couldn't care less he was there.

"That hardly equals the pleasure of molding hundreds of young minds," he said, smiling pleasantly. It was his same old charming Rutherford smile. She resisted the urge to poke him in the eye.

"How noble of you," she said coldly. "How unfortunate for them."

"You're not still mad at me, are you?" He looked surprised. "That was so long ago."

"The passage of time is not a reflection on character," said Frances. "That is an excuse that corrupt people hide behind, saying that they didn't know any better. You knew what you were doing. You didn't care. Am I supposed to be excited to see you?" Frances uttered this in a voice barely above a whisper, glancing around to make sure none of the students heard her. One watched her curiously: Rowan Makepeace. When she met Frances's gaze, she quickly redirected her eyes back to the book in front of her. Great. Just what she needed, more student speculation on her personal life.

"I'd hoped we could put all that behind us when you came to work here," said Rutherford regretfully. "Water under the bridge and all that. I came by to broker a sort of informal peace treaty. Didn't your landlady tell you?" Frances remembered Velma's questions about the tall, dark, and handsome stranger who'd stopped by. She'd summarily dismissed it without considering who it might be.

"That was you?" Frances stared.

"Yes, it was," he said, sounding pleased.

Frances lowered her face closer to his. "If I'd known that, I would have moved sooner." She rose to her feet and shoved her book in her bag. "Excuse me." She found a different table in the corner and sat with her back to him.

Maybe it was petty, she reflected, to hold him to the things he'd done as a teenager. She herself had been party to burning down a church, so who was she to judge? It was ironic, Frances thought, but it didn't make her remember him any more fondly.

Rather, she speculated on one of the few pieces of advice her aunt had ever given her (aside from her gospel truth regarding red lipstick). Remember, her aunt told her. No matter how much a bad man tells you he's changed, or improved, or come to Jesus or whatever the excuse is, remember the golden rule: once a devil, always a devil.

FRANCES SLOGGED her way through the freshly falling snow back to the girls' school in preparation for McBride's task force. She would be conducting room-by-room searches with Anna until they broke for lunch, then going back to the boys' school to teach her class. Then she'd return for dinner and bed. It was a ridiculous amount of work for something they were never going to find, thought Frances, resentful over being required to waste her time on such a fruitless endeavor. She remained close-mouthed about it when she met up with Anna at the end of the east wing. She was surprised when Anna handed her a skeleton key and told her to check Rowan's room first. She had been sure that Anna would be eager to search Rowan's room herself.

"Rowan seems to think I have an unfair bias against her," Anna admitted ruefully at the expression of confused surprise on Frances's face. "If I'm the one who searches her room, and I find something there, she'll insist that I planted it. No, really," she said as Frances started to protest. "She's made numerous complaints to the head-mistress and her parents against me. Claiming that I'm 'out to get her,' whatever that means. I am a bit hard on Rowan at times, I admit, but only because I know how much better she can be."

"These girls want allies, not coaches," said Frances, accepting the key. "It's very noble of you to want to better them, but it's something they'll only recognize from a distance, in hindsight. I wouldn't take it personally."

"I don't," said Anna. "Nonetheless, it's probably best if you do the honors."

Frances unlocked the door and opened it. She had just crossed the threshold when she glanced down at the desk nearest to the door and stopped dead in her tracks. Nothing was out of place or particularly out of the ordi-nary; not to anyone but Frances, that is. The meticulous neatness of the desk's contents—Post-It notes, paper-weight, day planner, desk calendar—made her certain it was Rowan's. Centered neatly on top of her blotter was Oscar Wilde's *The Picture of Dorian Gray.* Like the scent of Jane's favorite perfume hanging in the air, it instantly transported Frances to another place in her mind.

.   .   .

AP ENGLISH and Jane's obsession. They'd been assigned the book first term, and she couldn't stop talking about it.

"It makes perfect sense, complete and total sense," she kept saying over breakfast in the dining hall. "Youth is all that matters—youth, perfection, beauty. This is the most important time in our lives. We have a narrow window to experience perfection, and we must exploit it to our fullest advantage."

Elizabeth rolled her eyes. "It's really not that novel a concept," she mumbled into her sausage. Frances was startled to see her eating grease, then realized she was hungover, which was the only time Elizabeth ate grease—or anything at all.

"Wasn't Wilde put on trial for obscenity over it?" asked Haley, shoving down another forkful of eggs. She ran cross country in the fall and became a calorie-consumption machine.

"He was unjustly accused," mumbled Bethany into her World Cultures book, riddled with a rainbow of highlighter.

"Well, I realize that," said Haley defensively. "I was just clarifying."

"Haley, did you even do the reading?" Jane said impatiently. "This isn't just for school, you know. This is furthering us as people. It's expanding our reality, and our minds."

Frances bit her lip but refrained from contributing to the conversation. She'd recently done a report on Charles Manson for her American History independent study project. Her teacher had found the topic morbid, but reluctantly agreed. There were times when Jane reminded her of Manson: charismatic, influential. Dangerous.

"Can I see that?" she asked. Jane slid her copy of the book across the table. She studied the young man on the front cover of Jane's edition: austere, dignified, cold. He reminded her of Elizabeth.

"Reminds me of you," remarked Elizabeth, studying the cover at the same time that she was. Frances looked up and smiled, catching her gaze. It was like they could read each other's minds.

Jane watched them disapprovingly. She snatched the book back. "Dorian Gray realized things we can only dream about, stuck here in our prosaic little lives."

"Dorian Gray is not a real person," said Elizabeth calmly. "He's a character in a book, and you need to calm down. As usual." Elizabeth got up and dumped the remainder of her sausage in the trash. "I'm going back to bed."

"You'll miss calc!" gasped Bethany, scandalized.

Elizabeth shrugged, her classic little *oh well* shrug. "Take notes for me, will ya?" She shrugged her messenger bag onto her shoulder and headed for the exit.

"What should I tell Mr. Walczak?" called Bethany.

"Tell him I'm dead," said Elizabeth without turning around.

"Tell him she's skipping," said Jane disdainfully. "She's taking advantage of you, Bethany."

"It's nothing you don't do," Bethany mumbled, burying her face in her book again.

"What was that?" said Jane sharply.

"She said," Frances said slowly and clearly, startling

herself with the sound of her own voice. "That it's nothing you don't do. Which is perfectly accurate." She returned her attention to the plate of home fries and toast in front of her.

Jane studied Bethany, then Frances. Her expression wasn't hostile, merely curious. Assessing. "Okay," she said simply. "Whatever floats your boat." She got up and gathered her things before heading to the trashcan to dump her tray. "Later, haters."

"See you." Haley promptly returned her attention to her eggs, the moment of tension gone. Bethany glanced up from her book and caught Frances's eye.

Thank you, she mouthed, her expression grateful. Frances smiled slightly. She and Jane got along well enough, most of the time. But Frances was hugely touchy about what she perceived as Jane's proclivity to bully the others. Elizabeth would never put up with it, of course; she could dish it as well as she took it. But Bethany and Haley always struck her as vulnerable, Bethany especially. It bothered her. And for whatever reason, Jane always acquiesced.

"Gotta go, I'm late for morning practice," said Haley, jumping up from the table and taking off with her gear, cleats slung over one shoulder.

"I should get to calc," said Bethany, gathering up her books and notes.

"See you at lunch." Frances had a free period first thing, and so she took her time leaving the table. It wasn't until Bethany had gone that she reached for her things and realized that Jane had left her book behind. Frances picked it up and studied it again. She flipped absently through the pages, reading Jane's hastily scrawled notes in the margin. One in particular caught her attention:

Does anyone really matter? Anyone but ourselves?
Would there be anything finer than to experience
complete and utter annihilation
in our sad and limited lifetimes?

FRANCES CLOSED THE BOOK, disturbed. It was typical Prozac nation, pseudo intellectual, angsty stuff. But something about Jane always went a little beyond the ordinary teenage angst.

She shoved the book in her bag, resolving to give it back to Jane when she saw her at lunch. In the meantime, she had a very important secret rendezvous to attend on the other side of the lake.

ANNA HAD STARTED at the opposite end of the hall in Brandy's room while Frances unlocked the door to Rowan's suite. In many ways, it was nearly identical to the one she had inhabited during her time at Thackeray: the quilt folded neatly at the end of the bed, for that little touch of home. Posters tacked to the walls; fairy lights strung up around the windowsill. The cacophony of make-up scattered across a dresser, the oil spill of clothes oozing out of a closet across the floor. The only difference was the lack of a corkboard covered in prints from a disposable camera. All their pictures were online.

Rowan's space was fastidiously spotless in comparison to the rest of the room. Frances roamed around the room aimlessly at first, not even searching, but treating it more like a museum of other people's lives: Blair's expensive perfume on the dresser, her leopard-print towel. Tibbets' bookcase, bulging with science fiction and high fantasy. And Rowan's oddly sterile space. Reluctantly, Frances ran a hand along the underside of the mattress, hating the idea of violating their privacy, and for what? The unlikely notion that they might have caught and released a flock of birds at the start of Parents' Weekend?

Frances was startled when her hand hit the hard spine of a book, not unlike the yearbook she'd discovered in her own room. Seeds of doubt began to germinate in her mind. Maybe Anna and the headmistress were right. Maybe it was Frances who was mistaken. Or was it just a journal? Frances pulled the book out and dropped it with a little shriek.

There was no mistaking what the book was. It was the same black book they'd discovered in the library, all those years ago. The same book that led to the deaths of Bethany and Jane.

14

THE SECRET RITUAL

"*F*rances? Did you find anything?"

Frances shoved the book under her sweater as Anna rounded the corner and entered the room.

"No, nothing," she said in what she hoped sounded like a regretful tone. "Not yet, anyway."

"I'm sure they wouldn't be foolish enough to leave anything incriminating in here, especially when they knew their rooms would be searched." Jane's eyes swept the room with laser-like intensity. "Really, we'd need the combination to their gym lockers and access to their email accounts, if we wanted to be truly thorough. Both of which the headmistress remains reluctant to distribute. Something about violating their privacy."

"It's part of the honor system at Thackeray," said Frances, annoyed. Hack their email? Was she serious? "It's a sort of unspoken agreement that neither the faculty nor the headmistress will violate your privacy unless you give them a reason to."

"I would think the recent episodes would be reason enough, but apparently not," said Anna with a sigh.

"She's probably waiting until she has hard evidence against one student in particular," said Frances. "Avoiding a lawsuit. Even searching the rooms is pretty extreme."

"They're children," said Anna, sounding exasperated. "Teenagers, but still. That's even worse, as far as I'm concerned. They don't know what they're doing. They need guidance."

"Thackeray treats its students as young adults, under the theory that they'll be more likely to act that way," said Frances. She tightened her arms across her chest. She was aware it made her look even more defensive than she sounded already, but she felt the book slipping a little beneath her belted cardigan. She didn't even know why she was standing here arguing with Anna about this. She should be back in her room hiding it under the mattress. Or maybe someplace a little more imaginative, given how quickly she'd found it under Rowan's. Still, she hated to hear the school spoken of this way. "The theory goes that if we treat them like children, they'll act like children," Frances continued. Even after all these years, she felt an inexplicable need to defend the school.

"Or treat them as adults, and they'll act like criminals," Anna countered. "I would love to get my hands on whoever is responsible. This is taking up so much time and energy and effort that should be put into learning."

On this, at least, Frances felt they could agree. "Speaking of which, I have to teach a class at one," said Frances, edging towards the door. "Which doesn't give me long to get back."

"See you at dinner?" said Anna, already turning back to glance thoughtfully at the empty room.

"Sure, see you." Frances practically ran back to her room. She had only twenty minutes before she had to teach her class across the lake. It would take at least eighteen of them just to walk back to the boys' side. She hastily shoved the book under a pile of sweaters in the bottom drawer of her wardrobe.

BY THE TIME dinner rolled around, Frances was cold and exhausted. It was the fourth trip she'd made around the lake that day. If this went on for longer than a week, she would just have to say something to the headmistress, that was all. Maybe get some of the other teachers involved. Not that she wanted to form some sort of union; just to explain how taxing it was on both them and the students for the sake of a witch hunt.

But maybe without using the term witch hunt.

She had zero interest in sitting down to dinner and making polite small talk with the other teachers. All she'd been able to think about, since that afternoon, was the book. She couldn't keep the image of the book at the bottom of the wardrobe out of her head. Jane had refused to let the others read it, and they'd gotten mere glimpses of it over the few weeks that Jane had it in her possession. What was in it? What dark secrets did it conceal?

Frances grabbed an apple and a grab-and-go salad from the salad bar to take back to her room, so she'd have something for later that evening after the dining hall closed. She got a fresh black coffee from the teacher's lounge and hurried upstairs. She spent the rest of the day wondering, at the back of her mind, if the book would somehow vanish from the wardrobe before she had a chance to read it. It was an unreasonable thing to imagine, she knew, but hadn't it vanished (in a manner of speaking) from Rowan's room just that afternoon? It had disappeared because she'd taken it, but that's how easily the book changed hands. If she'd taken it in the first place, someone could easily sneak in and take it back.

Frances rifled through the sweaters in her drawer, feeling a sense of relief as her hand closed around the hard spine of the book. Her relief was immediately tempered by a sense of trepidation at what she might find once she opened it.

She took her coffee and the book over to her bed beneath the window and wrapped her throw blanket around her shoulders. The room had grown bitingly chilly, and she held her hand briefly over the radiator to make sure it was still working. It was, which made the cold seem inexplicable. Frances pushed this thought from her brain and what it might mean.

She glanced down at the book and ran her hand over the well-worn leather cover. It looked unchanged. The first thing she noticed was a dark red tassel peeking out of a section towards the back. Cracking the spine, she flipped back to that page and felt the cold wash over her in waves. It was the same ritual Jane had insisted they perform in the chapel the night of the fire.

Frances squinted at the page. Something was different. Jane had insisted the ritual would protect them and ensure good luck for their futures—that they would be accepted to only the best colleges, that they would pass all their mid-terms and finals with flying colors, that they would be surrounded by the best people and get the jobs of their dreams. It all sounded a little lofty to Frances, this idea that they could have whatever they wanted with no work on their part. These were all things that were attainable only if one worked at having them.

But Jane was utterly convinced. It was this certainty on her part that eventually caused Frances to relent. Not because she believed, but because she pitied Jane in thinking that a book could solve her problems. Whatever Jane's life was, she was even more close-mouthed about it than Frances was—which led her to assume that whatever Jane's life consisted of, it was probably bad. Otherwise, why begrudge her this strange belief that she could somehow magic it all away if she only spoke the right words?

Frances scanned the page. She could see where Jane had gotten her crackpot ideas from: the book suggested that if the reader wished to have everlasting fortune in all endeavors, the reader must bring a circle of four or more to a holy place, "a sacred ground," and light a candle for each person in the circle while speaking the incantation.

But there was a final requirement, one Jane had never mentioned. The book instructed the reader to bring a "sacrificial lamb." It said that a life must be given in order for a life to be eternally assured. While the reader could use a literal lamb and see an immediate return on the ritual in a superficial sense, in order to have true, undying, everlasting fortune, a human sacrifice was required.

A human sacrifice required. Frances slammed the book

shut and stared at the wall. Had Jane brought them to the chapel intending to sacrifice one of them? She thought of Bethany, trapped in the flames. Had Jane succeeded? And failed only at escaping herself?

Frances remembered the way the flames had raced down the pew as if following a trail. At the time, her macabre teenage imagination thought that maybe the ritual had worked, and there were evil spirits there that night—some dark shadow that fed on what they were doing and lit the church ablaze. How could a bunch of candles, even carelessly knocked over in their haste to escape, cause the whole church to go up like that? Unless someone had gone there ahead of time and doused the floors in gasoline.

Maybe Jane had intended for one of them to remain in the chapel that night, trapped in the flames as it burned to the ground. Maybe even all of them. Because if one life would guarantee her a lifetime of wealth and happiness, how much would she gain from four?

Frances pushed the thought from her head. Jane had treated them all badly in turn, it was true, but surely she hadn't meant for them to die. Surely she wasn't *that* insane, was she? Then again, there had always been something dark about Jane from the beginning. Frances noticed it, and she knew Elizabeth did, too. It was why they kept their distance. Frances had always thought there was something off, and Jane had only ever proved her right.

FOUR WEEKS before the chapel fire, a month before winter

vacation, Frances was getting ready for bed in the room she shared with Elizabeth. Elizabeth was already burrowed beneath her downy covers with her eye mask pulled over her face and her earplugs in to blot out all noise and light. Sensory deprivation, she called it. Frances grabbed her toothbrush and her toothpaste from her shower bucket and went down the hall to the bathroom.

After she brushed her teeth, she stopped in one of the stalls to use the bathroom before she went to bed. The temperature dropped below freezing most nights, and there was nothing worse than waking up in the dead of the night and having to creep down the ice-cold hallway to the bathroom.

Frances always chose the stall around the corner. It was set back in a shallow alcove. It gave her the illusion of privacy among eleven other girls, but it also rendered her invisible to anyone else in the bathroom at the same time. She had just slid the lock in place when the bathroom door swung inward. Frances listened as slippered foot-steps shuffled across the tile floor.

There were six rooms in the wing and twelve girls in the hall. Frances tried to guess by the sound of the foot-steps alone which one of them it was. She could usually recognize Bethany's hesitant tread and Haley's loping gallop with little to no effort. Elizabeth's footsteps were light like a fox on packed snow, barely audible. Jane just sounded like anybody else thudding thoughtlessly along, and so the person entering the bathroom could have been her—or anyone. But then Frances heard her voice.

"Soon, it will happen. Soon, we will never have to worry again. Soon, it will all make sense." Frances thought she must have come in with Bethany. Elizabeth was the only one of them with a cell phone, so it wasn't like she could have been talking to anyone else.

Jane kept up her rhythmic chanting about *soon this, soon that*, and Frances started getting uneasy. She looked under the door and saw only one pair of feet: the furry brown moccasin slippers that Jane wore before bed. Was she talking to herself? Frances hoped she wouldn't realize there was anyone else in the bathroom besides her. She was acting pretty weird.

The sink turned on, then off. Then the sound of the water being turned on and off repeated rhythmically, another six times while Jane chanted to herself. Did Jane have OCD? Frances read about it in one of her uncle's many onerous tomes, but this felt different than the case studies she'd read. There was something almost…unsettling about it.

Frances felt relieved when the water turned off for a final time and Jane ceased to chant. She waited, holding her breath, as Jane's shuffling footsteps made their way to the door. The door swung shut. Jane was gone. Frances made her way around the corner to the sink. She felt a little shaky. When she reached the mirror, she stopped and stared.

Someone—Jane—had drawn four tally marks across the mirror, four broad slashes in bright red lipstick.

FRANCES TURNED the memory over in her mind. Jane had been behaving oddly, but no more oddly than any young girl devising her own peculiar system of beliefs. It didn't mean she'd been planning to kill them. Even when Frances added it to what she discovered in the book. But it wasn't the only strange thing about Jane. As the memories came—first pebbles, then rocks, building slowly towards an avalanche—Frances began to wonder if she was the only one who noticed. She knew that she wasn't. The problem was, the only people who could corroborate her story were the last people who would ever want to talk about the past.

And the people who could confirm it with a complete certainty were now dead.

15

THE STRANGE THING ABOUT JANE

*F*rances tried Elizabeth first. Elizabeth would be harder to find because Elizabeth was like a ghost. She used exactly zero social media and had been prone towards secrecy even before she married some senator or another. They'd exchanged the occasional email over the years; nothing elaborate, just polite formalities. Once Elizabeth transferred, it was as if they both realized that they no longer had to remind one another of the tragedy that had taken place in their youth and were free to start their lives anew.

Frances highly doubted that Elizabeth had the same number she'd had since high school. But she also knew people who were religious about never changing their number, keeping it the way they'd cling to some other identifying aspect of themselves. As if it was part of who they were. Frances had never known Elizabeth to be sentimental about anything or want to make sure that the people she'd known back then would always have some way of reaching her, so she dialed the old number with little to no expectations.

Frances sat idly by her bedroom window, listening to the phone ring as she watched the morning snow accumulate on the ground. The light had a way of reflecting off the bright white snow early in the morning that made her feel like she was in a fairy tale. Or dead and in some kind of heaven. It usually depended on how morbid she felt. Today it was the latter.

"Hello?" The voice that answered the phone was guarded. It was also undoubtedly Elizabeth.

"Elizabeth?" She tried to keep the shock out of her voice. She had kept her number after all. "It's Frances. Frances Teller."

"Frances?" Elizabeth didn't bother to conceal the shock in hers. It had been at least ten years since they'd spoken last.

"I'm sorry to call you like this," said Frances. With Elizabeth, it was best never to mince words. "I know there's a lot of things you'd rather forget. I would, too. But I'm at Thackeray and I think it might come up again. For all of us."

"Where should we meet?" Elizabeth's tone was brisk. She didn't ask Frances to elaborate, nor vocalize any doubt as to what she was saying. It was almost as if she'd been waiting for a call like this. "I don't want to talk about this over the phone."

"Meet?" Frances was startled. She'd expected this would be like pulling teeth. Not only had Elizabeth agreed to meet her, she was the one instigating the meeting itself.

"Yes, meet." Elizabeth's voice was impatient. "Immediately. My husband is up for re-election, and we can't afford a scandal."

Of course. No wonder she was in such a hurry. "Um, maybe the nearest city for all of us? Maybe Montpelier?"

"Convenient for me, since I live here. Have you tried Haley yet?"

"Not yet, I was just going—"

"Good luck. I'm pretty sure all she does is get high and make things out of wire."

"She might get back to me. If she knows how important it is."

"That's true." Frances had forgotten Elizabeth's dry, sardonic sense of humor that she had once loved so well. "I find that people will often prioritize things, if they're frightened enough."

SHE TRIED HALEY NEXT, hoping that her luck would hold. She didn't have a phone number for her, but her contact information was listed on Haley's alma mater's website, where she was currently the artist-in-residence. She sent her the slightly cryptic message of, *At Thackeray. Past no longer past. Please contact ASAP. F.*

Given what Elizabeth had said, Frances didn't expect to hear back right away, or maybe at all. She had barely left the room for breakfast when her phone dinged with a new email notification.

The message was brief, and consisted of only two words:

When/where?

. . .

FRANCES CHOSE a coffee shop slightly off the beaten path in downtown Montpelier, figuring they would be less likely to be overheard. She got there early and chose a booth in the back, near the espresso machines. The sound of grinding beans would ideally obscure any conversation that took place.

Elizabeth arrived first, sweeping through the door in her billowing white coat and dark sunglasses. Frances had forgotten how heart-stoppingly beautiful she was: the arresting sight of her entering a room. Both the man at the front sitting by the window and the only barista behind the counter stopped what they were doing and momentarily stared before shaking themselves and resuming their respective activities, pretending not to notice her.

Elizabeth was so used to it she barely spared them a sideways glance. She strolled up to the booth Frances was seated in and plunked her simple Chanel clutch on the table before sliding in the booth across from her.

"Sounds like the shit's hit the proverbial fan," she said by way of greeting. "What are you doing back at Thackeray, anyway?"

"Teaching," said Frances, taking a small sip of her espresso.

Elizabeth snorted. Then she saw that Frances was serious.

"Oh, you're serious," she said. "I thought you were kidding."

"Why would I be kidding?" Frances said, annoyed.

"Because you hate everyone under the age of twenty-one and vowed never to return to Thackeray after graduation?" suggested Elizabeth, taking a drink of Frances's coffee with a familiarity that time had not served to lessen. "I'm quoting you here."

"It's not so bad." Frances wondered how her life looked through Elizabeth's eyes: back at Thackeray, one of the people they'd once disrespected and defied. Maybe she pitied her.

"Frances, why didn't you just find someone to lie to for the rest of your life?" Elizabeth got right to the point, blunt as always. "I did, and now I'm rich. Richer, anyway. I don't have to work. I don't have to think." She picked the clutch up and gave it a shake. It emitted a telltale rattle. "I don't even have to feel. I don't know why you persist on punishing yourself. You always have."

"I don't want to have to lie to anyone," said Frances. "I never met anyone worth lying to."

"Do you think that I did?" Elizabeth rolled her eyes. "It wasn't about finding someone worthwhile; it was mostly about finding someone I could tolerate without screaming or wanting to rip my hair out. Luckily, he's never home, so it's rarely an issue."

"How romantic," Frances said dryly.

"Since when do you care about romance?" Elizabeth glanced around. "Are we going to cut to the chase here, or are we waiting for the star quarterback?"

"I don't think she's athletic anymore."

"Frances, be serious. I was alluding to her illustrious past as Thackeray's varsity champion, and whatever else it was that she did before she discovered ayahuasca and painting. Speak of the devil." Elizbeth quirked an eyebrow and nodded towards the door.

Haley entered hesitantly, as if considering turning around and running in the other direction. She wore fishing boots and paint-splattered overalls under a black puffer coat. "And the award for worst-dressed at an impromptu reunion goes to…" Elizabeth intoned. Frances kicked her under the table.

Haley held up a finger and mouthed *one minute* as she went over to the counter. "Get me a macchiato, pretty please," Elizabeth called. Haley rolled her eyes and nodded. It was as if no time had passed since they'd seen each other last.

Elizabeth reached for her clutch. "Be right back," she promised Frances before gliding away towards the restroom. If Frances knew her old roommate, she had a date in the handicapped stall with the pharmacy she kept in her bag.

Haley came to the table with two steaming mugs. She slid into the booth across from Frances, right into Elizabeth's recently vacated spot.

"How are you?" She studied Frances seriously from behind her trendy, asymmetrical thick-framed glasses. Her hair was propped up in a messy bun atop her head. She wore no make-up. She looked like a very different person from the Haley that Frances had once knew, but her eyes were exactly the same. Thoughtful and a little bit pensive.

"I'm good." Frances smiled warmly. She and Haley had always gotten along, probably the best of all of them after Elizabeth and Frances, simply because they lived together. Bethany and Jane had what was very plainly a master-servant relationship, while Jane and

Elizabeth could barely stand each other. "How are you?"

"My art is going well," said Haley. "Which, to me, is all that matters." There was a brief silence while she considered what to say next. "Is it bad?"

"Not yet," said Frances. "Maybe soon. It might be too early to say."

"Don't start without me." Elizabeth collapsed back into the booth next to Haley and wrapped her hands around the fresh mug of coffee in front of her. "What's going on?"

"I found the book," Frances said. "The one Jane had."

Elizabeth and Haley stared. "The one from the library?" asked Haley.

"*Was* it from the library?" asked Frances. "Or did we just find it there?"

"Who knows where it came from?" Elizabeth sounded uncomfortable. "Who cares? It was just some old book that Jane dug up out of nowhere and used to channel all her depraved fantasies."

"I found it in a girl's room," said Frances. "With the same ritual marked that Jane was trying to perform."

"Maybe it's just a coincidence." Haley sounded fearful, as if trying to convince herself.

"I don't think it is." Frances elaborated more on the strange going-ons since she'd arrived at the school: the silhouette, the yearbook, the birds.

"You know what I think it is?" said Elizabeth once Frances had concluded. "I think one of those little brats found out you went to Thackeray the year of the fire. I think they're messing with everybody, trying to make them think there are ghosts. And now they're messing with you. Anyone can steal a copy of the yearbook, from any year, from the library. Have you checked to see if the library copy is missing yet?"

"No," Frances admitted. "I didn't think of it."

"Well, maybe you should." Elizabeth gave a satisfied little nod and leaned back against the padded booth.

"Of course McBride is using all this to instill a new totalitarian regime," Haley fumed. "Once a dictator, always a dictator."

"She's not a dictator." Elizabeth laughed. "She's just an old prune who has obviously not been with a man for a very long time. A human one, anyway."

"As opposed to what?" asked Frances. "A dead one?"

"I don't know," said Elizabeth thoughtfully. "She has that massive portrait of the first headmaster hanging on the wall. Maybe she's in love with him. In love with his ghost."

"Do you think the stories are real?" Haley said suddenly. She looked at Frances. "I mean, the stories your students told you?"

"About the ghosts?" Frances glanced down into her empty mug, regretting not having gotten a larger coffee to act as a buffer for this conversation. "I'm not sure what to believe."

"You two can't be serious." Elizabeth regarded them incredulously. "Ghosts? Are you kidding?"

"I saw something once," Haley said abruptly. "Before we graduated. And again, much later on. Just before I was about to graduate college. And right before my first gallery opening. Every time something good was about to happen. Something monumental."

Elizabeth was temporarily astonished into silence, her expression disbelieving. Frances watched Haley across the table. "What did you see?"

"A shadow, I thought. Of a girl. On my wall, in my room. I was the only one in it at the time. My roommate had gone home for the weekend. And this shadow was right in front of the desk, like somebody was sitting there. All night. I couldn't move, I couldn't stop watching it. Waiting for it to do something. I stayed that way till it got light out, and gradually it faded away."

Elizabeth shook her head. "That could have been a trick of the light."

Haley, used to ignoring Elizabeth, shook her head. "It was no trick. It looked like a girl, studying. Before I graduated, I was getting ready in the bathroom, fixing my hair. I saw Bethany in the mirror behind me, watching me. I turned around and there was nothing there."

Frances's mug clattered against the saucer. She glanced down and released it from her shaking hand, tucking it under the table in her lap. "And the last time?"

"It was the night before my first opening. I was really nervous, afraid I was going to get torn apart, that the reviews would be bad. It was the sculpture I made, about Bethany. It…came to life."

"Came to life?" asked Frances, perplexed. "In what way?"

"It was a fake garden with a path through it that led up to a wooden door, made to look like a cottage. You walked up to the door and put your eye against a keyhole, and I had this sort of kaleidoscope rigged up inside? But everyone kept coming up to me telling me about the girl crying behind the keyhole, and how it affected them. They all kept talking about the crying girl. *There was no crying girl.* It was a kaleidoscope. But they all saw it."

"Did you see it?" asked Frances.

"No," whispered Haley. "When I looked, I didn't see anything at all."

Even Elizabeth was silent now. Frances mulled this over. "Did she seem angry? Bethany?"

Haley looked relieved, like she thought they wouldn't believe her. "No, not angry. Just sad. It was almost as if she was…checking in."

"Oh, come on," objected Elizabeth. "You cannot possibly think you saw a ghost! It's entirely too far-fetched. I'm sure we've all had times where we've maybe…*imbibed* too much, and thought we saw something that we didn't, but that doesn't mean it was *real*."

Frances and Haley stared at Elizabeth. "What did you think you saw?" asked Haley.

"Nothing! Okay, well, maybe something. Once. Before I transferred, to NYU? I might have heard something in the bathroom at school. But I was definitely not sober, and I have always chalked it up to that and always will. Okay?"

"What did you hear?" Haley asked.

It was warm inside the coffee shop, the heat turned up high in the small space, but Elizabeth shivered and drew her coat around her tighter. "It was a girl, singing the same note over and over again."

Frances remembered the piano music drifting out of the rehearsal room.

"I was in the stall—the handicapped stall, the one you always tell me not to use,Haley—"

"What if somebody needs it? Somebody actually handicapped?"

"—and just when I threw open the door to tell whoever it was to stop singing that stupid song, whatever it was, it stopped. And I realized there was no one there." Elizabeth stared off into the distance, lost in her memory. Then she seemed to shake herself out of it. "Which doesn't *mean* anything. We were children. We weren't able to process what happened, we never let ourselves. Of course we saw things. Of course we assumed there were things there that weren't. Isn't there a condition for that?" Elizabeth looked pointedly at Frances.

"Post-traumatic stress can have a variety of unforeseen effects on both the body and the mind," said Frances. "I've considered the possibility that I might have experienced stress-induced auditory or visual hallucinations as the result of what happened the night of the fire. But what you described at your show concerns me," she addressed Haley. "For a group of people to see the same thing and then describe it to you, with no previous suggestion on your part of what they might see…it's extremely odd. I don't know what to make of that."

"I didn't either." Haley looked as though she wanted to crawl inside her coffee cup and drown.

"I can't possibly entertain the idea that we're somehow haunted," said Elizabeth, shaking her head. "I have three children under the age of five, which is every inch the living nightmare that it sounds. My husband is in the middle of his most hellish campaign to date. I do *not* have time to entertain ghosts. Even if they are real."

"I'm actually not that concerned about ghosts," said Frances. "Even assuming there is any truth to what we've experienced, what effect can a shadow from another place really cast over our lives? It could be little more than our own guilt. What I'm concerned about is the sort of mass psychosis that Jane was able to create in us all. Because I see it happening again, and I have to stop it. Before it's too late."

SONGS ABOUT JANE

"What do you mean?" asked Haley, a look of concern on her round features.

"Jane was a powerful, enigmatic figure in our lives who used her ability to influence others to control us," Frances explained. "There's currently another girl at Thackeray, not unlike Jane—highly intelligent, controlling, dictatorial—with two girls under her influence. They have the same book Jane did, with the same ritual marked. I have every reason to believe that she's going to attempt to do the same thing that Jane did. And now that I've seen the book—"

"You saw *the book*?" Elizabeth used elaborate air quotes to denote how sacred Jane had always treated it, never allowing any of the others to catch so much as a glimpse of its contents.

"Now that I've seen it," continued Frances. "I have every reason to believe this girl might believe she needs to harm one of her classmates for this 'ritual' to be fulfilled. I believe that's what Jane thought."

Haley paled. "You mean she really did set the fire on purpose?"

"And killed Bethany?" Elizabeth asked.

"Are either of you that surprised?" asked Frances.

They shook their heads. They were all rebellious, straining against the seams of their brocade and velvet prison in a relentless attempt to claw their way out. But it was Jane who was truly serious about it, in a way the others never could seem to touch. It was Jane who pushed hardest to break one more rule, to stay out after curfew one more night. The others were motivated by boredom or stress or some combination of the two, but it was like Jane needed to do bad things in order to feel whole. She was like a reverse-girl, thriving on breaking the rules rather than following them out of fear of being caught and facing serious repercussions, disappointing everyone.

"I need your help," said Frances. "I need to protect these girls now, in a way that we didn't back then. I need you to remember everything you can about Jane."

She was lonely. Or at least alone. That much Frances knew. Even when they were together, Jane was always somehow apart. Sometimes Frances glimpsed her in the hallways or crossing campus from the athletic field back to the dorm, and there was always something so solitary about her, like a shark gliding through the water. Jane was a lone wolf, even when she was surrounded by people. There was something very take-no-prisoners about her.

"It's weird," said Haley, ruminating over her coffee refill. "Because throughout high school, no matter what sport I played, I was always the captain. What's weird is that I didn't resent having to share it with her, even though I was the better player. She just seemed like more a leader somehow, you know? She made me doubt myself."

"Well, I never wanted to be friends with her," said Elizabeth snippily, stealing a sip of Haley's coffee. Her macchiato had been drained to the dregs and Frances's tiny espresso cup was long empty. "The two of you dragged me into it. Just because she shared her cigarette with you and made you laugh at assembly or was really good at hitting a ball with a stick—that didn't make her likable. Or a good person. You were so easily taken in by her."

"That's true," Frances mused. "You never seemed to give into it, really. But it wasn't just those things. If you'd had even a moment with her, you would know she had this way of making you feel...understood."

"Yes!" Haley's eyes lit up. "Like it was the two of you against the world."

"I had you for that," Elizabeth said to Frances. "I didn't need another ally."

"You were both so strong-willed, it was a miracle you got along at all," said Frances.

"We did it for you guys," said Elizabeth impatiently. "Just because we were teenagers didn't mean we were petty and worthless. It would have affected everyone negatively if we fought constantly and tried to drive each other out. You would have taken my side, Bethany would have taken Jane's, Haley would have tried to go back and forth like Switzerland. We respected one another; we just didn't like each other. At all."

"It's true," said Haley. "They always kind of circled each other, but never really drew blood."

And it was true, Frances remembered now. Elizabeth and Jane never did things on their own and rarely addressed each other directly, but still sat together and did everything together without trying to push the other out. Because it was what the others wanted.

"What about Bethany?" mused Haley. "What do you think did it for her?"

"Bethany was a person who liked being controlled," said Frances. "She needed to be told what to do in order to function. Did you ever see her room? Her closet? Her notebooks? She was a mess. Completely sloppy and disorganized, even though she was good at school. She just couldn't keep herself together. Jane kept her together. Jane told her what to do."

"Bethany was one of those girls who had no business being away from home at that age," Elizabeth said. "She still needed her mother. Probably until she left for college and then maybe she would have gotten it together with an RA breathing down her neck and some mindless major like communications or whatever. She just wanted to be taken care of."

It sickened Frances, remembering how vulnerable Bethany was. Who had she been kidding all this time? She didn't blame Bethany for what happened. She wasn't indifferent to her memories. It was devastating what had happened to Bethany, and the truth was that if she let herself remember how much so—even for a second—she might never get out of bed again.

"Bethany wanted a mother," recited Elizabeth. "Haley

wanted a teammate. You wanted…what did you want?" Elizabeth looked at Frances quizzically. "You never seemed to want anything."

"I never really talked about it." Frances debated whether or not to say anymore. Even after all these years, it somehow felt too personal to talk about, too dark to admit. "I wanted to burn the world down," she said after a moment of silence. "So did she."

"But why?" Haley looked startled. Elizabeth, who knew Frances better than anyone—even her aunt and uncle—regarded her somberly. She knew exactly why.

"Everything was taken from me," said Frances. "I hated the world and everyone in it: all the people who got to live happily ever after. She had it, too—that rage. I hid it. She didn't."

"Most of the time she did," said Elizabeth. "Until senior year, anyway."

"Something about that book pushed her over the edge," said Haley. "She was always kind of messed up, but then she became, like…*obsessed*."

"She did," said Elizabeth. "What was it about that book, anyway?" She turned to Frances. "What's *in* it?"

"For one thing, it's extremely old," said Frances. "It's either a limited edition or the only one of its kind that went to press. I've looked online, called rare book dealers and collectors over the years—and it doesn't seem to exist anywhere. Anywhere but wherever Jane found it and later left for someone else to find."

"In the library?" asked Haley.

"I don't think she really found it there in the first place," said Frances. She told them about the day she visited the spooky old bookshop in town, where the woman who predicted her future revealed that another girl had come in shortly before. "It's another one of my theories. Either she bought it there, or it was given to her. Then she pretended to 'stumble' across it in the library, so it could be all of ours together."

"Typical," snorted Elizabeth.

"She wanted it to influence us the way it influenced her," said Frances. "To pull us in. Something about the book's age and its strangeness made it seem real to her. She truly believed that if she performed these rituals as the book decreed, she would get everything she'd ever desired."

"What did she want?" asked Haley. "She never talked about it."

"She never talked about anything," said Frances. "What did any of us know about her life other than what little she told us? She had a father she never saw and a brother at Thackeray none of us met. That was pretty much it."

"I always thought that was weird," Haley mused. "Him being across the lake that whole time, but we never even saw him."

"I always thought it was because she didn't want him to fall in love with Elizabeth," said Frances. "She actually told me that once. When I asked."

"She wanted it easy," said Elizabeth. "I did, too. I popped pills so I could study later and longer. And be skinnier. I cut corners. I always have. I still do. But she was so ruthless about it. Like she thought there was one answer she could apply to everything. Most people just do cocaine and get on with it, but she was looking for, like…a philosophy. She talked about it in World Religion all the time. Finding this one great answer or whatever she thought it was."

"She thought she found it in that book," said Frances. "She thought she discovered the secret to everlasting happiness. But the book suggested that she sacrifice something—or someone. Maybe even multiple people."

"You really think she wanted to kill us?" said Haley with mounting horror.

"I think she considered it," said Frances. "Planned it out, even. But part of me still wants to believe that what happened in the chapel that night was an accident. That she wouldn't have gone through with it. Because she never meant for it to happen to her."

"That excuses nothing," said Elizabeth. "If she lured us down there to burn us alive, then she got what she deserved." Haley clapped a hand over her mouth. "Oh, come off it, Haley. You really mean to tell me that if she was planning to kill you, then you're actually sorry that she's dead?"

"I just can't believe she would do that to us," said Haley, ashen.

"Oh, I can," said Elizabeth. "You know why? Because she was completely and totally insane, that's why. She might have acted low-key about it, but that girl was a walking case study. Wasn't she?" Elizabeth turned to Frances. The expert.

"She displayed characteristics of a classic narcissistic personality," said Frances. "Signs of sociopathic and domineering behavior. I would say she started out borderline, when we were underclassmen. But then something pushed her over the edge."

"School pushed her over the edge," said Elizabeth dryly. "Do you know anyone that place *didn't* make insane? It was like living inside of a crockpot of eating disorders, tossing in the stress of school and organized sports, then stirring it with a big stick made out of Ritalin."

"It was a lot of pressure for girls so young to cope with," Frances acknowledged. "And there was very little release. It would make anyone a little…unhinged. Let alone someone who was already unstable to begin with."

"That's putting it mildly," said Elizabeth.

"Do you guys remember all the guest speakers?" said Haley. "Insanely successful people we couldn't fathom being at fifteen? It just made me feel even more inadequate."

"I thought it was worse when they were kind of lame," said Elizabeth. "Like becoming a tenured professor in Gender Studies at Sarah Lawrence was the most I could ever hope to accomplish. I wanted to move to New York and become Kate Moss, not some dowdy old bag wearing tweed, forgotten in a dusty old library someplace."

"The Olympic gold medalist from the US women's gymnastics team was the worst," said Haley. "I made myself throw up for a week after that one."

"You?" Frances was surprised. "You were always the most stable one of any of us."

"What bathroom did you use?" Elizabeth wanted to know. "I never heard you in there."

"Okay, so maybe it was only like a day," said Haley.

"Once. It just made me realize that I'd worked my entire life to maybe get a college scholarship—at the most. That was the best I could hope for: to be considered 'well-rounded.' I was never going to make it to the Olympics or even nationals—in anything—because I wasn't training ten or twelve hours a day, forcing my body to realize its fullest potential. It was so depressing, like everything I'd ever done had been in vain."

"It got you into Thackeray," Elizabeth pointed out.

"Lucky me," said Haley. They all laughed, then fell into a contemplative silence as the snow fell outside of the window. Elizabeth turned to Frances.

"Why'd you even want to go back, anyway?" she asked.

The truth was simple and obvious, yet too painful to admit, even to her oldest friends. It was the only home she'd ever known.

WALKING WITH A GHOST

$\mathcal{T}$hey parted with promises to keep in touch, insisting that Frances keep them apprised of what was happening at Thackeray. Everyone firmly agreed it was essential that they stay connected this time.

Frances had her doubts. They'd made the same promises the day they'd moved out of Thackeray, promises that eventually faltered over time and distance. They'd found other things and people to occupy their lives. Elizabeth had, anyway. Frances and Haley had remained largely solitary over the years, unsurprising given that two of their closest friends had been horribly killed in a fire at a young age. Frances could see her need to remain alone and unharmed reflected back at her in Haley.

Maybe they would, maybe they wouldn't. It was remarkable the ease with which the time had fallen away, and they'd become a unit again. Frances wanted to pretend that she wasn't alone in the world, but hadn't that always been the case? Before Thackeray, after Thackeray. What was four years compared to a lifetime?

"You've been avoiding me."

He appeared on the path from the parking lot, snow swirling around him and landing on his long black peacoat, startling Frances out of her own dark thoughts. Rutherford Hayes. She sighed.

"I'm not avoiding you." She slammed the door of her car and locked it, then briskly started up the path towards the dorm. Rutherford followed. "I'm not anything you. I literally haven't thought of you in years."

"I thought of you." Rutherford opened his umbrella over her head, shielding her from the fat white flakes that fell from the sky. "Many a time, with utmost regret."

"How tragic. Why didn't you just get Tinder like a normal person?" Frances wondered if he had actual business at the school or had been waiting to ambush her. Didn't he have anything better to do?

"What do you think about this business with the ghost?" he asked conversationally. "I'm actually here to talk to the headmistress about it. It's been a little oppressive on our end, having to accommodate over a hundred additional students, and I was nominated to bring it up with Nurse Ratched."

"It's a little oppressive on our end as well." Frances was half listening, but not really. Her thoughts still lay largely in a coffee shop in Montpelier. It took a moment for her to process the full effect of what he'd said. "Ghost? Why would you even bring that up?"

"It started the year after the fire," he said. He gave no indication that it might be a painful topic for Frances to broach, imparting information like a tour guide taking her around Thackeray. "Of course, everyone thought what was left of the chapel was haunted: an old place like this, a bunch of teenagers with cabin fever, keeping each awake. But then it grew more elaborate."

"Why?" asked Frances. She didn't know what else to say. She mostly just wished he would stop talking.

He shrugged. "Mythology? Ghoulish curiosity? Why do you think they went down there, anyway? Bethany and Jane?"

Frances shrugged. She had forgotten the public perception of their alibi. The story went that she, Elizabeth, and Haley were all in their beds that night. Only Jane and Bethany had gone down to the chapel. It was believable because they were roommates and theoretically might have snuck out on their own. Outside of that, everyone knew that the five of them went everywhere together.

"What difference does it make?" she asked. "They're dead."

This did not deter Rutherford in the slightest, not that she thought it would. Little deterred him, whether it was a wrathful email or a slap across the face. "But why, though? Why sneak into the chapel, of all places?"

"Maybe they were looking for a little religion," said Frances dryly. They were nearly to the front door and she was looking forward to shaking him off once they went inside.

He lowered his voice confidentially. "Everyone at the boys' school thought they were secretly together and looking for a place where they wouldn't get caught."

She stopped in the middle of the path. She didn't like that this business with the pranks—or an actual ghost—was bringing this up again. It felt too close, too dangerous.

"You know," she said slowly. "It's entirely possible."

"I knew it." He seemed excited by the prospect, not so much by the predictable fantasy of two high school girls having an illicit tryst in a boarding school chapel, but for the same reason deep dark dirt fascinated everyone in such a contained environment. It had been over two decades, and still the idea of two perfect prim Thackeray ladies burning down a church with their forbidden passion was thrilling news. Frances felt both disgusted and annoyed.

"Are you happy now?" she asked, opening the front door of the school. He lowered his umbrella and shook the snow off of it before they stepped inside.

"I'm sorry." He sounded genuinely contrite. "I forgot, they were your best friends, right?"

"Since when did you ever care about that?" Frances pivoted on her heel and took the opposite staircase to the east wing, leaving him at the foot of the one that led to the headmistress's office.

It made her sick to think of Bethany and Jane reduced to some pornographic narrative in the boys' school's sordid little rumor mill, though she supposed it was preferable to the possibility that Jane had been a homicidal maniac who had tried to murder all of them. Which led Frances to think, if there had been an accelerant used in the fire, shouldn't there have been an arson investigation? Probably not; not if the headmistress had anything to say about it.

Frances was so lost in thought she barely noticed Anna's door opening when she arrived at her own. She jumped and spun around at the sound of Anna's voice.

"Hello there. Where did you get off to today?" Anna asked.

"Montpelier," said Frances, already thinking about the hot bath and thick robe that awaited her in her room.

"Montpelier! Whatever for?" Anna smiled pleasantly enough, but her eyes were bright and inquisitive. What did she care where Frances went on her day off?

"I had some shopping to do," Frances said, returning Anna's smile. "Not many places to go around here."

"That's for sure," Anna agreed. She glanced down at Frances's empty hands. "What did you get? Anything good?"

"I got an eight ball and a pack of Camel Lights," Frances said brightly. "Do you want to come to my room?"

"What?" Anna stared at her, aghast.

Frances lowered her voice and glanced around conspiratorially. "Have you ever freebased before?"

"I—I don't think that's—" Anna looked sick. Frances laughed at her.

"I'm kidding," she said. "I was at the gynecologist. I was trying to be discreet about it. Obviously, I didn't buy anything. Besides a clean bill of health, of course."

"Oh," Anna said. Now she just looked horribly embarrassed. "Oh, I'm so sorry. I didn't mean to pry, I was just… making conversation. I'll just let you get to bed, then." She hurriedly turned and let herself into her room, shutting the door behind her. Frances almost felt bad but found that she didn't. Still laughing inside, she let herself into her room and locked the door behind her.

That was her thing with Jane, she thought. They both loved lying, and both were exceptionally good at it.

FRANCES WAS STARING up at the ceiling, watching the candlelight flicker and cast its strange shadows. Odd things were happening at the school, but what was causing them—and why? Did it even matter? Because what *was* happening for a complete certainty was the same thing that incited the tragedy of Frances's young life. (One of them, anyway.) A young girl with more energy than these walls could hold was attempting to channel that energy in dark and dangerous ways. How could Frances stop her? Before it was too late?

She could report her suspicions to the headmistress, of course; but what had Rowan done but hide a book beneath her bed? There was only so much she could reveal without implicating herself all those years ago. Maybe she should. It seemed selfish, under the circumstances, to conceal it. It also seemed senselessly pyrrhic to confess that she'd been in the chapel that night only to get fired and rendered unable to stop what was happening now. And she felt certain that she was the only one who could.

Rowan didn't seem to be quite the unstoppable force that Jane once had. Frances was twice her age and could view her more objectively as a confused child, rather than an enemy and an equal. It wasn't even Rowan who worried her so much as Tibbets.

Tibbets was a very different girl from Bethany, who was fearful, cringing, and toadying. She was sloppy and disorganized, but brilliant enough academically to make up for it. Tibbets was thoughtful, quiet, and inquisitive. She was an interesting student with a unique mind, and Frances was curious to see who she'd grow up to be. But Tibbets was clearly the most vulnerable in her ecosystem. Rowan and Blair were the lynx and the jaguar. Tibbets was the aardvark.

It would be Tibbets who Rowan planned to sacrifice, Tibbets who was in line for the funeral pyre. Of this Frances felt sure. Blair would probably go along with whatever Rowan said. She certainly wouldn't be brave or ethical enough to stand up to Rowan or stop her.

When would they try to do it? The school would be empty over Thanksgiving break, so that seemed like the most obvious and opportune time. Though they would have to come up with a pretty airtight excuse to get them out of going home for the weekend, or even staying for an extra day.

Jane had planned it out for weeks, starting a charity drive collecting canned goods and toys for families and children in need, then convincing the headmistress to let them stay through the first day of break to organize all the donations for distribution. Their families had been easy to placate. Who doesn't want their daughters helping the homeless at Christmas? Especially parents looking to bulk up those college apps.

Rowan, brilliant mind that she had, would likely come up with something similar. Then it would only be a matter of executing it. The girls were already masters at slipping in and out of bed undetected, so that wouldn't be an issue. What could Frances do between then and now to stop them?

It was on this question Frances was stuck when the lights flickered and popped, and again the room was plunged into darkness. It always seemed to happen when she was bathing. On a more positive note, this meant that she already had several candles lit.

Frances sighed and got out of the tub. Why was everyone so convinced this was the work of three girls? The building was literally two hundred years old, the wiring was faulty, it was late fall in Vermont and already snowing profusely. It could have been any number of reasons that weren't the handiwork of a band of bored vandals.

Frances had just finished tying her robe and slipping her feet into her fleecy fur-lined slippers when the knock at her door came. Anna, of course. Frances sighed. Anna was starting to remind her of someone: Charlotte Dumont, Haley's roommate before Angela Franklin. Charlotte got caught using black market test answers from an enterprising senior and subsequently expelled. It was ironic, because Charlotte was always so earnest—the first to raise her hand, ahead in every class. Eager to snitch and get everybody else in trouble; always wanting to know what everyone else was up to. Anna was like some nightmare mercenary Girl Scout, Charlotte 2.0.

She opened the door. To her surprise, it wasn't Anna. It was Tibbets.

"Ms. Teller?" Tibbets spoke in a voice barely above a whisper. "I think I saw something. In the bathroom."

"What did you see?" asked Frances. Behind Tibbets, she could see that the door to Anna's room was ajar. Frances imagined her rushing out to vanquish the nighttime fiends, as she had after the previous power outage.

"I'm not sure." Even in the darkness, Frances could see how pale Tibbets had gone, illuminated only by the light from her cell phone. "But it scared me. I may have just been imagining things, but I…I just wanted to know for sure."

"Of course." Frances shut the door behind her and tried to appear assured and in control of the situation. Internally, she recalled everything Haley and Elizabeth had said at lunch about the things they'd seen over the years and felt the first flutter of fear flickering at the edges of her consciousness.

She walked ahead of Tibbets down the hallway, slowing her footsteps so the frightened girl could stay close. Most of the wing (except for Anna) had slept through the power outage. The hallway was silent except for Tibbets' and Frances's cautious footsteps. When they reached the end of the hall, Frances cautiously pushed open the door to the bathroom.

"I think I'll—I'll wait out here," said Tibbets fearfully, hovering at the threshold of the doorway.

"That's fine," said Frances in what she hoped was a reassuring tone of voice. Inwardly, she was wracked by fears of her own. "Will you be okay out here?"

"Yes, I think so," said Tibbets in a small voice.

"Well, just call for me if you're not and I'll come right out," said Frances.

"All right, Ms. Teller." Tibbets watched her intently by

the light of her phone, as if it would be the last time she ever saw her (much to Frances's chagrin). Just before Frances entered the bathroom, she turned back.

"Tibbets," she said. "What exactly did you see?"

"I thought I saw someone," Tibbets replied. "I came out of the stall when the power went out, but I could see kind of a...silhouette, of a person. I called out, but they didn't say anything. I got scared, so I ran."

Maybe someone had somehow gotten a copy of the key to the cage that now held the circuit breaker box, threw the switch, and hid in the bathroom. It seemed elaborate and unlikely, as far as pranks went—why turn the power out at night while everyone was sleeping and unlikely to notice anything was awry? —but it was a possibility. Maybe Anna was more like Charlotte Dumont than she thought. Maybe she was the one behind the power outages. Frances repressed a little smile, in spite of her fear, at the ridiculous notion of Anna sneaking around in her bathrobe late at night in some bizarre revenge plot against the up-the-hill girls.

"Where did you see them?" she asked. "The person?"

"Sitting in the windowsill," Tibbets said.

Frances felt an unpleasant creeping sensation that started in the pit of her stomach and worked its way up her throat like acid reflux. *Sitting in the windowsill.* Jane's favorite spot. However unsettling the possibility of the ghost of Bethany was, it was nothing compared to encountering the malevolent spirit of Jane. Jane wouldn't be a sad ghost, crying in the corner and mourning her lost future. Jane would be vengeful, vindictive. A poltergeist.

Frances found that she had to force her feet to move

forward and will herself to open the door again after that. She shined the light of her phone at the window first, letting out the breath she was holding in one huge gust when she saw that there was nothing there. Next, she shined the light in every stall and every corner. She shined it under the sinks and across the floor. There was nothing there, either.

Frances exhaled with relief. Of course there was nothing there. Just a scared girl frightened by constant ghost stories, that was all. Frances pushed open the door to the bathroom and found a teary and shivering Tibbets waiting in the hallway.

"There was no one in the bathroom, Tibbets ," she said soothingly. "Just a trick of the light."

"Are you sure?" Tibbets looked troubled.

"I'm sure," Frances said. "If there had been, I would have run out of there screaming."

Tibbets managed a weak laugh. "Okay."

"Come on, I'll walk you back to your room."

Frances shined her light ahead along with Tibbets' light, brightening the dark hallway in front of them. She paused in front of the room that Tibbets shared with Rowan and Blair, waiting until she opened the door. Just before she disappeared inside, she surprised Frances with an impulsive hug.

"Thank you, Ms. Teller," she said. She quickly disappeared into the room and shut the door.

"You're welcome," Frances said to the door. "Good night."

She felt reassured as she walked back to her room. She'd helped someone. She'd done something for someone besides herself. It was a small thing, but a helpful thing, nonetheless. Maybe on some immortal scorecard, there was finally a tally mark in Frances's favor.

She saw no sign of Anna as she let herself into her room. The lights were still off, and Frances went straight to bed to avoid bumbling around and tripping in the dark. Under the covers, she stared sightlessly up at the ceiling, her mind racing. What had Tibbets seen? Or who? Had it really just been a figment of her imagination, or something else?

A sudden impulse made her get out of bed and hurry over to the wardrobe. She pulled open the doors and yanked the bottom drawer open, rummaging around the drawer. Her hands groped blindly beneath her many wooly sweaters.

The book was gone.

FIRE WITH FIRE

*W*ho had taken the book? She'd locked her door, hadn't she? She couldn't remember. Was it Anna? Or was it one of the girls, sneaking in while she'd helped Tibbets?

Frances hated to think that Tibbets could have been in on it: assigned to distract her and get her out of the room while Rowan entered. She wanted to believe the girls—if it had been them—had merely taken advantage of the blackout and Tibbets' absence from the room. Or maybe if she had acted knowingly, it had been under duress. Peer pressure, as it were.

But maybe it had all been orchestrated in advance: the perfect three-man job. One to throw the power, one to distract Frances, and one to sneak into the room and grab the book. Rowan and Blair could have easily snuck back in their rooms while Frances was in the bathroom with Tibbets. Maybe she was being naïve, convincing herself that the girls were in any way innocent. She hadn't been. Why would they be?

Frances was so lost in thought as she contemplated the many terrible possibilities of what had happened the previous evening that she didn't notice Rutherford Hayes until she nearly ran right into him on her way to the faculty lounge on the boys' side.

"Oh, it's you," she said, annoyed.

"How I've missed your dulcet tones," he replied, smiling. "On your way to class?"

"My class is at one," said Frances. "I'm on my way to get a doughnut from the lounge, if there are any left. What do you even teach, by the way?"

"Chemistry," he said with a little wink. Frances stared at him. "No, really!" He laughed. "I'm the chemistry teacher."

"You hated science," said Frances, mystified. "You complained about AP Physics every day."

"I hated high school physics, which is hardly physics at all," he corrected her. "I actually love science, in all its forms. Tell you what, I grabbed an extra bear claw this morning and hid it in my desk. Walk with me to class, and it's yours."

Frances harbored a very serious sugar addiction and mainlined a steady infusion of it from sunup to sundown, like an intravenous drip. Regardless of Rutherford's past transgressions, all could be temporarily overlooked in exchange for the fat glazed doughnut currently languishing in his desk drawer. Especially when compared to the sad cardboard box empty of everything but crumbs that inevitably awaited her in the faculty lounge. Without a word, she turned and matched his step. He smiled, pleased.

"The boys and girls are still sitting on opposite sides of the room," he said conversationally as they walked.

"Old habits," said Frances shortly.

"I find it bizarre. I mean, I know we got pretty serious about the senior week color wars, but I for one would have been thrilled if you guys got shipped over here for a month or two. It's like they actually hate each other now."

"Maybe they just pretend to, so we won't realize they're using social media to coordinate an attack against us—by pretending to be ghosts," said Frances dryly.

"Don't even joke about that. You got here after the latest school shooting drill. An hour and a half of standing around in the cold."

"Does that even happen at private schools?" asked Frances. "I thought that was only public schools."

"Don't let Anna-from-down-the-hill hear you say that," snorted Rutherford.

"Making new friends, are we?" Frances asked.

"I ran into her in the faculty lounge this morning and she gave me a death glare. I didn't even say anything! Or do anything! It was like she resented me for being alive."

"Maybe you used the last of the nondairy creamer," suggested Frances.

Rutherford shook his head. "I'm telling you; it was weird. Like she knew something about me she didn't like. I've never even met the woman."

"She's a bit of an odd one," Frances admitted. "I can't quite get a read on her. She seems to vacillate between resenting the students and taking her job deeply personally. Her job on the task force, anyway."

"That's never going to work," said Rutherford. "No

student is dumb enough to keep incriminating evidence in their rooms. What does McBride think establishing a 'task force' is going to accomplish, anyway?"

"You know McBride," said Frances. "As long as she feels like she's doing something, it's the same as actually doing something. What did she say during your meeting with her, anyway?"

"She told me in no uncertain terms to stay out of it," he said, shaking his head. "That it was up to her 'to determine whether the inconvenience for the students and teachers outweighed the desired outcome,' whatever that means."

"Catching the culprits and making an example out of them, I'd imagine," said Frances.

"Never going to happen," he said. "Here we are." He opened the door for her. The students were already at their desks, setting up for the day's lab. Rowan and Blair, outfitted in oversized plastic goggles, glanced up curiously as Frances entered.

She looked around the room, taking in the almost comical separation of the boys and girls: primly self-divided along either side of the aisle like a Senate hearing. She watched for a moment as they worked studiously away in their aprons and thick black rubber gloves, thinking about how glad she was that she would never return to high school again.

Sometimes she still had nightmares about it. Different from the ones about the fire, or Bethany and Jane; separate from her feelings about Thackeray in general. They were the kind of ordinary, mundane nightmares where she found herself having to go back and repeat her senior year, earning a math or science credit that she'd failed, being trapped in the endless cycle of useless classes all over again.

"Mr. Hayes?" Rutherford glanced up from his desk drawer to the back of the room, where Tibbets was working with Brandy. "Our Bunsen burner's not working."

"Hold on, I'll be right there." Rutherford bustled down the center aisle, as if concerned they'd blow themselves up if he didn't reach them in time. "I've got it." He leaned over it and appeared puzzled. "That's odd," Frances heard him saying. "This thing is brand new. We just got these in —" Rutherford's words were cut short by his sudden scream as the fire leapt up, singing his eyebrows right off his face. Tibbets and Brandy jumped back with little shrieks as Rutherford threw himself to the floor, his signature bouffant smoking.

Frances rushed over and threw her sweater over his head in case he was still on fire. After rolling briefly back and forth on the floor, he got shakily to his feet, removing the sweater from his face. His eyes were a little bit wild and his head released an acrid smell of smoke and burnt hair, but he seemed to be otherwise none the worse for the wear—aside from his now-missing widow's peak.

"You should go to the nurse," Frances said firmly over his protests. He seemed fine, but his scalp was red and the still-burnt smell lingering in the air was unsettling. "I'll take over your class for you."

Rutherford rubbed his face, looking disoriented. "All right," he finally agreed. Half-hearted applause followed his exit as if to encourage him, then awkwardly tapered off. Frances went to the front of the room and regarded the bewildered teenagers, bug-eyed in their plastic goggles.

"All right, everyone," she said briskly. "What do you say to a study hall?"

THE HEADMISTRESS CALLED A VERY ominous-sounding assembly for the next morning to take place on the girls' side. Frances had a hard time believing that the headmistress truly thought the Bunsen burner incident was the fault of one of the girls but was willing to believe anything about the headmistress at this point.

"I don't know," Anna mused over her apple at breakfast. "You said it was Tibbets' Bunsen burner this happened with?"

"Tibbets and Brandy," said Frances impatiently. "You cannot possibly think that Tibbets rigged that burner to burn off Rutherford Hayes' facial hair."

"Maybe not," conceded Anna. "But maybe Rowan did, to try and get revenge on Brandy. And it backfired and got Rutherford instead."

Frances just shook her head. She had her own theories about what happened in the chem lab, but none she would ever say out loud. Maybe someone—someone unseen —*had* been getting revenge on Rutherford. But certainly no one that Anna would ever suspect.

"WE SHOULD LIGHT RUTHERFORD ON FIRE," said Jane casually, tossing Elizabeth's snow globe from France up into the air and catching it. Frances watched Jane without really seeing her, then suddenly shot out her hand and grabbed it, setting it carefully down on Elizabeth's desk. It was one of the last trips she'd taken with her parents before their marriage turned sour. Now they barely inhabited the same house, let alone took vacations together.

"I think we'd probably get caught," said Frances.

"Elizabeth told you, right?" Jane asked in an offhand tone. Too offhand. "About what he said to her?"

"She told me everything." Frances and Elizabeth were always scrupulous about never giving Jane—or anyone—a window to drive a wedge between them. Elizabeth called Frances over to her iMac G3 the second Rutherford IM'd her on AIM. They watched as he progressed from casually asking her about something inane to trying to convince her to meet him in the boathouse. As livid, hurt, and humiliated as she was, there was a part of her that almost pitied him as they sat side-by-side and watched him embarrass himself, confessing increasingly lurid fantasies he harbored about her; about both of them.

She copied the conversation and pasted it to a fresh email, sending it from her address. She wished she could have seen his expression after the voice intoned YOU'VE GOT MAIL and he clicked on the letter-in-the-mailbox icon only to see his words repeated from her address. But that was revenge in the technological era. The bomb went off far away, out of view.

They printed the conversation out afterward and pasted it to the walls of the girls' bathrooms. Eventually, the story made its way across the lake and Rutherford stopped showing up at the girls' field hockey games. The other boys became mysteriously cagey when talking to anyone from the girls' school on AIM. Someone had apparently proposed a moratorium on dating them and decreed dating only girls from Hyde, the day school several towns away, but that lasted about a week.

"Well, she wasn't *going* to." Jane watched Frances, her expression avid. Frances gazed back at her, expressionless. What was she talking about? She'd been there the whole time.

"That wasn't the first time they talked," continued Jane. "She told me he came on to her before and she was actually considering it, until I pointed out how utterly vile that would be." Jane gave the snow globe a little flick of her thumb, watching it roll across the desk and catching it at the last second before it rolled off the edge and shattered on the floor. "She'll deny it, wait and see."

Frances felt a flicker of doubt in her brain. Had they spoken before? No. Elizabeth would never lie to her. Frances remembered Elizabeth's words after Frances had told her that Jane planned to steal the test answers for the AP Bio midterm: *Jane lies.*

"She wouldn't do that," Frances said flatly.

Jane gave a little shrug. "Whatever you tell yourself to sleep at night. It's cute how close you guys are. You're like a little pair of Siamese twins or something."

Elizabeth walked into the room. Her small shoulders were stooped under her heavy bookbag. Seeing Jane leaning against her desk, her eyes flicked over her in a way that clearly said *get off my stuff* as she crossed the room, dropped her bag, and flopped onto her bed. Jane gave a slow, lazy smile and backed out of the room with a little wave of her fingers.

"Later, haters." She closed the door behind her. Frances looked over at Elizabeth's bed, where she was staring fixedly at the pages of YM without reading it.

"Tell me what's wrong right now," she said. "I'm not dealing with you sulking around here for the next week and a half making me guess what I supposedly did because you think I should already know."

"I'm not mad." Elizabeth rolled over so she was facing Frances. "I overheard her before I came in. I heard you defend me. I'm just upset that she's trying to turn you against me."

"But why, though?" Frances asked. "That's what I don't get."

"Because she knows she can't control me, that she has no influence over me, and it drives her insane," said Elizabeth, her somber, heart-shaped face propped on her hand. "All that girl wants is to control people. It's crazy to me how none of you can see it. We should all back away slowly and forget that she exists. She's like a pipe bomb. Bethany is probably doomed, of course, but it's not too late for the rest of us."

Looking back on Elizabeth's words now filled Frances with a kind of mute horror. Bethany *had* been doomed. But maybe it wasn't too late for the rest of them.

AT ASSEMBLY THE NEXT MORNING, the headmistress watched them with her standard severe expression, shifting restlessly in their seats as they settled in, murmuring and whispering about what punishment might await them now.

"As some of you may already know, there was an... incident on the boys' campus yesterday," the headmistress began. In the back row, Rowan was clearly repressing laughter while Tibbets rolled her eyes and resumed reading her book. Blair played with her hair and snapped her gum. Frances turned her eyes back to the front.

"I am by no means suggesting that one of you is responsible for what to me was obviously the case of a malfunctioning piece of equipment," the headmistress continued. Frances was surprised. This was a new tack on her part. "The headmaster, however, disagrees. He feels that we have simply transferred our problems to the other side of the lake and is concerned that whoever perpetuated the pranks on this side is determined to continue their reign of terror at the boys' school. Therefore, you will be returning to your regularly scheduled classes on this side as of today."

An excited flurry of whispering broke out among the gathered crowd. The headmistress waited for the buzz to die down before she continued. "It occurs to me now that I may have been approaching this in a way less conducive to apprehending the culprit, and that I might provide a more powerful, positive incentive," she said. "Therefore, in exchange for any information leading to the party or parties responsible for the unfortunate pranks, I will provide a personal letter of recommendation to any and all colleges of that person's choosing. We will also offer, as further incentive, a full GPA point towards any class at the end of the semester for information leading to the apprehension of the party—or parties —responsible."

Gasps of excitement could be heard rippling throughout the auditorium. Frances also spied more than a few stern expressions on teachers she knew to be tough graders, who would be less than pleased at the idea that a girl could earn a "free" full GPA point in such a nefarious way.

Frances was less than pleased herself. One of Thackeray's mottos was *loyalty and honor, above all else.* The girls were taught to be loyal—to the school, to each other, to themselves. To act always, above all else, with integrity and honorable intentions.

Now the headmistress was setting them loose on each other, encouraging them to inform on their own classmates by enticing them with an unheard-of incentive. One that would prove irresistible to any student under massive pressure and performing poorly in at least one class they simply didn't have the faculty for, which likely described each and every one of them. It was like the Golden Ticket in a Wonka Bar, thought Frances, only far more twisted and manipulative.

Anna appeared at Frances's side, eyes gleaming. "I give it an hour before they all turn on each other," she said gleefully.

Frances glanced at the other teacher. She realized fully for the first time how avidly she disliked her.

"Excuse me," she said as she walked away.

19

AFTER THE FIRE

*T*hey ran through the woods. When they reached the edge, they could see the first students trickling out through a side door to investigate the sound of sirens, the smell of smoke. They all had hoodies on over their pajama bottoms, just like the three who had just fled the woods. With a little twitch of her head, Elizabeth signaled for them to join the back of a group wandering, confused, out onto the snow-covered hill. As if they'd just woken up like everybody else and wanted to see what the commotion was all about.

Frances's eyes scanned the crowd. She didn't see Jane or Bethany. *They're back inside, they're already back in their room*, she told herself. *Jane is smart. They went straight back so they could pretend they slept through the whole thing.*

A frightened freshman turned to see them standing silently at the back of the group. "Do you know what happened?" she asked, her eyes wide and round.

"No idea," said Elizabeth shortly. The freshman turned away.

From their vantage point, it was easy to see the tower of flames shooting out of the chapel. The girls on the hill watched in silent horror as the inferno raged. Sirens wailed as the first fire truck made its way up the drive.

"I hope no one's in there," said the freshman girl worriedly.

Haley promptly doubled over and threw up on the freshly fallen snow. The girls closest to her jumped back, eliciting cries of disgust. Frances and Elizabeth quickly flanked her and held her upright, marching her back to the dorm. Haley's door stood open. Her roommate had rushed out with the others to find out what was going on.

"Get into bed and act like you have no idea what's going on," Elizabeth instructed her. "When your roommate comes back and asks where you were when she woke up, tell her you were in the bathroom. You went outside to see what was going on and came back in because you were cold. If you can't sleep, come down to my room and I'll give you a pill."

Haley, pale and shaking, nodded her head. She went into her room and promptly pulled the covers over her head. Elizabeth closed the door behind her.

They walked to the end of the hallway to their room in silence. Frances looked at Bethany and Jane's door: closed, dark. *Empty*, she thought with a sick feeling. She stopped and knocked softly on the door, placing her ear to the wood. Nothing.

"Jane?" she called softly. "Bethany?" No one answered.

Frances tried to keep the unimaginably horrible thought from surfacing in her mind. They weren't here because they were still in the chapel. And if they were still in the chapel…

No. Jane had Bethany perfectly trained, like a circus animal. They wouldn't come to the door because if someone saw them all together like this, in the hallway, maybe they'd put two and two together and realize that these were the girls responsible for the raging conflagration downstairs. They would stay in their rooms until dawn, and come out stretching and sleepy, feigning disorientation: *what's going on? What happened?*

Frances turned to see Elizabeth regarding her somberly. Later Frances realized that Elizabeth already knew what Frances was trying so hard to deny. Elizabeth opened the door to their room and waited for Frances to go through it first.

"Where are they?" Frances said as soon as the door was closed and locked behind them. Elizabeth didn't answer. "They made it out, right?" Frances said. "They were right behind us."

"I don't know, Frances. But if they didn't…"

"Don't say that!" Frances was stricken. She couldn't entertain the possibility that they were still in that building. The flames had been so high…

"Look," said Elizabeth. "We need to get one thing perfectly clear, right now: whatever happens, we keep quiet. I know we agreed in the woods, but you and I need to discuss this. Because if the worst has happened, if they're still in that chapel—I know you don't want to think about it, Frances, but we have to resign ourselves to the possibility that it might have happened—then Haley is going to fall apart. *Unless* we stay strong for her and present a perfectly united front. If even one of us cracks, we won't just be thrown out of school. We'll go to prison. We'll probably be tried as adults, and we'll probably go to jail for a very long time. The rest of our lives will be ruined. We'll never go to college; we'll never get jobs. You'll spend the rest of your life explaining to anyone that you try to date that you have a felony arson conviction and probably one for involuntary manslaughter, too. And then you'll just have to hope they love you, anyway. Which they won't. Do you understand?"

"The fire was an accident," said Frances, breaking out into a cold sweat. "I mean, we were there, I know we started it—"

"*We* didn't start anything," Elizabeth interrupted her. "Jane kicked over the candle, I saw it. And it may have been an accident, but what were we doing out of bed in the middle of the night in the chapel in the first place? Then it just *happened* to burn down while we were in it? Even if we explain, what will we say? Our friend wanted to perform a ritual to grant us everlasting happiness or whatever it was supposed to do? Imagine the headlines: Crazed Teens Burn Down Church, Pretending to Be Witches. They'll say we saw *The Craft* too many times and went insane. The townies will have a field day with the rich brats up the hill who set the Lord's house on fire. It will go public. It will become a massive story. Even my family doesn't have enough money and influence to keep this out of the papers. And look, Frances, I know you might not want to believe this, but one candle falling over —or being kicked—does not burn an entire church down. Do you understand? There is a reason it went up like it did. We'll get charged with arson. And if they didn't make it out, arson will be the least of our worries."

"What do you mean?" asked Frances, sickened. Even as she asked, she could see where Elizabeth's logic made a kind of sense. How did a single pillar candle from Pottery Barn ignite an entire building?

"She did something down there," said Elizabeth grimly. "She must have. Before we even got there. I've been telling you this for years, Frances, and I know you think I was just being catty or whatever, but there's something seriously wrong with Jane. If the chapel caught fire tonight, it was only because she wanted it to. You know how seriously she's been taking this stuff. She probably thought she was an actual witch or something. And we were like her little coven. I think she wanted to burn it down."

"She didn't want to kill us," Frances whispered.

"Maybe not," said Elizabeth. "But if they're dead—" Frances emitted a choked sob and Elizabeth continued to talk over her, "—if they're dead, it's because of Jane. And I am *not* spending the rest of my life with an arson charge and another for involuntary manslaughter hanging over my head because Jane was a psychopath who tried to kill us all."

Was. Not *is.* Elizabeth thought they were still in the chapel. Elizabeth thought they were dead.

She could be wrong, Frances thought mechanically to herself. She was wrong, definitely. Jane would never make a mistake like that. Jane would never get caught.

"Why are you being so quiet?" Elizabeth asked. "What are you thinking about, Frances?"

"This is going to come back to us," said Frances. "We

can stay quiet, Elizabeth, and we will. But no matter what, this is going to follow us for the rest of our lives."

THAT NIGHT WAS THE LONGEST—AND worst—of Frances's life. Waiting to hear for a complete certainty what she already knew and still told herself that she didn't.

The headmistress called for an early assembly to take place before breakfast. Frances knew it was about the fire, but in the back of her mind, she suspected there was worse news to be shared that the headmistress didn't want to spread through the dining hall before she could impart that information herself. Frances pushed the thought away.

Elizabeth made an elaborate show of knocking on Jane and Bethany's door on their way to the assembly. Frances watched her, sickened. She knew exactly what Elizabeth was doing. Frances trailed along behind her, silent and ill, while she asked every person they saw in the hall on their way out if they'd seen Bethany or Jane. None of them had.

Haley's door opened just as they got to the end of the east wing. Her eyes were wide and wild. Elizabeth wrapped a hand around her arm in a vise-like grip as she reached into her hoodie pouch with her other hand.

"Take this," she hissed at Haley. Haley didn't even ask what it was. She tossed it in her mouth and swallowed without even stopping at the water fountain. It was this small gesture that imparted the magnitude of what had happened upon Frances. Not the impending assembly and whatever terrible news awaited them, or the sight of the fire last night. It was the sight of anti-smoking, anti-drug

Haley Lee dry swallowing a Valium without a second thought. *This is going to be bad*, thought Frances. *Really, really bad.*

The girls filed into the auditorium with the rest of the school and took seats in the back. It was where they always sat. Frances tried not to look at the two empty seats beside them. Elizabeth did, and made a big point of it.

"Where are they?" she asked loudly. "I've asked everyone, and no one seems to know where they are."

Frances didn't answer. Haley, doubled over in her seat with her head in her hands, gave a low moan. Elizabeth kicked her. She rummaged around in her bag and pulled out a bottle of Evian, shoving it at Haley.

"Drink this so it kicks in faster," she said.

Haley obeyed. By the time the last girl entered the auditorium and took a seat, Haley was slumped over in her chair, eyes glazed.

The headmistress looked more serious than Frances had ever seen her. She approached the podium and adjusted the microphone. Every face was raised expectantly towards her for news about the fire.

"As most of you already know, there was a terrible fire in the chapel last night," McBride began. "The firefighters arrived and put out the blaze, but the structure was burned to the ground." Several cries of dismay went up. The chapel was even older than the school itself, and it was a fixture of campus life. "But I am afraid that is not the worst news I have to impart." Frances' stomach dropped like a stone.

"I am afraid—" Here the headmistress stopped. She

took off her glasses and pinched the bridge of her nose. She was crying.

And that was when Frances knew. She knew beyond any doubt. The impregnable, austere headmistress—whom the girls often joked was actually a cyborg sent from the future—was in tears. Frances realized she was already crying before the headmistress got out her next words. Elizabeth reached over and pinched her. Frances slapped her hand, hard.

"Two of our students were in the chapel last night, and were caught in the fire," the headmistress said in a choked voice. "Jane Wilcox and Bethany Jones. I am devasted to tell you that they passed away."

Several cries sounded, followed by a wail. Haley's head snapped up. She started to cry. Frances buried her face in her hands. Elizabeth moved her hair in front of her face, as was her custom when she wanted to conceal whatever emotion she feared would betray her normally stalwart expression.

"Classes will be suspended for the rest of the week, and grief counselors will be made available," McBride continued in a shaking voice. "Anyone who would like to call their families and return home during this time is welcome to do so. My door is open to each and every one of you. This is the greatest tragedy to occur at this school, during my time or any other. Please know that we will get through this together, as Thackeray women. We will mourn. We will grieve. But there will someday be a dawn at the end of this long night."

Elizabeth was pale, her jaw clenched tightly as she got up and racewalked out of the auditorium. Frances and

Haley got up and ran after her. Ms. Holloway the art teacher moved away from the wall and seemed on the brink of following them, her eyes filled with concern. Frances and Haley broke out in a dead run in the hallway outside the auditorium. Elizabeth had already vanished, but they knew where to find her.

Snow fell in the clearing. A thin beam of light penetrated the forest canopy, shining down through the bare branches on them. *It's Bethany*, Frances thought for one wild moment. *It's Bethany, she can see us from heaven, she's sending us a message.* Then she thought, *No, it's God, shining a spotlight on the guilty, telling us we're going to hell.* This seemed the more likely prospect of the two, given the circumstances.

"It wasn't our fault." Elizabeth lit her cigarette with a shaking hand. "We didn't kill them. We didn't burn down the chapel. Jane did."

"How is this not our fault, Elizabeth?" Frances demanded. She took one of Elizabeth's cigarettes and lit it off the one in her hand. "We were *there*. We could have *stopped* it. We could have gone back for them; we could have *saved* them—"

"Bullshit." Elizabeth's voice was cold. This was how she survived: her parents, school, her life. That coldness. She iced everything out, from the strongest emotion to the worst situation imaginable. "If w had gone back, we would have died, too. They died because of a stupid stunt that Jane pulled that could have gotten us all killed. We're lucky to be alive. The least we can do is prevent it from ruining the rest of our lives. Do you think Bethany would want that?"

"She would want to be alive right now." Tears shone on Haley's cheeks. "She would want to be here with us."

"Obviously she would want to be here, Haley." Elizabeth's tone softened. "No one is disputing that. But she's not. And we are. It's time to survive. Jane brought this down on all of us, but she's gone now, and she can never hurt anyone again."

"What do you mean?" whispered Haley.

"Elizabeth thinks that Jane set the fire," said Frances.

Haley was shocked. "No," she said. "She wouldn't."

"Think about it, Hales," said Elizabeth patiently. "Why did the church burn down so quickly? Do you think a candle falling over could do that? Just one?"

"I thought maybe it worked," Haley whispered. "The ritual. I thought it was because of that."

"I thought that, too," Frances admitted.

"There *was* no ritual," said Elizabeth grimly. "Just an evil girl who wanted to hurt her friends. Well, she took Bethany, but she can never take us. Understand? It will be the three of us, like it was at the beginning. Before she came along and fucked everything up. We stick together. No matter what."

Haley took a cigarette from Elizabeth and lit it off of Frances's. They stood in a circle, quietly smoking, until it was time to go back to the hell that awaited them inside. Frances watched Haley smoke and thought grimly, *Doomed. We're all doomed.*

. . .

THE FOLLOWING WEEK passed in a kind of fog. Haley went back to Ocean City until the memorial services. Elizabeth stayed in bed in a pill-induced haze. When she was awake, she seemed to be in a kind of fog.

Frances found a different way of coping. She never told the others that she continued secretly seeing Rutherford even after the incident with Elizabeth. It was too shameful and pathetic to ever admit out loud. But as loathsome as he was, he was also familiar and that made him feel safe. And all she wanted right now was to feel safe. Even though she knew that in reality, she'd never be safe again.

Rutherford had been gently but persistently badgering her for months now. He didn't have a lot of leverage, given that he'd tried to cheat on her with her best friend and roommate, so Frances found him easy to ignore. She didn't want to remember Rutherford Hayes as the person she lost her virginity to.

But now she'd crossed into some kind of netherworld, a state between waking and dreams, even during the day when she was ostensibly awake. She no longer felt like herself. She felt like a ghost moving through the world, watching all the other girls do everything normally—grieve, study, practice, eat, talk. She watched them from behind the wall that had formed inside her. On one side was the person she had been before the fire—dreamy, pensive, often morse about her family, but still hopeful that the future held something beautiful for her, some-thing better. That it held something like this for all of them. That she'd meet someone, and he would become the family that she'd never truly have.

Now, she would never be the same again. She would never again be innocent. Not only did she no longer feel hopeful, she didn't feel that she deserved to ever hope for anything again.

She vaguely wondered if this was the way that Bethany and Jane now felt. Assuming they felt anything at all, wherever they were. Assuming they were even anywhere.

In the boathouse, she took off his jacket, then his tie. When she unbuttoned his shirt, he paused and looked at her, startled. "Are you sure?" he said uncertainly.

She could see that it seemed like an odd time for her to suddenly reconsider her stance on sleeping with him. This was the one week he hadn't said anything to her about sex. When they met up at night after curfew, he held her for hours, saying nothing. It was the first time she was certain he actually did care about her, in his own messed-up Rutherford way. He was there for her in whatever capacity she needed. And in that moment, the only thing she needed was to feel anything but the way she felt.

"I'm sure," she said as she unbuckled his belt. Later on, it became one more piece of incontrovertible proof of her own guilt: when she told herself over and over for the next two decades that she was worthless, beyond redemption. Her friends died in a fire in front of her, a fire she had a hand in causing, and three days later she had sex in a boathouse with a guy she was pretty sure she didn't even love.

But it was the first time she ever felt in control. And when she left the boathouse, she found that she wasn't worried about what Rutherford thought or how he felt, whether or not anyone would find out and what they would think of her if they did, or about anything at all. She didn't care. Not about him, not about anyone. She just had the peculiar sensation of floating, of drifting away watching herself from the outside.

It felt a little bit like power. She felt a little bit like Jane.

20

THE GHOST OF BETHANY JONES

*O*ver the coming days, the students seemed to eye each other keenly in classes and the corridors. It was as if they were all waiting for someone to slip up and reveal their identity as the person responsible for the power outages, the silhouette on the wall, the birds in the foyer. The atmosphere was one of paranoia and suspicion.

Frances was distraught. The environment of the school in general was tense at times, filled as it was with teenagers whose emotions and hormones ran high. But she had never seen it like this before.

Anna had to separate two girls in the cafeteria who were exchanging heated, wild accusations in the lunch line. Frances had numerous appointments with girls voicing their ethical dilemmas over whether or not to bring their speculation on who the culprit might be to the headmistress, sessions which inevitably devolved into their anxiety over grades and the one class they couldn't seem to keep up in.

Apart and above it all were Rowan, Blair, and Tibbets.

They sat by themselves in the cafeteria in an isolated triangle, solemnly watching the outbreaks of tension. In class, they were quiet while the others peppered Frances with questions about whether or not the headmistress's offer was sincere.

Frances mulled their detachment and what it might entail. Were they, and they alone, separate from the recent hysteria because they already knew who the culprits were? Or did they simply not care about the head-mistress's incentives, which more closely resembled bribes?

Frances had another appointment with Tibbets, which she thought might be her opportunity to find out. She scrolled through her email while she waited for her to arrive. Most of it was irrelevant, but there was an email—sent to both her and Haley—from Elizabeth. The subject read simply *Checking In* and the body consisted of a simple, *Everything okay?* Frances smiled slightly. She was composing her response when a timid knock issued from the other side of the door.

"Come in," Frances called. She usually left the door open, but her last student session had been with an anguished field hockey player trying desperately to get into Harvard with a B in Spanish. She had dissolved into tears and rushed out melodramatically, slamming the door shut behind her.

Tibbets slipped in, as if she was trying to be invisible. Her small frame was dwarfed by her oversized backpack, filled with heavy AP books in every subject. Frances felt thankful again that she was no longer in school and never would be again. She waited while Tibbets settled in, sitting in the chair across from her. She was quiet, staring down at her hands.

"How are you, Tibbets?" Frances greeted her warmly. "Are you doing okay?"

"Not really," Tibbets admitted. "To be honest, I'm really afraid."

"What are you afraid of?" Frances asked.

Tibbets was quiet for a moment, as if considering saying anything more. Finally, she looked up and said, "I'm afraid of Rowan."

"What makes you say that?" said Frances carefully. Maybe Rowan was the one forcing Tibbets and Blair to sneak around after hours, much the way Jane had once forcefully controlled her, Elizabeth, and Haley. And Bethany.

"I feel like I can't say no to her," said Tibbets fretfully. "It's like she has this hold over me, and over Blair. I don't know why. It's not like she has anything on us, it's just like…sometimes I wish we weren't friends, but it feels impossible to get away from her. Like she's my family."

She could have been describing Jane. "I know what you mean," said Frances sympathetically. "In a small and claustrophobic space like this one, much of our interactions seem unavoidable and involuntary."

"Have you ever known someone like that?" Tibbets asked.

"I did," said Frances. "When I was your age."

"How did you deal with her?"

"I didn't," said Frances. "She died."

Tibbets looked stricken. Frances kicked herself

inwardly, remembering how sensitive some of the students were; how fragile.

"It was an accident, of course," she continued in a rush. "But I'd be lying if I said part of me wasn't a little bit… relieved." It was the first time she'd ever said it out loud.

Tibbets looked fascinated. "Because you knew that you'd never have her looking over your shoulder ever again?"

"Well, yes." She felt like she'd opened a Pandora's box she should have left untouched. "I was devastated by the knowledge that my friend was gone, but relieved that she could no longer control or influence me anymore."

"Your friend," started Tibbets, then stopped.

"Yes?" Frances said encouragingly.

"Do you think she was…dangerous?" Tibbets' eyes were bright behind her thick glasses.

Frances studied her, aware that they were talking about Rowan, and yet remembering Jane.

"I think she was," she said.

"If you could go back, would you have tried to stop her? Turned her in?"

"I would," said Frances. "There are a number of things I would have done differently, knowing what I know now. But that's the real burn of it, isn't it? You know when you know, and not a moment before."

"And what do you know now? That you didn't back then?" asked Tibbets.

"That I was a coward," she said. "That I should have done everything I could to stop her. If I had, she might still be alive today." She gave Tibbets a searching look, and the girl immediately looked away.

"Tibbets," she said. "Is there anything you want to tell me?"

Tibbets was silent a moment, considering. At last, she met Frances's gaze.

"No, Ms. Teller," she said. "Not today."

FRANCES FOUND it hard to fall asleep that night. She restlessly turned back and forth, running through all the events that had taken place since she arrived at Thackeray, transposing them onto her memories from the past. Tibbets' fearful face followed by Bethany's. Rowan's arrogant eyebrow arch melted into Jane's insolent smirk. The book back then and the same book now.

Maybe she should act on what she'd told Tibbets earlier, that she wished she'd had the courage to say something. She'd been afraid back then of all the wrong things: of what people might say about her if she told on a friend; of losing her other friends. Things that seemed of paramount importance at the time but couldn't be pettier in the wake of what she'd ultimately lost.

Would the headmistress take her seriously? What could she even say? That she found a book, the same one her dead classmate once religiously carried, and now believed that a new group of girls was planning to set part of the school on fire? Frances could only imagine how that conversation would go. She had no doubt in her mind the headmistress wouldn't believe her, and what could she do even if she did? She couldn't suspend Rowan for having a book, nor for Frances's speculation on what she might do with it.

Frances punched her pillow and rolled over again. Maybe she could appeal to Anna, enlist her help? But Anna was so irrational and militant about cracking down on the girls. She seemed less interested in helping them than she was in prosecuting them.

Frances's thoughts raced for so long it was difficult to pinpoint when they finally tapered off and she slipped into unconsciousness. At first, her dreams were the simple garden variety manifestations of her current stress—Rutherford following her around campus in a toupee to cover his burnt hair while a line of girls trailed behind him, complaining about their grades. As Frances's dream self rounded the lake, she saw her: in the woods, in the distance, at the tree line. Bethany. She watched Frances solemnly. She wore a thin white nightgown and had no shoes on her feet. It was what she wore to the chapel under her parka that night. She'd had snow boots on then.

"Aren't your feet cold?" Frances asked as she wandered up to her. She glanced behind her. Rutherford and the girls were gone. She glanced down. She wore her Thackeray uniform. She reached up to touch her hair, which was pulled back in its customary black headband.

"I can't feel them anymore." Bethany reached out a hand to her. Frances reached out and took it. They floated up and over the school grounds, looking down. Students threaded their way across the paths like ants. Around them, the sky rapidly darkened, as if time itself was shifting. The stars were bright in the clear winter sky. Frances found that she could no longer feel the cold, either.

All at once, she heard the dull roar of fire erupt from the roof of the chapel a short distance away. Bethany took her hand and pointed. The side door burst open and three hooded figures ran down the path into the night, disappearing into the woods. As Frances watched, Bethany pointed again.

The front door opened. A fourth hooded figure strolled down the steps, casual and languid, as if it had all the time in the world. As soon as it hit the sidewalk, the figure broke into a sprint, running down the steep and snowy hill toward the front gate. Bethany glided after it, towing Frances along after her.

They followed the figure through the gate and down the winding drive that led to the main road. The figure ran without stopping, nor even growing winded, all the way to the small square that comprised all the businesses in town—all five of them. It stopped at the train depot and went to the tracks, waiting.

They floated gently down to the platform as the headlights appeared on the track. The train pulled into the station and the figure pushed its dark hood back. It was Jane. She watched as the train pulled in and pulled to a stop with a hiss of brakes. She reached into the front pocket of her sweatshirt and pulled out a ticket. She boarded the open door of the train. The ghost of teenage Frances watched alongside the ghost of Bethany Jones. Jane took a seat out the window and looked out as the train left the station.

She smiled.

FRANCES WOKE with a startled gasp to the pitch-dark cold room. She fumbled on the nightstand for the lamp and turned it on. She could see her scared reflection in the mirror across the room.

It was a dream, but it hadn't felt like one. It had at first, retaining all the usual nightmarish abstract qualities of a dream, but then it had shifted. It felt real. It felt the way it had felt the night of the fire at the chapel, but as if she was watching from the outside, looking in. What had it meant? Had Bethany been trying to show her something?

If it was just a dream, it was Frances's worst nightmare: that Jane had planned everything, that she'd murdered Bethany and was still alive, out there somewhere. Hadn't that always lingered, in the back of her mind, as a possibility? She found it hard to believe that Jane, wily and calculating as she was, could have truly been careless enough to burn down the church with herself inside of it.

And if it was a message from Bethany, what was she trying to tell her? That Jane was alive after all these years, and had simply escaped? That she'd vanished into the night? But why?

Because she believed the ritual was real. She believed that if she sacrificed one of her friends—or maybe even all of them—she would be afforded with eternal wealth and happiness. She believed it so strongly it had been worth killing for, worth leaving town over and going into hiding, maybe leaving the country.

Frances was more awake than ever. If she did choose to read this as anything but a dream, she'd be opening the door on the possibility that she believed in ghosts, believed that one was trying to communicate with her and send her messages about the living—messages that affected her present-day reality. To do so would be honoring what was almost certainly a delusion, which was problematic enough even prior to factoring in the possibility of acting on that delusion. It was not a road that Frances wanted to go down.

But if there was even a kernel of a possibility that it could be true—that the spirit of Bethany still resided within the school's walls, her last home, and wanted Frances to know the truth—then that meant that not only was there likely another Jane trying to repeat the same evil with a new group of girls, but that maybe Frances herself was still in danger from her oldest and cruelest of opponents.

Frances rolled over and turned the light off again. She would call the others tomorrow. She would raise the possibility that Jane had made it out of the chapel that night and see what they said. Maybe they would have an idea about how to prove it—or disprove it. Maybe they would reassure her that she was completely insane to entertain such an idea. Yes, that was it. That was very likely what would happen.

Frances's eyes were falling shut when she saw the figure at the foot of her bed, watching her. Frances froze from her head to her toes. *Bethany*. The figure was perfectly still. The feeling Frances got was not one of accusation or recrimination. It was more like the feeling she had when she saw her parents: one of protection.

Frances reached slowly for the light, wondering if the vision would hold. As her fingers closed around the switch, she blinked. The figure was gone when she opened her eyes, before her hand even reached the light.

21

FRANCES THE MUTE

rances set up a group FaceTime appointment with Elizabeth and Haley. The other two weren't free until the next evening, and Frances waited impatiently all day throughout meals and her class while she replayed the dream in her mind. Once she was safely squared away in her room with her laptop, shortly before she'd arranged to make the call, she became apprehensive. What if they didn't believe her? What if they thought she was crazy?

She concluded that if none of them had judged Haley for her haunted art installation, there was no reason for them to judge Frances for having an oddly lucid dream about their dead friend. She clicked on the icon and added both contacts. Haley answered right away, popping up on screen. Elizabeth took longer and looked hassled when she did appear.

"The whole point of a nanny is supposed to be that I don't have to deal with my children when I don't want to," she said by way of greeting. "Looks like someone is getting fired. Again."

"You have a nanny?" asked Haley curiously.

"Obviously I have a nanny. I want a life," she answered sardonically. "And I still barely have one regardless. So, what's happening at Thackeray?"

Frances bit her lip, then decided the best way to explain it would just be to come out and say it. "I saw the shadow of a girl in my room," she said. "Before that, I had a dream about Bethany. But not just about her, it was like I was there, and she was trying to tell me something. It was the night of the fire. I saw us run into the woods. Then I watched Jane walk out of the church, get on a train, and leave town."

"What do you think it means?" asked Haley.

"I don't know what to think," admitted Frances. "I mean, being back here is bringing up a lot of bad memories. It could easily be a story invented by my subconscious. Of course I wish she had lived."

"Scary thought," murmured Elizabeth.

"She was a difficult person, but I'd obviously much rather that she was alive today," said Frances.

"Even if she tried to kill us?" asked Haley.

"We don't know that," said Frances. "It was purely speculation on my part. It might have been an accident—Bethany, the fire, everything."

"The Jane you described in the dream doesn't seem like she was running from an accident," countered Haley. "It sounds like it went exactly as planned."

"Maybe it was just a dream," said Elizabeth doubtfully. "What did you eat before bed?"

"Do you guys remember her memorial service?" asked Frances, ignoring the question. "That's the other thing that's been bothering me."

A look of recognition crossed Haley's face, followed by a sudden dawning of fear. Elizabeth remained mystified.

"Honestly, no," she said. "I was on an awful lot of Valium."

"I remember," said Haley. "It was like Bethany's, but…different."

"How was it different?" demanded Elizabeth. "What are you talking about?"

"It was strange," said Frances, remembering. "It was like she hadn't really died."

BETHANY'S SERVICE had been a nightmare: weeping, wailing relatives, Mrs. Jones resolute, Mr. Jones melting into a tearful puddle every other minute. They piled into the bathroom in a tight knot of black dresses and sheer tights, clunky black Steve Madden shoes clicking on the tile floor. "Are those Jane's clogs?" Frances asked, staring at Elizabeth's feet.

"So what?" she said defensively. "It's not like she's gonna need them, where she's going." Haley gasped. Elizabeth smiled meanly. "And by that, I mean hell." She pulled a flask out of her bag, took a swig, and offered it to the others. Haley, pale and drawn from crying constantly, shook her head silently. Frances took it wordlessly.

It would have looked incredibly suspicious if none of them had showed up the memorial services, though none of them wanted to go. It made it all too real: the guilt and fear, the devastation of the certain knowledge that neither Bethany nor Jane would be returning to the dorm after that nightmare weekend was over. Mercifully, the services were virtually back-to-back—one on Saturday and the next on Sunday—so they didn't have one hovering over their heads for days on end after the first one was complete. Though if Jane's was anything like Bethany's, Frances doubted she would make it through with her sanity intact.

They tried to escape right after the service, calling a cab to take them to Burlington to Jane's family's house, but Elizabeth's cell phone was dead, and they got cornered on the way to the pay phone by Bethany's dad. He bombarded them with questions about Bethany, since he'd last seen her over spring break: was she happy? Had something happened? What was she doing in the chapel that night? It was that roommate of hers, wasn't it? He'd always had a bad feeling about her. Didn't they? Was there something they wanted to tell him? Something they thought he should know?

Haley looked stricken. Frances was ashen and close-mouthed. Elizabeth looked like she was on the brink of slapping him across the face when Mrs. Jones appeared, closing her hand over his arm in her vise-like grip.

"Let the girls be now, Harold," she said gently. "They're going through it, too." She acknowledged them with a brief nod. "It's worse for the young," was all she said as she turned away. Being comforted by Bethany's mom was the worst thing of all. In the bushes outside of the funeral home, Elizabeth was violently sick while

Frances and Haley held her hair back. Sympathetic onlookers looked away tactfully, as if it was merely an expression of the deepest grief.

AT JANE'S HOUSE, her tense and silent family huddled in dark clothes in the living and dining rooms, holding drinks and little plates of food that no one ate. The service was being held at the house and they took turns speaking about Jane.

There was neither a casket nor an urn for either Bethany or Jane. The church had been burnt to a cinder, and details (like what remained to identify either of them) were shielded from the girls, lest they be any more traumatized than they were. School had been closed for a week, and then re-opened with grief counselors available all day. It was a small school, and most were genuinely stricken by the loss, but some of the more elaborate displays of mourning in the hallways by girls who barely knew or liked either Bethany or Jane left Frances incensed. For some, it was just an opportunity to wallow in their existing over-the-top-emotions, have something to talk about passionately, or to get out of class, assignments, reading, tests. *I'm too upset to focus right now* became the catch phrase of the day.

At both Bethany's service and Jane's house, there was a framed eight-by-ten senior photo placed prominently at the front of the room. At Jane's house, it was on the piano. Her hair was swept to one side and she held a rose. Frances remembered how Jane told her the only reason she was smiling was because she was high.

It was the first and only time Frances ever saw Jane's brother, silent in his dark and tweedy suit with slicked-back hair. Frances caught herself thinking idly and inappropriately how good-looking he was, and that it was unsurprising that Jane had never wanted any of them to meet him. Elizabeth would have pursued him without a second thought.

Someone had given Elizabeth a plastic cup of wine, which she'd been liberally refilling in the hour since they'd gotten there. Even Haley had caved at this point and shared it with her. Frances had a clear plastic cup of what looked like water but was actually vodka. They were lined up on the piano bench like a single organism. The heat of the room and their warm bodies pressed on her. She felt like she was going to pass out.

She excused herself when Jane's aunt finished talking and stumbled through the throng of bodies towards the mercifully empty hallway, sucking in a quick exhale of recycled air. The hallway smelled like a pine-scented Glade plug-in, and the sickening smell seemed in that moment to represent her agonized misery. All the doors were closed, and she swayed from side to side, confused. Instead of opening the first one she saw, she kept walking, inexplicably drawn towards the door at the end of the hallway. She'd just raised her hand to the knob when an arm shot out in front of her, blocking her path. She looked up into the dark, bottomless eyes of Jane's brother.

"What are you doing?" She could smell whiskey on his breath as he backed her up against the wall outside the door. She felt a pulse of fear—and a second, much sharper one of undeniable excitement.

"Looking for the bathroom." Her voice came out high and tight.

"The bathroom's that way." He pointed at the opposite end of the hall, to the door closest to the living room. She held her breath to see what he would do. He eased back; his breathing slowed. He made his way down the hallway to the only open door, a dark blue painted room across from the one at the end, and shut the door behind him.

Frances turned away from both doors and listed drunkenly down the hall back towards the living room.

In Jane's backyard, the three of them sat on a wooden picnic table, sharing a cigarette Elizabeth extracted from a crumpled soft pack of Marlboro Menthols she'd unearthed from the bottom of her Paul Frank bag. The smiling monkeys on their pale blue background were incongruous with the rest of her dark and subdued ensemble, but she'd been too hung over that morning to find her black clutch at the hotel and Frances didn't feel like finding it for her.

The air was crisp and cold, a welcome respite from the stuffy air inside. The silence was a gift after overhearing hordes of Jane's relatives discuss her for the last two hours straight while they tried to blend in and seem invisible.

The three were quiet. Haley jumped slightly as the patio door slid open behind them. Elizabeth turned around as Frances stared into the pool at the dry dead leaves skimming the surface. She looked at the monkeys on Elizabeth's purse and thought they were like that: Elizabeth with her hand over her eyes, Haley's over her ears, and Frances's over her mouth.

Frances heard footsteps approach and when he pulled back the nearby Adirondack chair and slumped over in it, she saw that it was Jane's brother. What was his name? Bexley or Baxter or something like that. A family name, Jane said.

Frances glanced up and saw Elizabeth watching him keenly. Frances recalled her earlier observation. He looked back at her and wordlessly held out a hand. She handed him her lighter. His fingers grazed hers lightly and there was a familiarity behind the gesture. Frances knew then, though she couldn't have explained how she knew, that there was something between them—before that day, something had happened. Haley, looking up at his even, streamlined features with her mouth open in a slight O, didn't seem to notice anything.

No one spoke. They smoked in silence. When he finished, he threw the butt into the pool and went inside. Elizabeth carefully ground hers out on the bottom of Jane's clog and dropped it in a flowerpot filled with dry dead leaves. Frances waited tensely to see if it would catch on fire. It didn't.

She resolved to ask Elizabeth what had happened between her and Jane's brother at the hotel that night. But Elizabeth spent the night on the bathroom floor on her side next to the toilet, sound asleep with one of the white hotel robes twisted around her slim coltish frame. Frances covered her with a towel and let her sleep.

· · ·

"I FORGOT ABOUT THAT," marveled Elizabeth when Frances had finished her recap of the second worst weekend of their lives.

"That's hardly surprising," said Frances dryly.

"Wow, I was really messed up that weekend, wasn't I?" she said.

"You were a masterpiece," said Haley, shaking her head. "Like a Picasso—just disconnected body parts and facial features floating through space. But also kind of beautiful, like his Blue period."

"Thank you for the art metaphor, Haley, but getting back to the point, don't you guys think that's weird?" said Frances. "First of all, there was nothing left of either of them. Which is horrifying to think about, but that means there was also nothing left to prove for a complete certainty that both of them were dead. Secondly, what was in that room at the end of the hall? Why wouldn't he let me go in?"

"His iguanas?" ventured Elizabeth.

"His what?" said Haley.

"He kept iguanas," she said. "Like, a lot of them. In terrariums. He was really into, you know, reptiles."

"How do you know that?" Frances said suspiciously.

"We saw each other in secret," Elizabeth admitted. "For like, half of senior year. Jane found out about it right before her stupid ritual, so truth be told it was probably me she was planning to kill. She never said anything, but she came down to breakfast one day and I knew. I could just tell that she knew somehow, even though all she did was look at me. It was the way she looked at me."

"How did she look at you?" asked Haley.

"With this look of like, disgust. Like 'of course you did that, Elizabeth. I'm not even surprised.' Then she ate her potatoes or whatever."

"I didn't know about this," said Haley in total surprise. "How didn't I know about it?"

"I didn't know about it, either," said Frances. She was shocked, even after all these years, that Elizabeth had actually kept a secret from her.

"We didn't know *every*thing about each other," said Elizabeth, annoyed. "Jane and I once got drunk and made out at Homecoming, for example."

"What?" gasped Haley, scandalized. As if it had just happened.

"It was a hate-kiss," she explained. "Like we were trying to stab each other with our tongues. Trying to outdo each other. Teenage girl stuff."

"I never did that," said Haley, staring.

"Wait, wasn't that the year that Madonna kissed Britney at the VMAs?"

"Probably," said Elizabeth. "Not to digress."

"So, we agree?" said Frances. "Jane might still be alive and out there somewhere, waiting. Biding her time."

"Whoa, whoa, let's not get ahead of ourselves," interjected Elizabeth. "I never said I agreed with that."

"I believe it," said Haley quietly.

"Say she is," repeated Frances. "She's obviously been playing dead for the last twenty years. But what if she's the one who's been sneaking into the school, doing all this stuff, moving the book around?"

"But why?" asked Haley.

"What if she's planning to do the ritual again?"

Frances said. "Only this time, take three new victims with her?"

"Well, you're definitely the first in line, if that's the case," said Elizabeth. "I hate to put it to you that way, but you're there, Frances. Maybe you should get out."

"You need to leave," Haley agreed. "All this stuff that's happening—I don't know, it's just a bad place, you know? I was so excited to leave for school, and then whenever I came home and saw all my old friends, they just seemed so ordinary, you know? The stuff they talked about, their plans. It was like Thackeray was the real world and everything else was just window dressing. But now, I think it was depraved. I think it made people go crazy. I think that Jane was one of them. And this other girl, this Rain?"

"Rowan," said Frances.

"It sounds like she's the same," said Haley.

"And if Jane has escaped from some secret sanitarium or wherever her parents had her stashed like Michael Myers all these years, you're definitely high on her list, Frances," said Elizabeth. "You and Thackeray. I know you like teaching and all—" she said this rather dubiously— "but maybe you should just take a nice little sabbatical and lie low for a while, till this all blows over."

"We did that before, and where did that get us?" asked Frances.

"Haley has herself a nice art career. And I know you haven't seen it, but I live in an extremely large house. And you have—you have your teaching," Elizabeth concluded lamely in spite of just questioning Frances's vocation only seconds before. "We have reasonably nice lives, for three teenage murderers. Maybe we should try to keep it that way."

"We're not murderers!" exclaimed Haley. Frances glanced at her closed door, paranoid, and put her earbuds in. "It was an accident."

"An accident we ran away from," said Frances. "Don't you guys see? We never stopped. We're still running. Maybe it's time we finally confront the past. Before it confronts us."

"Speak for yourself," said Elizabeth. "Look, Fran, if you want to come hide out at my house until this little coven of yours graduates, I'm happy to accommodate you. But I'm of the belief that we should let sleeping dogs lie."

"I agree," said Haley. "You're welcome to stay with me, too. But I just don't think there's anything we can do."

"Okay." Frances sighed. Admittedly, she had no viable solution worked out. "But will you just do me one favor?" She directed this at Elizabeth.

"What is it?" she asked warily.

"Call Jane's brother," she said, continuing over Elizabeth's protests. "Call him and ask about Jane. I don't think he'll tell you anything, but just…let me know how he reacts."

"Okay, okay." Elizabeth never could say no to Frances. "But if I wake up with a vengeful zombie ghost crawling across my bedroom, I'm sending her straight to you."

22

THE CALM BEFORE THE STORM

*T*he week of Thanksgiving break, there was a blizzard warning. It gave Frances flashbacks to the winter break the chapel burned down. The first major storm had come early this year, and there was a flurry of packing and updated travel plans to try and get out of Thackeray before it hit.

The headmistress yielded to an onslaught of calls from concerned parents and agreed to let the girls out a day early, ahead of the storm. Frances was unsurprised to learn that Rowan, Blair, and Tibbets were all unable to change their travel plans at the last minute and would have to stay at school an extra day. She had no doubt in her mind that the roads would become impassable and travel impossible, stranding the trio at school for the entirety of the break: subsequently providing Rowan with ample opportunity to perform the ritual.

Frances felt as though she could see the approaching disaster on the horizon with no real way to stop it. She considered both Haley and Elizabeth's words as she sat in her room the Monday before break. Maybe she *should* just leave. What was she thinking, staying in a dangerous situation just to watch history play out the same way twice? What made her think she could stop it? She hadn't been able to the first time; why should things be any different now?

Frances crossed the room and threw open the wardrobe. She started throwing everything she could find into her open suitcase at the bottom. Wasn't this what she had always done? Had it ever failed to solve the problem (at least, in an immediate sense)? She would just tell the headmistress there was a grave illness in the family she must attend to—her sick aunt, as usual. By now, the woman had been afflicted with everything from pancreatic cancer to lupus.

A knock at the door. Frances halted her hurried attempt at escape and glanced over her shoulder at the door. Anna, no doubt. Exasperated, she crossed the room and threw open the door. It was Tibbets.

"I'm sorry to bother you, Ms. Teller," she began, as her gaze wandered over the room and landed on the wardrobe. Tibbets' expression shifted from one of serious reserve to outright dismay. "You're leaving? I thought you were staying at the school over the holiday."

Frances was flooded with shame. To have a witness to her cowardice felt like more than she could stand. "Not yet," she said evasively. "Probably just overnight, on Thanksgiving Day." Lying to Tibbets felt, if it was possible, even more shameful than fleeing in broad daylight with a litany of flimsy excuses.

Relief flooded Tibbets' face. "Will you be back on Friday?" she asked.

"Friday?" asked Frances. "Why? What's on Friday?"

Tibbets flushed. "It looks like I won't be able to go home this weekend," she stammered, looking flustered. "I mean, at all. My mom wasn't able to afford to have my ticket changed and I've been watching the radar—it looks like flights are going to be grounded. I just didn't be want to be here alone all weekend…I'm afraid."

Frances glanced up and down the hallway to see if anyone else was coming. "What are you afraid of, Tibbets?" she asked.

Tibbets gazed down at the floor, shamefaced. "Ghosts, I guess." She looked up pleadingly at Frances. "It's just so scary here, and that's with everyone here in the dorm. I don't want to stay by myself."

"What about Rowan, and Blair?" Frances asked. "Are they both leaving?"

Tibbets snorted. "I'm sure Rowan's father will just send his helicopter pilot or whatever," she said with contempt. "Blair's mom will probably buy the roads and have them salted by her own personal fleet of snowplow drivers. They don't know what it's like, to struggle. They don't know what it's like to be alone."

This last statement made Frances's heart feel like it was caving in. Hadn't she felt completely alone at Thackeray, while all the other girls had families who cared, families who could swoop in to rescue them at a moment's notice? What kind of person would she be to allow a young girl to suffer the same fate out of her own cowardice? When was she finally going to stop running?

"To be honest with you, Tibbets, I've never much cared for my family," said Frances. It was the first honest thing she'd said all day. "I probably won't be leaving at all."

Tibbets looked as though she'd been given a stay of execution. "Oh, good," was all she said. "I'm glad. Thank you, Ms. Teller." Even as she backed away down the hallway, her eyes never left Frances's face.

Frances turned back to her closet and closed the doors. As they clicked shut, there was a finality to the sound, if only in Frances's mind. It demarcated the difference between her inclination to flee, and her resolve to stay and fight instead.

It was the difference between her past self, a frightened girl who put up walls and the person she thought could be now instead: a woman who stood up for the vulnerable and protected the ones who couldn't protect themselves. The person she wished she'd been all those years ago, for Bethany. She only hoped it would be enough to save Tibbets now.

MONDAY'S LUNCH in the dining hall was a tense affair. Many of the students were still looking shiftily at one other, hoping for some telling slip-up that would award someone with the leverage required for the headmistress's reward/bribe. Other students, particularly the underclassmen, were simply keyed up at the thought of break and escaping the oppressive, high-pressured environment of school for several days.

Frances had taken to eating in the cafeteria with the art teachers in order to avoid the petulant gossip of the faculty lounge, who discussed not only each other but the students with rabid enthusiasm. She found something particularly petty about listening to a bunch of adults with degrees, ostensibly in charge of the student body's mental advancement and overall well-being, discussing them with the same viciousness the students themselves used to decry one another. The art and music teachers mostly just talked about what movies they'd seen and various exhibitions at the MOMA they planned to attend.

Frances was an island at the end of their table, wrapped up in her thoughts of what she could do to stop whatever Rowan had planned for Thanksgiving break. The most obvious solution would be to get into the girls' room and take the book back, though she didn't think it would be hidden in the same place she'd found it before— no one was that dumb. Somehow, she didn't think it would stop Rowan, anyway. She probably had back-up scans on her laptop or had memorized the whole thing by now. Short of locking the girls in their rooms over break or reporting them to the headmistress—reporting what, exactly? —she had little but speculation and circumstantial evidence to go on.

Frances was startled from her pensive malaise when Anna plunked herself down on the bench beside her. She looked over to see the other woman gnawing on an apple and regarding her cheerfully.

"You're staying over the weekend too, I hear," she said by way of greeting. "I heard the funny bunch is going to be around, so I figure this is my chance to catch them in the act. Who else can it possibly be if anything happens when there's nobody else around?"

"I thought Rowan and Blair were going home for the holidays," said Frances, sipping her rapidly cooling coffee. "I thought just Tibbets will be here."

"Don't be fooled," scoffed Anna. "The headmistress has already heard from the Makepeaces that they'll be vacationing in Spain—must be nice—without Rowan, and Blair is being punished for her various 'disciplinary issues' by being forced to remain at school and work on college applications. If you can believe that. They're probably in their room right now, celebrating."

"I don't know if that's something they would necessarily celebrate," said Frances doubtfully, imagining how terrible it would be to be left behind by your own family on the holidays. And after meeting Blair's mom, it didn't surprise her in the least to hear she'd instructed her daughter to remain at school over break in order to get ahead.

"Are you kidding?" Anna laughed. "I'm sure that Rowan insisted her parents go without her and had them call the headmistress to tell her whatever she told them to say." Briefly, Frances remembered Martina Makepeace's claim of how controlling her daughter was. "Although it wouldn't surprise me in the least if Blair was so bad her family didn't want her around to sully their holidays." Frances was amazed at her cruelty in breaking the girls down. Why had she even wanted to become a teacher? She seemed to really hate children.

"Maybe," Frances said, finishing her coffee and setting the empty mug on the table, as if to signify the end of the conversation. Which, for her, it was. "But luckily, we'll both be here to keep an eye on them, won't we?" She got to her feet, fixing Anna with a pleasant expression.

"Why, yes," Anna said, looking back at her keenly. "We certainly will."

AFTER HER UNSETTLING exchange with Anna in the dining hall, Frances went back to her office to call Elizabeth and ask if she'd been able to garner any new information from Jane's brother. Given her memories of Baxter—Bixby? — as a teenager, her hopes were not high. She was surprised by Elizabeth's frantic expression when she connected with her via FaceTime.

"I can't talk long," Elizabeth whispered, casting a glance over her shoulder. "The campaign manager's here and she is a *nightmare*. She scrutinizes everything we do for the slightest single misstep, so talking to my best friend from high school with whom I may have inadvertently murdered two people will not be high on her list of approved activities."

"Did you talk to him? Bixby?"

"Baxter. Yeah, I was actually just going to call you— just a minute, I'll be right there! Sorry. I was going to call you. It was one of the stranger conversations I've had in a while."

"Strange?" Frances was instantly on alert. "In what way?"

"He *lost* it. He's always had an anger management problem, Baxter—it was mostly the reason we broke up, in addition to the ghost of his evil sister metaphorically haunting our relationship—but this was unreal."

"What did he say?"

"We haven't spoken for literal years, so it was kind of out of the blue when I called, and he sounded guarded as usual—which is pretty much the norm for him. I had no idea how to subtly broach the topic of whether Jane was secretly still alive after being declared dead for the last twenty or so years, so I just asked him outright if Jane got out of the fire that night, because I needed to know. There was just this long, spooky pause, so long that I thought he'd hung up, and then he was just like, what did you say? I repeated the question and he said that if I ever asked him anything like that again—or anyone, anywhere, ever—he would find me, and he would kill me. Like seriously straight up murder me! Who *talks* like that? Does he even know who my husband is? That whole family is a bunch of homicidal maniacs, I swear to God."

"So he definitely has something to hide, then," said Frances grimly.

"I would say that it seems like a given," Elizabeth said. "Although I don't know if it's anything as extreme as Jane hiding out in some halfway house somewhere, crouched in wait for her opportunity for revenge. He was always extremely touchy about so much as bringing up her name, after she died. Frances, you're getting out of there, right? Please tell me you're not considering staying. Don't be a hero."

"I'm getting out of here," said Frances. No point in worrying her unnecessarily. Especially during a campaign.

"Good. I know you want to help them, but you've got to admit there's only so much you can do. I find it highly unlikely that any girl today could be as crazy as Jane was. I'm sure they'll refrain from burning down the library in your absence, if it makes you feel any better."

"Of course," said Frances, her mind already elsewhere. "Would it be all right if I gave you a call after the holidays? I'm on my way to my aunt and uncle's place, unfortunately."

"Yes, definitely," said Elizabeth. "Call me anytime. I might not answer right away, if I'm up to my neck in some dinner or appearance or whatever, but I'll get back to you as soon as I can." There was a brief pause, then she added, "And please know that you'll always have a place at my table."

Frances felt deeply and unexpectedly moved. She took a shaky breath inward to calm herself before she replied.

"Thank you, Elizabeth," she said. "I'll keep that in mind."

THE FIRST FLAKES of snow were beginning to fall as Frances moved her car from the parking lot, where it would almost certainly be buried for days on end, to the carriage house. As she made her way from her car back to the dorm, a burly, towering figure swaddled in a puffy parka joined her on the walkway.

"Hello there," said Tom with a cheery, mittened wave.

"Hi, Tom." Frances smiled. Here was one of the few interactions she could possibly have on this campus that wasn't fraught with implications. "How's it going?"

"Getting ready to head home for dinner with my mom." He rolled his eyes. "She's sure to interrogate me about meeting a nice woman and coming up with some grandchildren."

Frances tried to picture Gretel Hildebrand as a cookie-baking, crocheting, kindly old grandma and found that she could not. "Could you maybe invent someone to pacify her, for the time being?" Frances suggested.

He laughed. "If I make up a girl I'm supposedly seeing, she'll want to meet her by Christmas dinner," he said. "No, my mother is quite the detective. Right now, she's helping me solve the case of the missing kerosene."

A slow, creeping sense of horror spread over her. "You're missing kerosene?"

"I keep quite a bit of it in the shed in the back of the cottage, for all these power outages we've been having," he explained. "The headmistress does like her oil lamps. Why any of the students would want to steal something like that is beyond me. Mom thinks they're a bunch of vandals, probably planning another fire." He shook his head. "Me, I think it was townies. Some drunk boys from down the hill. I should know; I used to be one." He laughed again. They'd reached the front steps of the school and he held open the door for Frances. "Going to tell the headmistress now. Wish me luck."

"Good luck." Frances forced a laugh and watched as he made his way up the winding double staircase towards the headmistress's office. Frances turned and ran up the opposite stairs, thinking only that she must come up with a plan. If someone had stolen kerosene from the gardening shed, that someone was almost certainly planning to start a fire. And Frances had a strong idea of just who that someone was.

23

HOME FOR THE HOLIDAYS

*D*uring Frances's final class before the school broke early for Thanksgiving, the girls seemed inattentive, exhausted, and subdued. Frances recognized the signs of checking out early for vacation, though she suspected it was more than the usual nerves over college applications and midterms affecting the students. The alleged haunting seemed to be taking a toll on them, as they'd confessed her first day of class that they truly believed there were ghosts in the hall. It was a substantial added stress to the already overwhelming strain of their considerable workload.

Frances tried to keep her lecture as light as possible for the final class, asking the students if they had anything in particular they wished to discuss prior to going home: worries, anxieties, or concerns they were welcome to vocalize. She knew there were many in class who would have benefited from a one-on-one session but either didn't make the time or considered visiting the school guidance counselor the province of crazy girls and something they should avoid.

The students regarded her bleary-eyed, and for a moment her question was met with only silence. Then Rowan—the only one of them who'd remained bright-eyed and alert up to this point—raised her hand.

"Yes, Rowan?" Frances said encouragingly, wanting to combat the sudden onslaught of side-eye that the girl's action received from her classmates. She wondered what they knew, or suspected, about Rowan. Or if it was, as Liddy Carlton had suggested, simply jealousy.

"I was wondering what you thought of ethics," said Rowan, fixing Frances with a serious stare.

"What about ethics in particular?" asked Frances. "Aristotle's *Nicomachean Ethics*? The three types of ethics? It's a pretty broad field. I'm afraid you'll have to narrow it down for me."

"Do you think there's any point to them?" she asked. "In even having ethics at all?"

"I would say that a civilized society is based on its ethics," said Frances, troubled by the question. She spoke contemplatively, careful not to reveal that the question disturbed her. Children were often amoral, without the benefit of experience to guide their decisions, but few of them questioned whether there was any point to contemplating right or wrong. "Without them, we would descend into anarchy."

"Most would say that the Nazis were highly unethical, but they were also highly organized," countered Rowan. "I don't see how you can say that ethics automatically leads to chaos."

"Only you would find a way to defend the Nazis, Rowan." From the back row, Brandy laughed.

"Even the Nazis imagined they were acting according to a higher ideal, however monstrous it was," said Frances. "Most people, even when practicing evil, believe that they're doing it for a reason, even if that reason exists nowhere but the inside of their own minds."

"Nazis are bad. Ethics are good. And you, as usual, are trying too hard." Tibbets looked up from her book and glanced over at Rowan. Frances stared. It was a remark she would have expected from Blair, not Tibbets. "Stop gunning for the Harvard rec, Row. For one day. Seriously, no one cares." Tibbets' eyes flicked back down to her book. Blair stifled an unpleasant laugh. Rowan looked stricken, her eyes flicking back down to her notebook. Frances felt an immediate and inexplicable impulse to reassure her.

"Rowan raises an interesting question," she said. Rowan looked back up at her. Tibbets arched an eyebrow without looking up. "How do we convince ourselves to act ethically, according to our convictions, when it seems so easy to do bad—and get away with it?"

"That's what I meant," said Rowan feverishly, latching onto this lifesaver in the sea of her decriers.

"I would argue that we have to live with the consequences of our actions," said Frances. "We have the rest of our lives to contemplate the repercussions of the decisions we make, and having a system of ethics to guide us can prevent us from making the wrong ones." She glanced around the room. Most of the girls were staring at her with a kind of glazed determination, hearing little, but resolved to get through the class. Brandy looked dubious. Blair was asleep. But Tibbets and Rowan watched her avidly, with the attention a predator devotes to prey. Frances glanced uncomfortably out of the window, aware she might have revealed too much.

"Of course, ethics are highly subjective to the individual, and that's only the opinion of one person," she continued. "And on that note, I feel that it's my ethical duty to release you for the break. After the term you've had so far, I feel that you all have earned it."

Sighs of relief broke out over the room like little brush fires. The girls hurriedly gathered their things and rushed from the room, as if afraid she might change her mind and call them back for a pop quiz. Rowan glanced up at her as she left, giving her a small smile. Frances slouched in her chair behind her desk, relieved as they were to see them go. She glanced around the room and saw that only Tibbets remained.

"You don't actually believe all that, do you?" Tibbets asked her as she slowly gathered her books.

"We have to believe in something, don't we?" Frances watched her. Her concern for the girl was mounting. The stress was beginning to show. She wished Tibbets would just confess whatever it was on her mind before she finally cracked. Before the ritual commenced, and history repeated itself.

"I don't know about that, Ms. Teller." She paused at the doorway and regarded her. Her expression was not one of either worry or fear, but seemed bright, almost mischievous. "I don't believe in anything at all, and I seem to be doing just fine." She disappeared through the open doorway. Frances stared after her. Was there anything more frightening, she thought, than a teenage girl?

THE NEXT DAY, the girls traipsed down the hill to their waiting parents, who helped them with their things. They loaded up their SUVs and luxury sedans as the snow began to fall in earnest. Frances watched the school empty and the snow swirl in the courtyard with mounting trepidation. Whatever was going to happen would happen this weekend. Of this she felt sure.

As the final girl caught a Lyft into town to catch her train, Frances turned to go inside. She felt like she was being watched. She glanced up at the windows of the east wing and swore she saw a face in the window, but by the time she looked more closely, the face had vanished.

Frances shivered. Partially it was the cold, but mostly it was the feeling Tibbets had described: the feeling of hauntedness. It was starting to take a toll on her, especially combined with her relatively certainty that she knew just who was doing the haunting.

THE NEXT DAY WAS THANKSGIVING. The headmistress had arranged for the remaining faculty (Frances, Anna, and Harmony Carruthers) to attend dinner with her and the remaining students (Rowan, Blair, Tibbets, Brandy, and an international student from Beijing) in the dining hall. Frances was not particularly looking forward to the dinner, as it entailed a number of awkward dynamics to navigate: Rowan and Tibbets, who were apparently quarreling; Rowan and Brandy, who were mortal enemies; herself and Anna, who were not exactly the best of friends; and the headmistress herself, who was an awkward person to be around under any circumstances—let alone a formal holiday dinner, an occasion normally reserved for immediate family.

Frances sighed as she buttoned up her most conservative cardigan over a neutral palette of taupe and mauve. Why had she wanted to subject herself to this again? The polite, forced conversations. The sterile hallways, the puritanical rituals. She had always had a tendency to idealize places in her mind, since she had few people in her life to idealize (besides the friends of her youth). She had a tendency to remember only the good and none of the bad. How else could she have imagined it would be a good idea to return to the sight of her greatest personal tragedy?

Subconsciously, she theorized, she must have wanted to return here because she'd never dealt with the past. Since she refused to do so in any other present she'd lived, she must have realized, on some level, that it would take being confronted with the situation directly in order to move on.

Yes, that's probably it, Frances, she said sarcastically to herself. This is all an elaborate attempt on the part of your subconscious mind to come to terms with your past. She shook her head. It was something she'd tell a patient, all the while feeling with complete certainty that she'd never engage in such a behavior herself. Well, look at her now.

Frances waited at the door until she heard Anna's door

open and close, her footsteps receding down the hallway. Modest, low-heeled pumps by the sound of it. She really couldn't stand Anna, in a way that felt petty and juvenile but no less true for it. Having to walk down to dinner with her and listen to her defame the students was one more Thanksgiving injustice she simply couldn't bear, on top of having to look at the headmistress over turkey and mashed potatoes for the next two hours. Were they serving it in courses, or all at once? If it was all at once, she could probably easily sneak away after forty-five minutes: just excuse herself as if to go to the bathroom, and never return. She'd felt a food coma coming on, she would say.

Frances was unpleasantly startled when she ran into Anna on the stairwell, staring at her phone's screen.

"Oh, hello," she said, struggling to sound pleasantly surprised. "I thought you'd gone down to dinner already."

"I was just on my way there," said Anna cheerfully. "We can walk together."

"Great." Frances forced a smile. Had she been waiting for her there? Frances forced this paranoid thought from her brain. She was getting as bad as the girls.

"What's it like here, over Thanksgiving?" asked Anna conversationally.

"I'm not sure," said Frances absently. "I never really stayed. I always went to my roommate's house."

"I always hated Thanksgiving," said Anna confidentially. Frances wondered if she thought they were friends and felt guilty for adamantly despising her. "My father and brother yelling at each other, and me hiding in my room under the bed."

"What did your mom do?" asked Frances, for lack of anything better to say to this awkward and deeply personal revelation. She could think of few darker holiday memories to share than a child cowering under a bed while half her family came to blows. Even Frances just holed up in her room with a book while under the care of her largely loveless guardians.

"Drank in her room." Anna smiled pleasantly, as if there was nothing unique about this holiday experience. "What about yours?"

"Dead," Frances said shortly. This was a surefire way to shut down any unwanted attempt at getting to know her better. She waited for the kneejerk response of *oh I'm sorry* followed by an awkward silence.

"I wish my family had been dead," said Anna, opening the door to the cafeteria for her. "It would have saved me the trouble of having to kill them."

Frances stopped and stared at her. She laughed in Frances's face. "I'm just kidding! It would have saved me a lot of awkward holiday meals. In you go."

Frances entered the dining hall, shaking her head. Was everyone at Thackeray insane? Looking up and sighting the lavishly decorated table in the center of the hall, at the head of which sat the headmistress, surrounded by a stuffed goose and five miserable girls, Frances realized it was about to get a lot worse.

DINNER FOR EIGHT

*F*rances stared at the stuffed goose on the table. *I know just how you feel,* she thought. She was seated in between Harmony Carruthers and Anna, across the table from Blair, who had lifted an eyebrow in greeting when she sat down. Blair was between Tibbets and Rowan, who steadfastly stared down at their respective plates, determinedly ignoring one another. The headmistress was seated at the head of the table across from Xiang Li, who appeared wistful to escape back to her room.

Frances filled her crystal goblet of wine noticeably fuller than the other teachers. Blair saw it and winked. Frances thought how much she reminded her of a young Elizabeth and promptly downed half her wine.

The headmistress clinked primly on her glass. The table fell silent. Everyone looked up expectantly. Frances checked her watch: *forty-three minutes to go.*

"In spite of our recent difficulties, I would just like to say how thankful I am to see all of your bright, smiling faces gathered around," McBride intoned. Frances felt confused. Was this like the end of *A Christmas Story*, when Ebenezer Scrooge awakens a changed man?

"I am so privileged, and yes, thankful, to oversee such a wonderful and heartfelt institution as ours. I am grateful, as always, for Thackeray—and for all of you here." The headmistress raised her glass and the others followed suit: Rowan with a solemn expression, Tibbets looking annoyed, Blair stifling a laugh, Harmony looking disgruntled, and Anna with an expression of utmost seriousness. Xiang didn't raise her glass at all and merely fixed the headmistress with a bored expression.

Frances stifled a laugh until she realized she hadn't bothered to pick up her glass, either. The headmistress shot her a dirty look and she quickly raised it. Xiang sighed, rolled her eyes, and did the same.

The headmistress took a sip of her non-alcoholic sparkling champagne, then looked expectantly at Harmony, who looked confused. Did she actually expect them to go around the table and give thanks? Frances took the opportunity to drain her glass.

Harmony cleared her throat nervously. "Ahem. Ah, yes. I'm grateful for my husband understanding that I needed to miss Thanksgiving dinner this year in order to help supervise the remaining students at Thackeray. Given that there are so many of them, I can see why it was necessary."

Frances stared at her, in awe of her brutal candor. Judging by the flush of her cheeks, Harmony had started early that day. Anna wore a look of startled disapproval. Rowan looked insulted. Tibbets sniggered into her napkin while Blair choked back a laugh. The headmistress pressed her lips together in a prim line.

"As I told you before, you are perfectly free to excuse yourself early," she said stiffly. "I simply wished to provide our remaining students, separated from their families over the holidays, with the maximum degree of support. Anna? What about you?"

Anna sat up straighter. "I'm thankful to you, Headmistress, for giving me an opportunity to teach here at Thackeray. I'm thankful to you girls, for making every day worthwhile. And to my fellow teachers, for bringing me into the fold." She tapped her glass against Frances's. It wobbled dangerously for a moment and Frances frantically grabbed it to keep it from tipping over. She'd never needed a glass of wine more.

Frances drained the glass. After Harmony's display of open defiance, she was tempted to refuse. The holidays were miserable for her and she hated to even acknowledge them, let alone be forced to do so. But she wanted to at least attempt to set a good example for the girls at the table with her.

"I'm thankful for old friends," she said finally, draining her glass. Harmony discreetly passed her the bottle of wine. Frances gratefully accepted.

"Hear, hear." The headmistress nodded sagely and turned her attention to Xiang. Xiang simply shook her head. Even the headmistress was unwilling to force an unwanted custom on an international student whose parents were paying out of pocket. She shifted her attention to the girls on the opposite side of the table from Frances. "Rowan?"

Rowan's face was serious in the candlelight. "I'm thankful for my friends." She looked at Blair and then Tibbets, waiting until Tibbets acknowledged her gaze. "I'm thankful for my teachers, and I'm thankful for Thackeray."

"That was lovely, Rowan." The headmistress beamed. *See, it's not so hard to be good.* "What about you, Blair?"

"I'm thankful that my mother decided to bang her Swedish masseuse this year instead of subjecting me and my father to yet another folly of a fake Thanksgiving where we all pretend," said Blair.

The headmistress closed her eyes, pained. "While we are deeply sorry to hear of your family troubles, Blair, I would prefer that you not air your private grievances at the dinner table. Is there something a little more positive you'd like to focus on? Your choral performance, perhaps?"

Blair stared at her like she was crazy. "I'm not *in* chorus."

"I am." Tibbets looked up. The candlelight glinted off her glasses and Frances couldn't see her eyes. "I had a solo in the spring concert."

"That's right." The headmistress looked pleased, as if she hadn't just mixed her up with Blair. "You have a lovely voice. Soprano, if I'm not mistaken."

"Alto." Tibbets cleared her throat. Frances, slightly buzzed, wondered if she planned to sing. "I'm thankful for my alto singing voice. I'm thankful for my friends—most of the time." She shot Rowan a look. "I'm thankful for my teachers, and Thackeray. And for you, Headmistress. For putting up with us." She smiled sweetly at McBride, who looked touched.

Frances studied her. What was she up to? Just the previous afternoon, she claimed to see no reason for basic human decency. Today she loved everyone. Was it hormones? Mood swings?

"Why, thank you, Tibbets." The headmistress ignored Blair, who was pretending to gag over her plate of roast goose. "Does anyone have anything they'd like to talk about?"

Silence reigned the table.

"The fire extinguisher is missing from the library," said Xiang.

The headmistress sighed. "I'll have Tom check on it when he returns tomorrow morning."

"What if there is a fire?" asked Xiang. "What will you do then?"

Frances choked into her wine. Blair watched her curiously. The headmistress blanched. "In the highly unlikely event that there is a fire in the library tonight, Xiang, I shall put it out myself, with the extinguisher from my office," said McBride.

"What if you do not arrive in time?" asked Xiang. "What then?"

"Then the library will burn to the ground," said Blair gleefully. "And we'll never have to study again."

"That is not going to happen," the headmistress snapped, finally losing her composure. "Now: does anyone have anything *pleasant* they would like to discuss?"

"I saw a family of deer at the edge of the woods today,"

volunteered Anna. "I took a picture of them on my phone." She passed it around the table to unanimous *oohs* and *ahs.* Everyone loved the family of deer. On this, they could agree.

"They look like a painting," murmured Rowan. She hurriedly passed the phone to Blair, blinking. "Will you excuse me for a moment?" She got up from the table and rushed off towards the bathroom.

"Someone misses her crappy excuse for a family," said Blair in a sing-song voice. Tibbets elbowed her in the ribs. "What? She'd be much happier if she just wrote them off like I did."

"You should never write off family, Blair," said Anna seriously. Frances recalled her odd comment at the door. She seemed to vacillate between being borderline malicious and Hallmark sincere. Frances couldn't figure her out. She found that she didn't want to. In the back of her mind, she was thinking of leaving at the end of the term. She would pack her things and this time, she would never return. The girls would try, and fail, to do what the book said because none of them were insane or audacious enough to light the school on fire. She would sit outside their room all night to ensure that they weren't. She would take the extinguisher from the common room and put it in the library.

Then they'll just burn down the common room instead, an unpleasant voice pointed out. It sounded like something Jane would say. Frances rubbed her temple.

"Are you all right?" Frances looked up to see Tibbets regarding her with concern.

"Yes, I'll be fine," she said, forcing a smile.

McBride gave her a little nod. She liked the sight of a

stalwart Thackeray girl powering through. "You're welcome to go back to your room and lie down, Frances." Frances sighed with relief and started to stand. "After dessert is served," the headmistress concluded.

Frances slumped back into her seat as the head-mistress lifted the cover from the pumpkin pie.

BACK IN THE EAST WING, Frances fought the tryptophan coursing through her body, threatening to lull her into a deep and bottomless goose-induced sleep. She must remain vigilant in case anything should happen tonight. That was why she'd borrowed the skeleton key from Anna and moved into the room across the hall from Rowan, Tibbets, and Blair. Anna had looked surprised, then pleased, when she'd asked.

"Good to see you're finally coming around," she'd said approvingly. "Wish I'd thought of it myself. We'll catch them for sure if they try anything tonight."

Frances didn't think they would. When Tibbets came to her room to ask if she would stay for the break, she'd seemed most concerned about Frances leaving on Friday. Friday was the day that frightened Tibbets, whatever she claimed about ghosts.

Frances got up and put a small wedge of wood between the door and the jamb. The hallway light cast a sliver on the floor. Now she was certain to hear if their door opened. Which she would, anyway, because she was definitely not going to sleep.

She put in her earbuds and found a loud playlist of riot grrrl songs out of 90s Seattle. She stared at the ceiling. It was like the soundtrack to her high school existence. She imagined she saw it all play out in a montage projected onto the ceiling: the seemingly endless field hockey practices, meals in the dining hall, trips over break and weekends at the mall. At least it seemed endless, until one day it ended. It wasn't that she wanted to stay in high school forever, but part of her wished she could have reached out and hit the pause button that final term, before everything went so horribly wrong.

Frances didn't know how long she watched the movie of her mind while suspended in a twilight state, halfway between sleep and waking. She was jolted up out of her subconscious by a thud in the hallway. She jumped out of bed before she was fully awake, already race-walking to the door as she rubbed her eyes. The thud repeated itself.

Frances peered into the hallway. She didn't see anyone, or anything. The noise issued again from down the hall. Her gaze wandered after the source of the sound. She watched and waited, perfectly still. She heard it again.

The thud seemed to come from behind the wall. Frances felt the hair rise on the back of her neck. *What was behind the wall?* It seemed to be clearly a question of *what* and not *who*.

Frances wanted nothing more than to go back to bed and pull the covers over her head, but she knew she had to pursue the sound to its source. She had to learn the truth. This was her opportunity to find out for a complete certainty if the bizarre occurrences had been the product of mortal mischief or paranormal activity.

She moved down the hallway, her heart in her throat. She could think of more than a few horrifying possibilities of what might be behind the wall and found herself imagining every awful thing from every horror movie she'd ever seen. She found herself waiting for something to come tearing its way through the wallpaper, grabbing her in its sharp talons and sucking her into the walls of Thackeray, never to be seen again.

Instead, the rhythmic thumps merely continued down the hallway, leading her to the staircase. Frances paused on the landing. She waited. The sounds resumed. Now they sounded like footsteps, making their methodical way downstairs. She repressed her fear and the inevitable questions of whether or not she was having a breakdown and finally going insane, once and for all—and if not, whose footsteps were they?

Frances followed the sounds all the way down the sweeping staircase. There was another brief pause, and then the sounds resumed: the click of boot heels across the foyer, disappearing into the quiet study room. Frances clicked the flashlight app on her phone and shined it ahead of her. She found she had to force herself into the darkened room.

As always, the window in the corner had been opened. This time, rather than simply sliding it shut, Frances examined it more closely. She peered outside, down at the ground below the window. No footsteps in the fallen snow. She examined the window ledge. Along the sill, she saw the letters carved into the wood: *BFJ*. Bethany Franklin Jones.

This had been Bethany's favorite study carrel. It was the farthest one from the door to the common room, and she was able to eat food she filched from the kitchens undetected. Food was strictly forbidden in the study room, not that Bethany had ever let that deter her. Frances sat at the desk at which Bethany had once sat.

She shined her light on its surface. Cold air billowed through the window in gusts, frozen air and a little bit of snow. She left the window open, though she couldn't have explained why, if asked. Not that she would be. There was no one else here tonight. No other human being, anyway.

There was nothing carved onto the surface of the desk. She ran her hand alongside the underside of the ledge, then the bottom. She flinched when she came across the inevitable wad of hardened, petrified gum. In the center, there was something else: she almost missed it, as it was nearly flat, flush against the underside of the desk. She leaned over and shined her light on it. She could just make out the outline of a square of paper. There was a note taped to the underside of the desk.

Frances crouched under the desk on her knees and pried the paper off with her thumbnail as carefully as she could. The paper was old, soft and fragile. The tape gave way with little effort. As her hand closed around it, the window crashed shut with a bang.

Frances jumped and hit her head on the underside of the desk, cursing. She quickly crawled out from under it and fled the study room. She ran up the stairs, back to the room across from Rowan and the other girls. She locked the door behind her.

Frances turned on the pink crystal salt lamp on the nightstand. The light was dim and suffuse, and she impatiently tapped the floor switch on the standard IKEA paper lamp in every dorm on the hall. She curled up in the armchair in the corner and carefully examined the slip of paper as if it was an ancient scroll.

Here Frances stopped dead and simply stared: on the underside of the note, the side that was flush against the desk, were scrawled four simple letters written in Bethany's hand: *JANE.*

BLACK FRIDAY

*F*rances's hand shook as she unfolded the note. It was a wrench to see Bethany's round, loopy left-handed scrawl after all these years. Her eyes scanned the page.

J,

I DON'T THINK *we should do this. I know you hate Elizabeth, but this is crazy. Really crazy. We could get in a lot of trouble. If we get caught in the chapel, we could get kicked out of school. If someone gets hurt—if Elizabeth gets hurt—we could go to jail. I don't want to go to jail. I know you think the book is real. But I don't. I don't want to do this, and I don't think you should, either.*

B

FRANCES REFOLDED the note and looked up with unseeing eyes. All she saw was the past.

It was Elizabeth (not Bethany) who Jane had wanted to sacrifice. And Bethany knew about it. Apparently, she had tried to stop Jane, to no avail. Frances wondered if Jane had seen the note, or simply dismissed it and re-taped it to the underside of the desk so she could pretend she hadn't.

Frances imagined how she would have felt if it had been Elizabeth, her best friend and roommate, who had died that night. She thought of everything that happened since—from taking care of Elizabeth during the memorial services to their college days to seeing her again more recently—and felt grateful for the time she had with her. And it made her look at Bethany and Jane through new eyes.

They weren't the odd couple she thought they were, one bumbling and sycophantic. It wasn't that Bethany was easily controlled while Jane was a devious mastermind. Bethany wasn't a naïve and helpless puppet, but someone who had been in on Jane's secrets. Still, she had tried to stop her at the last minute. Was that what had gone wrong in the chapel? Had Bethany died trying to stop Jane in order to save Elizabeth?

Dawn was breaking, filling the room with weak gray light. Frances's resolve hardened. It was time, she decided, to tell the headmistress. The girls must be stopped. This couldn't happen again. If Frances didn't know how to stop them, she would appeal to a higher authority. Maybe the headmistress would separate them for the remainder of break and have each of them under supervision by one of the teachers. Frances didn't know. She only knew that she was in over her head, and the past could not be permitted to repeat itself.

After she locked the room behind her and set off down the hallway, Frances rehearsed what she planned to say when she arrived at the headmistress's office. She would tell her about the missing kerosene that disappeared from Tom's shed. She would confess that the chapel fire had been no accident, and that it had been started by a student. And that she, Frances, had witnessed it.

She would tell her about the book and explain that it had fallen into the hands of the very girls the head mistress suspected of causing all the recent trouble, and that she believed the girls had the same plan that Jane once had. Then she would be at the headmistress's mercy. Frances didn't care if she was fired, she only wanted to know that action would be taken.

"Frances? Where are you going?" Frances stopped at the top of the stairs. Anna, of course. Did she have her under surveillance? How did she always seem to appear at the most inopportune of times?

Frances reluctantly turned to see Anna approaching her from the corridor, already dressed for the day. Frances was still in sweatpants and a Thackeray hoodie. She glanced at the round porthole window over the landing. The sun had yet to rise, and the inside of the school was still dark. What was Anna doing? Was she going to wait in line at Best Buy to get a TV?

"I'm going to the headmistress's office," said Frances. If she was finally going to start being an adult, she would have to fully rely on other adults to control the situation. "I believe the girls have hatched a dangerous plan."

"So it is them, then." Anna's eyes gleamed as she drew closer. "What is it? What did you find?"

"I have to take this to the headmistress," said Frances firmly, sidestepping the question. "Then we can determine where to go from there. I think they need to be separated—Tibbets from the other two. After we separate them, they need to be monitored. At all times."

Anna nodded. "I'm so glad you see what I see," she said. "I feel like no one takes me seriously, as an outsider. I've been reluctant to fully voice my suspicions. Let me go to the headmistress while you keep an eye on the girls. They listen to you. You have a better chance of stopping them."

Frances hesitated. She knew things that Anna didn't, things she needed to tell the headmistress in person—in confidence. "I really need to talk to her myself," she hedged.

"I'll ask her to call everyone in for a meeting," said Anna eagerly. "I'll explain that you've acquired new evidence. You'll speak to her first, and then she can call the girls in once she's determined what to do with them. If I watch them, they'll probably lock me in my room again. They'll slip through my fingers and get away by the time you get back, I'm sure of it."

Frances raised her eyebrows. "They locked you in your room?"

"It's been known to happen," said Anna bitterly. "Just

watch them. I'll be back in ten minutes. It's time we put this to an end."

Relief washed over Frances, as much as she tried to push it away. If Anna went to the headmistress instead of Frances, she wouldn't have to confess to her involvement in the fire. Action would be taken, they would all prevent disaster, and maybe Frances could go on living her relatively quiet life. It seemed selfish and somehow unlikely, but Anna had given her such a clear out. Frances found in that moment that she wanted very badly to accept her help.

"All right," she said. "But please, hurry."

"Of course." Anna reached out and squeezed her arm. "I'll be right back." Anna rushed off in the direction of the headmistress's office.

Frances turned and went back the way she came. She paused at the door of the girls' room, listening. It was silent. She began to pace the corridor. Was she mistaken, getting Anna involved? Neither the headmistress nor Anna seemed as concerned with the girls' welfare as they were with their own image—the headmistress's upstanding image of Thackeray, and Anna's image of herself as competent in the headmistress's eyes.

How much of this would be about punishment rather than stopping them, and helping them? Even if they were separated, suspended, punished, it wouldn't stop them from ultimately trying to execute the plan they had already put into motion.

The plan they had put into motion.

Frances stopped and looked at the still and silent door. She had been so sure she would know if they left. Anna, on the other hand, had been certain they had another means of escaping their room—maybe even through the window. Frances put an ear to the door. She heard nothing within. She removed the skeleton key from the front pouch of her hoodie and slid it into the lock. She turned it and pushed open the door.

Part of her wished for nothing more than to see the girls' sleeping faces against the pillow. But the larger part of her was not surprised to see their beds were empty. Rowan's had been made neatly in her wake; the sheets tucked neatly into hospital corners. Blair's duvet was thrown carelessly back, half on the floor. Tibbets contained a misshapen lump that for a moment, Frances thought might be her. But it was only her pillows gathered in a shadowy bunch on top of her comforter.

The window was slightly ajar. Through it slipped a thin stream of ice-cold air. Frances pictured it: how easy it would be to return to the shed behind Tom's and boost his extension ladder after dinner, leaving it propped against the wall beneath the window. But where would they have gone? Surely not somewhere out on the grounds, not during a storm of this magnitude. They must have snuck out the window and circled around. But to where?

The library. The fire extinguisher had disappeared from the library earlier. Rowan wouldn't have wanted anyone to have a way to put out the fire. Her questions about ethics had a new and darker meaning now. Was it unethical to sacrifice a friend if it meant eternal success? Never disappointing your parents and teachers or succumbing to failure ever again? Frances feared that she'd already drawn that conclusion for herself, and she'd taken her best friends along for the ride.

Frances hurried off in the direction of the library. Just as she set off down the corridor, the power went out. She stopped and glanced up. The sun had not yet risen, and the windowless hallways were plunged in darkness. Cursing, she accessed the flashlight app on her phone and resumed her trek.

Shadows seemed to loom out of nowhere, as if they had a life of their own. Then one in particular drew her eye. It loomed large at the end of the corridor, in the shape of a girl: a silhouette, like the one that had appeared on the staircase when Frances first arrived at the school.

Frances halted, standing stock still as the silhouette beckoned. Slowly, she moved forward. The silhouette glided along the wall ahead of her, leading her towards the library. When they were nearly there, the shadow stopped. It seemed to lift itself from the wall and resolve its shadowy form into a more solid shape. Frances stared at the shadowy figure of Bethany, standing in the hallway.

Guilt crashed over her in waves. "I'm sorry," she said, gazing at the figure of her old friend.

Bethany only smiled slightly. She raised her hand, pointing. It wasn't the main entrance of the library she pointed to, but the door that led to the back of the stacks. She raised her spectral hand to her mouth, placing one finger over her lips. Frances understood without asking, without needing anything more to be said.

She killed the light on her phone and slipped into the back entrance as quietly as she could, letting the door close by inches until it clicked shut with barely a sound.

She waited for her eyes to adjust. She went to the end of the aisle and peered around to the main room of the library. There was no one there. But she didn't have long to wait.

It couldn't have been more than a minute before the main door of the library clanged open in the darkness, which was instantly disrupted by a series of three narrow beams. The lights swung wildly and erratically back and forth in the darkness, illuminating the floors and ceilings, then the shelves. Frances ducked back into her hiding place and waited.

"She's not here yet," came Rowan's impatient voice, followed by the zipper of a backpack. Who wasn't there? Were they waiting for Frances? Was she the sacrifice?

"She'll be here." Blair's voice was calm. "We just have to wait."

"Well, I guess we can get started while we do." Tibbets' voice was dubious. "Do you have the candles? And the matches?"

"I have everything right here," said Rowan. "Do you have the book?"

"Obviously I have the book." Tibbets' voice was cold. "After you nearly lost it for all of us."

"I didn't know what to do!" Rowan protested defensively. "It's not like we have an abundance of hiding places at our disposal. I didn't think they were going to search our room that day; I thought they were doing the underclassmen's rooms first."

"They don't suspect the underclassmen of doing anything wrong," said Tibbets patiently. "They think we're responsible for everything."

"Only because they don't believe in ghosts," Blair pointed out.

"It doesn't matter what they think about us now," said Rowan. "What matters is we finally have a chance to do it. After this, we don't have to worry about anything anymore."

Frances realized this was it: her opportunity to do what she should have done all those years ago. To stop this disaster before it was ever even put into motion. Not everyone got a shot at redemption, but here was hers—literally staring her right in the face. Frances stepped out of the stacks.

A flash of motion caught the corner of her eye, and she turned. It was Bethany. Silvery, translucent, and weeping. She remembered Haley's words in the coffee shop: *they all kept talking about the crying girl...*

Bethany looked at Frances and shook her head. Frances realized at that moment that Bethany had been here, all along. Maybe she'd never left. Maybe to her, no time had passed. And the outages, the shadows on the wall, the open window by her favorite study carrel leading her to the note about Jane had been warnings: Bethany was trying to protect her. The same way Haley and Elizabeth had when they told her to leave—to get out and save herself.

But Frances had done that before. The end result was that she'd never truly been able to leave Thackeray. She might have physically departed the grounds in a way the friends she'd lost that night never could, but she was still here, in her mind. Trapped, just like Bethany. And it was here she would always remain unless she found a way to put the past right.

Frances walked out of the stacks to confront the girls. They'd set their flashlights up in the center of a nearby table, beams pointed straight up at the ceiling.

"I know what you're doing," Frances said as she walked towards them down the aisle between the bookshelves. "I know you think this is a good idea, but trust me when I tell you that it's not. I speak from personal experience on this one."

Rowan glanced up, her expression startled. Blair jumped about a mile, knocking over one of the flashlights. Tibbets remained still, her face fixed on Frances, that peculiar glint from her glasses obscuring her eyes and making her appear sightless. Frances had the sudden thought that they were like the three blind mice.

"I don't want you to get in trouble," Frances said. "Ms. Raines has gone to fetch the headmistress, but if you stop right now, I doubt you'll get more than a slap on the wrist for being out of bed after hours. If you'll give me the book, and give up on your quest, you can say you've been sneaking out of bed to spend extra hours in the library studying, maybe working on your college applications. I'll attest to the stress you've all been under, as you've spoken to me about it in the past. But please believe me when I say that nothing makes everything all better."

Rowan's confused expression resolved itself. "I don't think you understand, Ms. Teller," she said.

"I do understand." Frances stopped when she reached the table, covered by their ring of lights. "More than you can ever imagine. That fire that was set here, twenty-one years ago? It was the result of the very act you're trying to perform. That book has been around longer than you know. You're not the first people to find that book and to fall under its spell. It happened to some very good friends of mine who are no longer here as a result. It happened to me."

Tibbets spoke up next. "We know that, Ms. Teller," she said gently. "We already know."

"What?" Frances was perplexed. How could they possibly know?

"It's not us." Rowan watched her gravely. "Not *just* us, I mean."

"What are you talking about?" Frances was getting upset. She was the adult; they were the children. It was her job to reassure them, to exhibit control over the situation. Instead, it was like they were the ones comforting her, as if she was the child instead of them. They stood in a semi-circle, exuding an eerie calm, watching her with identical expressions of sympathy.

The door swung open. Frances whirled around and breathed a sigh of relief. Anna, the last American Girl Scout. If Frances's authority wasn't enough to intimidate the girls into submission, maybe the authority of two teachers would be.

Anna glanced curiously around, taking in the sight of the three eerily motionless girls with Frances in front of them. "Well, well," she said. "It seems I got here just in time."

"Anna," said Frances relieved. "Did you see the head-mistress?"

"Yes, I did," Anna said gravely. "Fortunately, she didn't see me." She laughed. "She never even saw it coming."

"What are you talking about?" Frances heard the odd tone of her voice, like the one outside the dining hall on Thanksgiving. "Saw what coming?"

"Saw it when I hit her over the head and left her tied up on the floor of the office," Anna said conversationally.

Frances stared. "Now is really not the time for jokes—" she started.

"But I'm not joking, Miss Teller," said Anna seriously. "Frances." Something about the way she said her name stopped Frances cold. There was something so familiar about it. "I've been waiting a long time for this."

Frances's mind was reeling, putting the pieces together even as she struggled to reject them. No, surely not. It wasn't possible. What had Tom said, about the townies?

"Please don't hurt the girls," said Frances. "If this is a down-the-hill thing..."

"Oh, Frances." Anna regarded her with amused contempt. Contempt, and something else: much like the girls, who now watched quietly, Anna's expression contained a little a bit of sympathy. "I can't believe you bought my bumbling townie routine! You were always sharp as a tack. I thought I'd never get by you, with you living across the hallway like that. I overestimated you. Or maybe I underestimated what a good plastic surgeon can do."

Frances's heart raced. She stared at Anna Raines, realization dawning on her. "Jane?" she said weakly.

Anna's smile broadened into a wide, malicious grin. She was Anna no more. Even the contacts and dyed hair couldn't conceal the secret she hid within. Her features might have been reconstructed, reconfigured, and enhanced, but there was no mistaking the deep twin wells of madness in her eyes.

"Now, Frances," said Jane. "Is that any way to greet an old friend?"

THE FACE BEHIND THE MASK

rances stared into the new face of her oldest enemy and former friend. Different nose, new chin, colored contacts, hair dyed and straightened, lip and cheek injections. Even with all the work, she might have still spied the faintest traces of the old Jane beneath the layers of cosmetic work, but Jane was dead— or at least she had been, up until a moment ago. Frances had never gone looking for the face of a dead girl in the one of the woman across the hall she'd done her best to ignore.

Now she felt sickened by her own blindness. It was a feeling familiar to her, one she'd often felt around Jane: that feeling of being swindled, of having the rug pulled out from under her feet. She'd think she had a handle on things only to realize that no—it was Jane who was one step ahead of her, who could predict her every move before she even made it. Tonight was no exception.

Frances thought of Bethany in the aisle, weeping. Trying to stop her from making this terrible mistake. The same one, no doubt, made by Bethany herself all those years ago. What was she doing back here? Why had she waited, all of this time?

"You were wrong about the book, you know," said Jane, sitting on the table like it was old times, like they'd never left Thackeray. She glanced at the girls and made a little gesture with her hand. They all sat obediently in the nearest chairs and waited. It was as if she had brainwashed them. She probably had. She'd done it before.

"What do you mean?" said Frances mechanically. All she could think of was to keep her talking. If there was one thing she knew about Jane, it was how much she loved to brag about her accomplishments.

"Some things *do* make it all better," said Jane. "What you don't realize, Frances, was that the ritual did, in fact, work. You would know that, had you taken it more seriously than you did. You were never really down for the cause, were you? Always just along for the ride. Living vicariously through the rest of us, because you'd forgotten how to live." Jane snorted. "Or because you were too afraid. But I was always serious. The ritual required a sacrifice, and so I performed one. I intended it to be Elizabeth, of course. She was always undermining me. Trying to turn the rest of you against me. Then she went after my brother—no doubt purely out of spite. Then Bethany developed a conscience, after years of doing everything I told her to. Suddenly she was Jiminy Cricket. She kept trying to stop me; to stop it from happening. But you can't stop a boulder from rolling down a hill, once it gathers enough momentum. Anything that gets in its way will be crushed. And I had all the momentum in the world." Jane smiled dreamily. "It was like I could feel it flowing through me, you know? Like I just knew. The same way these girls know there are forces here beyond anything the books on those shelves can explain."

The girls watched her, transfixed. Frances realized that while she'd been reassuring them about their grades and the pressure their parents were putting on them, Anna had been getting into their heads on a whole other level. She'd pretended with Frances that she avidly disliked them and considered them little more than suspects, but she'd been playing Frances from minute one.

"It can give you anything you want," Jane said. Her eyes were shining in the dim light. "It gave me anything I wanted. For a while, I worried that it hadn't worked. The book said that I had to set an intention, and I intended to kill Elizabeth. Then Bethany freaked out at the last second and tried to stop me. She kicked over one of the candles, to distract me. What she didn't realize was that I snuck into the chapel earlier and soaked the floors in gasoline. I needed an accelerant. I needed to make sure that Elizabeth didn't make it out in time, and that the place would go up fast. Even faster than I could have imagined, it seemed. You guys freaked out and ran. I anticipated that; that was when I planned to tackle Elizabeth. I'd say later on that she was running in the wrong direction, and I was trying to save her. But tragically, she only thought I was trying to start a fight with her. She scratched me and ran into the smoke, and I only just got out in time. But it ended up being Bethany who fought me. Who jumped on me and stopped me from reaching Elizabeth. I tried to get her off of me, but she was heavy, you know? So when I finally shook her off, it was almost too late. I would have gotten her out—I really didn't want anything to happen to her, you know—but I could barely see, let alone breathe. I went for the first exit I could find, and I never saw her again."

Bethany had been a hero. Frances replayed the scene in the chapel that night with this new information in her mind. It was Bethany who tried to stop Jane when none of them had, Bethany who stopped her from hurting Elizabeth. She had known what Jane planned to do; it was true. She should have said something sooner. But she had tried to save them, in the end.

"What about the marks on the mirror?" Frances asked. Someone had to come looking for them. They had to. "I saw them. There were four of them. I thought you planned to kill all of us."

"I considered it," Jane said cheerfully. "If one person could grant me eternal wealth and prosperity, imagined what I'd get from four! But I couldn't go through with it, honestly. I lived with Bethany for four years; I liked you and Haley. I didn't want that kind of blood on my hands."

"Just Elizabeth's," said Frances bitterly.

"Look, Frances," said Jane impatiently. "I know she was your bestest buddy and all, but it's not like she was some kind of saint. She popped pills and never ate, and she was mean to people. And she *did* sleep with your boyfriend. She told you he came on to her after the fact, because she felt guilty, but it happened. She was ruthless. Maybe even as ruthless as me."

Frances didn't know or care whether or not Jane was telling the truth. It was decades ago; who cared if Elizabeth slept with Rutherford? It was easy to make mistakes, where Rutherford was concerned. If she hadn't told her, it had only been to preserve their friendship, which she must have known would have ended otherwise. It was pretty amoral, but weren't they all? They'd all gone along with Jane, right up until the end.

"I don't understand," said Frances slowly. "Why are you so convinced that it worked, Jane? What evidence can you possibly have?"

"What *evidence?*" Jane stared at her incredulously. "Frances, how can you possibly be so naïve? Look at what happened for everyone in the chapel that night: Haley became a famous artist. Elizabeth married a senator and lives in some mansion on a hill. You know the most she could ever hope for was to marry for money. I left Thackeray and went straight to Vegas, after I stopped back home for my own funeral. Which was amusing, to say the least. I watched you all in the backyard, crying over me like you had nothing to do with it. I couldn't tell if you were just drunk or guilty or actually sad because you thought I was really dead. Anyway, I won a bunch of money. I played the lottery. It was like I was invincible or something. I had enough money to start over, get a new face, a new name, a new life. Go wherever I wanted and do whatever I felt like. It was like *The Picture of Dorian Gray*. Remember when we read that? For AP English? The part when he travels all over and basks in his immortality?"

"He sells his soul," said Frances. "The picture grows more warped and evil over time because it's the deterioration of who he is inside. Who he could have been."

"Rather a moot point, I'd say," said Jane. "When you're rich, who gives a shit about the person you could have been? What does that even mean? I could have worked the rest of my life and never seen that kind of money. I liked Bethany and all, but I have to say—it was kind of worth it."

Frances felt disgust rise in her throat like bile. Jane was like a bad penny she couldn't throw away. She just kept coming back.

"Why did you come back here, Jane?" she asked. "Why are you even here?"

"It seems my luck has run out." Jane sighed. "I wasn't exactly frugal, unfortunately. I wasn't aware there were any limitations or terms on the power the book had bestowed on me. I blew through my cash, then my savings. It wasn't like I could go out and get a job; I was supposed to be dead. I didn't even finish high school. I tried to gamble again, tried playing the numbers. No such luck. That feeling that I'd felt, it was gone. That was when I knew: I had to do it again. This time, I'd make sure it stuck. And now here we are." She smiled broadly at Frances, then the girls.

"Ms. Raines?" Rowan spoke up. She looked uncertain. "What exactly are we going to do? I thought you said we just needed to read from the book? That the thing about the sacrifice was, like…optional, or whatever."

"That it was like, optional or whatever." Jane mimicked her cruelly. "Don't be an idiot, Rowan. I thought you were the one who was fascinated by the possibility that we can get whatever we want, be whoever we want, if we're only willing to sacrifice. Isn't that what you wrote about, in your essay? That was how I chose you; you know. Your essays for class."

Frances thought of the copy of *Dorian Gray* she'd seen on Jane's desk when she was masquerading as Ms. Raines. Jane's other bible, after the book. The smell of Cool Water cologne in the hall. Some things never changed. And some ghosts just wouldn't stay buried.

"Rowan's made it perfectly clear that she would do anything for a little bit of power," explained Jane. "Blair said she admired Dorian, for not being weak and for taking what he wanted. And Tibbets?" Jane smiled fondly at the girl. "Yours was my favorite essay of all." Tibbets remained silent, saying nothing.

Blair, on the other hand, was starting to look sick. "Ms. Raines—Jane—whoever you are, I never agreed to kill anyone. I mean, I thought it was a little weird in the first place, but I was willing to try it just to see what happened. But I'm not going to kill a teacher. That's completely beyond."

"Well, Blair, unless you'd like me to kill you instead, then you're just going to have to go along with it," said Jane patiently. Blair looked stricken. "Otherwise, it will be your word against ours, and you can do the time for everyone. Like Frances here." Her eyes flicked back to Frances. "You never experienced the power, did you? Never benefited from Bethany's sacrifice. Because you didn't believe, you didn't want it enough. You rejected it. Out of guilt, to wear your little hair sweater or whatever. You could have had anything you wanted."

"I didn't want anything," said Frances. "The only things I wanted could have never been given to me by a book."

Jane snorted. "What, your family back?" she mocked Frances. "*We* were your family. I was. Me. You were an ingrate. You couldn't see what was right in front of your face."

Now Rowan was starting to look uncomfortable. "Ms. Raines, I don't want to hurt Ms. Teller," she said. "Isn't there another way?"

"'Fraid not," said Jane breezily. "It's my way or the highway. And at this point, I'm afraid you girls don't have a lot of say in the matter. I'm going to perform the ritual. Then I'm going to light this place up. If you'd like to stay and get burned to a crisp with Ms. Teller here, that's your business."

She turned to Frances. "What do you say, old friend?" She smiled broadly. "Once more, for old time's sake?"

A FRIEND IN NEED

A Friend in Need

*F*rances's eyes flicked towards the window. It was getting lighter now. The library was filled with gray-blue light. The headmistress was tied up, Xiang Li was slumbering peacefully in her room, and Harmony Carruthers had gone home to her husband. Tom was with his mother. But what about the other side of the lake? What about Rutherford? There had to be at least one person left who could intervene.

But there was no one. Frances knew this as surely as she knew that the person standing in front of her was the last person she ever thought she'd see again, the last person she'd ever wanted to see. She'd tried to repress the past, to bury it so that it could never harm her again, and now it was back.

So this was what she got for running away from her problems.

"Jane," said Frances urgently. Yes, she was unstable and

dangerous, but hadn't they been friends once, all those years ago? "You've got to stop this. You can't run forever. These girls have a chance. Don't ruin their lives the way we ruined ours." She was careful not to accuse her. That wouldn't lead to any favorable results.

"Frances, Frances." Jane laughed. Had she ever laughed, as Anna? Frances felt certain that if she had, she would have known immediately that it was Jane all along. Her laugh was unmistakable—mocking and grating all at once. "Are you trying to *reason* with me? You can't possibly imagine that will have any effect. I've made up my mind, and so have they. Haven't you?" Jane cast a pointed glance around the table.

Blair looked too afraid to move. Rowan pressed her lips together, silent. Frances imagined her weighing her options: rebel, be murdered and never go to Harvard, or go along with her captor. Tibbets continued gazing into the distance, as if in another place. Frances wondered if she'd gone catatonic.

"They don't want this," Frances said firmly. "They don't want to go through with it. And I won't let you."

Jane rolled her eyes. "What, you think this is a choice?" She reached into her bag and Frances saw the gun. It glinted in the breaking dawn, metal and menacing. Jane raised her eyebrows. "Everyone participates. Or school's out—for good." She laughed again. That guttural, horrible laugh. She was positively relishing this. She aimed at the girls, gesturing. "Put the candles on the table and light them up. I'll tell you what to do from there."

The girls obediently rose and followed Jane's orders.

Frances considered the odds of her being able to over-power Jane without getting shot.

"Don't even think about it," Jane said, tapping the gun lightly on the table. "I can still read your mind, even after all these years." She smiled. "I'd forgotten how much I enjoyed your company, you know. You always had the most cynical sense of humor. Like when I tried to catch you lying about going shopping and what you'd bought. 'An eight ball and a pack of Camel Lights,' you said. It was so hard to keep a straight face! I almost wanted to tell you then. So we could reminisce. But of course, it wouldn't have been that way. I had to remain buttoned-up school-marm Anna, the walking conscience. How ironic."

Frances remained silent. How easily she'd deceived her all these months. She'd never realized what was looking her right in the face.

Jane glanced over at the girls. "Can you hurry up? I thought you were supposed to be the best and the bright-est. My god, you're slow."

The girls hurried to finish lighting the candles. Frances's heart hurt at her own worthlessness. Her one task was to protect them, and she couldn't even manage that.

Jane gestured with the gun again. "All right, get in a circle. Frances, you're next to me. I want you close by. You and Rowan get on either side of me. The four of you will hold hands and repeat after me."

Jane stood behind Frances with the gun at her back. Frances gently took hold of Rowan's and Tibbets' hand while Tibbets held Blair's. She knew then that she really had never made it out of the chapel that night.

"Repeat after me," Jane instructed.

As she descended into the lengthy string of gibberish, made-up nonsense words and the girls mechanically repeated after her like robots, Frances glanced over Rowan. Her expression was stricken, her eyes filled with grief. *I'm sorry,* she mouthed to Frances. Frances squeezed her hand. She gave a slight nod towards the wall. Rowan's eyes followed her, landing on the fire alarm on the far wall, then widened. She nodded.

Frances glanced over her shoulder. Jane's eyes were closed. Her head was tipped back, and her expression was one of rapture, ecstasy. Frances squeezed Rowan's hand again and she ran for the wall.

Frances grabbed Jane around the waist, tackling her to the ground. The gun flew out of Jane's hand, skidding across the wood floor. She screamed and rolled over on top of Frances, wrapping her hands around her throat. Frances clawed at her face as she choked her, kneeing her in the mid-section and knocking her to the side.

A high-pitched clanging sounded. Rowan had reached the alarm. Frances clambered to her hands and knees. Blair was frozen in place, hugging her arms to her chest, looking lost. Tibbets stared at the candles on the table as if hypnotized. Rowan looked at Frances, scared and uncertain of what to do next.

"Run," Frances said. "Run to the headmistress's office, and—" Her words were cut off when Jane's arm looped around her neck, bending her head backward. Jane's other hand shot out and grabbed one of the candles on the table.

"Make one move," she said calmly. "And I will torch this place and everyone inside of it. Including myself.

Don't test me. I've done it before." She pointed at the table. "Sit."

Tibbets immediately sat down at the table. Blair moved quickly to sit down beside her. Slowly, reluctantly, Rowan drifted over from the wall and sat next to Blair. Jane pushed Frances roughly into the chair next to Blair.

"Ever the problem child, Frances," said Jane, shaking her head. "You just don't know when to quit, do you? Maybe we should end the party early." She raised the gun to Frances's head. "There's nothing in the book that says you actually have to die in the fire, after all."

"No!" shouted Rowan. "Don't do it."

"What's this?" Jane raised an eyebrow. "I'm sensing an insurgency here. Maybe I should get rid of you, too." She aimed the gun at Rowan.

"Please," said Frances urgently. "Don't hurt the girls. If you're going to hurt anyone, Jane, please just make sure it's me."

Jane rolled her eyes. "Just make sure it's me," she mimicked Frances. "Since when did you become such a martyr, Fran? That was always more Bethany's thing than yours." Something behind Frances seemed to catch her attention. Her eyes widened. For a moment she stood stock still, her gaze fixed and frozen on whatever she had seen. Then she seemed to shake herself and come to her senses. Frances glanced behind her. She thought she saw the fleeting glimpse of something glimmering in the stacks. Then it was gone.

"Now, where was I?" she said.

"I believe you were about to put the gun down and

back away from them slowly," a cold voice came from the door.

Frances looked up to see Elizabeth in the doorway, with Haley right behind her. Elizabeth held a gun that was easily twice the size of Jane's. Frances remembered vaguely reading somewhere that her husband had a lot of backing from the NRA.

Jane swiveled her head slowly around like an owl's. It was both unnatural and unholy. It was a sight that Frances would see in her nightmares for a long time to come.

"Where did you come from?" she hissed. She aimed the gun at Elizabeth, who didn't budge.

"I've been talking to your brother," said Elizabeth, entering the library and slowly advancing on Jane. "He didn't want to speak to me at first, but then I showed up at your house with my friend here—" she nodded at her gun—"and he suddenly got very candid. I knew you'd come back here to finish what you started, Jane. You always were predictable that way."

"I'm not going to stop," said Jane. "I don't care if every single one of you dies."

"I know," said Elizabeth regretfully, just before she pulled the trigger.

The noise of the shot rent the library in two. Jane dropped like a stone. The girls screamed and crawled under the table. Haley rushed over to check on them. Frances ran to Jane's side, where she lay on the kerosene-soaked floor, clutching her arm and howling. Elizabeth walked over to the table and blew out the candles.

"Just like old times," she said grimly. "I knew there was a reason I never wanted to see this place again."

.   .   .

THEY WRAPPED Jane's arm as best they could and locked her in the library with the skeleton key Frances found in Jane's coat pocket. Frances was uneasy about tying her up, but Elizabeth was certain she would escape if they didn't.

"It's better for her not to move anyway, with that injury," Haley pointed out gently as they bound her hands and feet. The girls waited in a still, silent row behind them, pale with shock.

"How did you know?" asked Frances as they stepped into the hallway while she locked the library door behind them.

"I knew you'd try to be noble, Frances," said Elizabeth. "I wasn't happy with what I learned from Baxter, which was nothing. I decided to be a little more persuasive. Maybe he accepted that she needed to be stopped. I knew she'd come here first. I should have called the police, but what could I have said? A dead girl has risen and returned to take more victims? I called Haley, and she was already on her way here."

"I had a dream," said Haley, looking pale and shaken. "It was about Bethany. We were back at Thackeray, and I saw a woman. She was Jane, but not Jane. It was so real. I woke up in a cold sweat and drove here in the storm. The roads were bad, just barely passable. I had this sense of urgency, like I had to get to you before she did. Before it was too late."

"Can you take them to the headmistress's office?" Frances asked, gesturing to Rowan and Blair. There was a little trickle of blood at Tibbets' temple. She'd been injured in the fray. "I want to take Tibbets to the infirmary and find something to put on her head while we wait for the firefighters and EMTs to get here. You guys should call the police while you're there, too."

"Of course," said Haley, putting a reassuring hand on Rowan's shoulder. She jumped and looked up guiltily. "It's okay," said Haley softly. "It's going to be okay now."

Elizabeth ushered Blair, her younger self, down the hallway after Haley and Rowan. Frances took a good hard look at Tibbets, who still looked dazed and somewhat detached.

"Are you okay?" The fire alarm clanged ceaselessly in the library. Frances led Tibbets in the opposite direction of the others, towards the nurse's office and away from the noise. "Let me see that."

Tibbets held still while Frances examined her forehead. She couldn't find the source of the cut, but the power was still out, and the hallway was dark. There would be more light in the nurse's office. She led the young woman down the hallway and into the corridor off the east wing.

"Do you want to tell me what happened?" Frances asked as she unlocked the door of the nurse's office with the skeleton key. "Maybe what you were trying to tell me before? It's okay now, Tibbets. It's safe."

"I know," said Tibbets in a toneless monotone. "Maybe I should wait till my mom's lawyer gets here or something."

"I'm not the police." Frances rummaged through the cabinets with her back to Tibbets, searching for bandages and antiseptic. "This is strictly off-the-record."

"Is it?" Tibbets sounded odd. Frances wondered how severe her head injury was. Maybe the girl was just in shock. In the glass front of the cabinet, she caught a fleeting glimpse of a shadow—her reflection?

The dim shadow of a girl sat on the cot beside Tibbets, quietly watching. Frances closed her eyes. She knew if she opened them and turned around, there would be nothing next to Tibbets. But she found herself unable to. Would she ever *not* see Bethany? Hadn't they done enough for her to finally rest in peace?

Bethany's reflection turned slowly to look at Tibbets. Her profile was fixed and riveted, staring at the girl the same age that Bethany would be forever. Frances's eyes shifted from Bethany's reflection to Tibbets. She saw that the girl had a scalpel in her hand.

Frances whirled around, groping on the counter until her hand wrapped around a pair of medical scissors. Could she really stab Tibbets? She might not have a choice.

They faced off on either side of the narrow infirmary, Tibbets on her cot and Frances at the counter. The pair regarded each other warily.

"Can you put that down, Ms. Teller?" said Tibbets quietly. "Before you ruin everything?"

28

THE LYNX AND THE JAGUAR

*F*rances lowered the scissors. Tibbets didn't seem like she was in any hurry to stab her; not yet, anyway.

"But Tibbets, why?" she said sadly. "Jane—Ms. Raines —isn't here anymore. You don't have to do this."

Tibbets sighed, world-weary. She clenched the scalpel tightly at her side. Her whole body was tense as a cat waiting to spring on its prey.

"It was never about Ms. Raines, Ms. Teller," she explained patiently. "Or Jane, or whatever she wants to call herself. She might have showed me the book, but she showed me much more than that. She showed me how to free myself: from her, from Rowan and Blair—from everyone. From my parents' fights, the headmistress and the stupid rules in this place. All the stuff I'm supposed to care about but don't. Grades. College. It's all so arbitrary, really."

Frances watched her. How had she hidden this for so

long? There had been signs, of course; cracks in the pavement that had started to appear. Her odd behavior in class. Just now in the library when she sat so passively, watching the scene play out even as Rowan and Blair started to crumble. Or had she been playing Frances all along?

"All those times you met with me," said Frances slowly, piecing it together. "About Rowan…"

"It was never about Rowan," said Tibbets. "Anna told me to keep you distracted. She said you would be wary of our aims. I thought it was just because you were the new guidance counselor. A teacher of psychology, more observant of the human condition. Ms. Raines never saw fit to fill us in on the truth—not that I ever trusted her, anyway. She was clearly operating with some kind of ulterior motive. Rowan and Blair were so easily taken in: Ms. Raines this, and Ms. Raines that. They thought her ideas were so brilliant. I considered her a bit of a dilettante, frankly. A fraud. But she did deliver the book, and the book was invaluable. I didn't know what her motivations were. I didn't care."

"So that night you came to my room," said Frances gently, hoping to keep her calm. Her eyes darted around for something, anything she could use to overpower the girl without seriously hurting her. "That was a hoax?"

"I needed to distract you while the others got the book back," she said. "They knew I was the smartest. Smarter than Rowan, even. They did what I told them to do. I used to be the scapegoat of the three of us, the joke: Tibbets who can't get a guy, Tibbets always with her nose in the book. But when Ms. Raines came, they started to respect me. They finally started to see." She smiled dreamily. "I hid the book under Rowan's mattress before the searches. I knew I could easily steal it back. I was friends with her, but as long as everyone thought she was the ringleader, no one was really looking at me."

"What did Jane—Ms. Raines—tell you to do?" asked Frances. It seemed important to piece together what had been Tibbets and what had been Jane. Maybe there was still some way she could talk the girl down from this ledge.

"She didn't *tell* me to do anything," said Tibbets impatiently. She twisted the scalpel back and forth between her fingers, an odd glint in her eye. "I decided on my own. I wanted to do it. It was after our *Dorian Gray* essays. Ms. Raines said she wanted to form a literary club. A sort of secret society. She said she liked our ideas—mine and Rowan's and Blair's. The second book she assigned, and only to us, was *the* book. She said it reminded her of the book in *Dorian Gray*. She wanted to know what we thought of it. The ritual, in particular. I was the one who asked her if it was real. She told me that it was."

"And she asked you to perform it?" Frances asked quietly.

"No! *I* asked her if we could. Whether or not she thought that we should try it. And she said that she would help us, if we did. But it was my idea. And you ruined it." Tibbets's grip around the scalpel tightened. "But it's not too late. All it requires is a sacrifice. Just one. And I have you here. I could still make it happen."

"It won't work," said Frances. "Tibbets, the police are on their way. You'll go to jail. What everlasting fortune do you expect to find there? You'll waste the most promising years of your life. Whatever Jane told you about the power of that book—it's not real. She had some luck and made it about that. But it wasn't. It's your will, what you manifest. If you manifest violence now, it will bring you nothing but pain."

"I don't believe you," said Tibbets calmly. "It's time. It's finally *my* time, to get what I want." She raised the scalpel.

Frances glanced behind her at the reflection in the glass. Bethany's ghostly form, still seated next to Tibbets, pointed to the counter behind her. Frances turned away from Tibbets even as she snarled, "What are you doing? *What do you keep looking at?*"

Frances's hand closed around the bottle of rubbing alcohol she'd taken out to disinfect Tibbets' cut. She popped the top open and turned as Tibbets rose and charged her with the scalpel. She flung the alcohol into her face and Tibbets screamed as it hit her eyes, doubling over with pain.

Tibbets was many things: deeply intelligent, astute, and too sensitive for her own good. She was also completely insane. But she was neither strong nor athletic. Frances wrestled her to the floor. She bound her wrists and ankles with ace bandages from the cabinets.

It took awhile. She wanted to make sure they would at least hold until the police arrived. Like Jane, she would have to lock her up alone in the room and feared the girl might hurt herself if she got loose.

"You're ruining it," Tibbets whimpered. Even after the display of violence and insanity Frances had just witnessed, she felt a strong surge of pity for the girl. "This is my one chance! My only chance."

"I know," said Frances, pushing her hair back from her forehead, the way her own mother had once done for her —so long ago she could scarcely remember it now. "I know."

THE HEADMISTRESS WAS DISORIENTED from the blow to her head. It took awhile to sort things out. She couldn't understand how earnest Anna Raines could be the same girl who died twenty-one years ago. She was taken away by the EMTs, who were considerably delayed by the storm.

Jane and Tibbets were also taken to the hospital and kept under police supervision. Frances, Elizabeth, Haley, Rowan and Blair all delivered statements after Frances had called the girls' parents. The Makepeaces did not, in fact, have a helicopter sent to pick up Rowan—but they did have a private plane chartered, scheduled to arrive once the worst of the storm had cleared.

Frances, Haley, and Elizabeth stayed overnight at the school one final time, together. After the police, the fire department, and the EMTs departed; after they walked the girls back to their room to wait for their parents, they returned to Elizabeth and Frances's old room at the end of the east wing. Frances still had the skeleton key Anna had stolen from the headmistress. She let them in.

The room was empty. It was one of two in the east

wing that had no boarders this term, and though over twenty years had passed, and the room was absent all their things, something about the air inside remained unchanged. Frances went over to the window and pushed back the curtain, gazing out at the freshly fallen snow in the grounds.

Elizabeth regarded the four walls in which they'd spent four years of their youth. "It's like we never left," she said.

"I always envied you guys," said Haley wistfully, coming to stand beside Frances at the window. "Getting to live together. I didn't like either of my roommates the entire time I was here."

"You shouldn't have," said Elizabeth. "It was like being in a womb with your Siamese twin. Eventually, we became the same person."

"I always liked it," Frances admitted. "That feeling of never being alone."

"I did, too." She came to join Frances and Haley at the window. "It made it that much harder when I didn't have it anymore."

"Maybe this time we could actually keep in touch," ventured Haley.

"I'm pretty sure once you save each other's lives, it's kind of a mandate," said Elizabeth.

"Do you see that?" Frances said suddenly.

In the distance, at the edge of the lake, was the shimmering figure of a girl with long dark hair. She seemed to waver in and out of focus as Frances squinted against the mid-morning glare of the bright sun against the snow. Haley gripped Frances's arm.

"I see her, too," she whispered.

"Is it her?" asked Elizabeth.

They crowded around the window as they stared. In the distance, the girl looked back at them. She lifted a hand. With a slow twitch of her fingers, she gradually vanished from sight.

29

COMMENCEMENT

$\mathcal{I}$t was spring at Thackeray. The rolling lawn was vast and verdant as heaven. The final traces of snow and ice had melted weeks ago, and the buds were on the trees. Flowers were on the brink of bursting into bloom. The surface of the lake was still and smooth as glass.

Frances looked out the window over the campus she'd once called home. She'd packed the last of her things away into her old steamer trunk. She was leaving again. But this time, she wasn't running away.

She'd surprised herself by staying for the spring term. After Elizabeth, Haley, and the girls had left, she'd planned to pack her things at once. She thought she wouldn't be able to get out of Thackeray fast enough. Especially after the headmistress had summoned her to her office.

"Frances, I can't thank you enough for what you did in the library that night, protecting those girls," McBride began. "Haley and Elizabeth as well. It's as I always say: once a lady of Thackeray, always a lady of Thackeray."

"I appreciate that, Headmistress," Frances said. "But you should really know that I'm not the best example of a Thackeray woman. Haley or Elizabeth, either." She took a deep breath. It was time. It was time twenty-one years ago, and it had been eating away at her ever since. It was finally time to come clean and tell the truth. Only then could she be absolved. "We were in the chapel that night, the night that it burnt down. All of us, along with Bethany and Jane. We could have stopped it, and we didn't. And then it was too late."

The headmistress gazed at her for a long moment. For a moment, Frances wondered if McBride was going to throw the heavy-looking paperweight on her desk right at Frances's head. But that wasn't it at all.

"I know," she said gravely.

"You what?" said Frances, startled. "I'm sorry, did you just say you know?"

"I've always known," said McBride, swiveling her chair to look out the window. "I knew the moment I heard. You were always inseparable, the five of you. It was unusual: young women in cliques, there's often tension. Even the most close-knit of groups tend not to last all four years, unless it's for survival purposes. But you girls were like a family. I knew that if Bethany and Jane had been in the chapel that night, that meant the rest of you had, as well."

"Why didn't you say anything?" asked Frances, shocked. "Why weren't we punished?"

"Two girls were dead," said McBride grimly. "Two promising young lives ended in the blink of an eye. Why add three more? You girls were on your way to college, followed by promising careers. What good would it have done? It would have been a stain that would have followed you for the rest of your lives. A stain on both you and on Thackeray. I said nothing. Questions were asked. I silenced them." McBride regarded Frances from across the desk. She had seen so much more than Frances had ever realized.

"I don't know what to say," said Frances awkwardly.

"Don't say anything," said McBride. "Not about then, and not about now. It is the only practice that has kept me in this position for the last thirty years. In my experience, silence is the best policy."

"Are you asking me to cover up what happened at the school over Thanksgiving weekend?" asked Frances.

"Frances, I would never ask you to engage in a conspiracy," said McBride. "That is beneath you, it is beneath me, and it's beneath the school. I am merely asking that you consider putting yourself, your future, and the futures of the young women involved ahead of anything else."

"Ahead of the truth?" asked Frances.

"Our society is built on little white lies," said the headmistress. "If everyone woke up one morning and simultaneously told the truth, it would crumble before our very eyes. It is our job as educators to prioritize the students above all else. I'll leave it to you to determine what truth should best be told, in this scenario."

"Yes, Headmistress," said Frances quietly. She didn't agree with what the older woman had said; to her, it sounded like spinning the facts in a way favored by politicians and petty crooks. But she supposed that McBride hadn't gotten where she was—and stayed there for three decades—without picking up a few tricks of her own. Frances chose to respect the headmistress without buying into her philosophy. But she did wish, on a very fundamental level, to protect the girls.

Tibbets had been institutionalized. It wasn't the harsh and sterile fate of a rambling lunatic in the street; her father had shelled out a considerable sum to place her in a posh, comfortable "recuperation facility" in the mountains of upstate Oregon. From what Frances had seen of Tibbets' madness, she felt certain that not even the most expensive facility could hold a mind that large, that dangerous—but no one had asked Frances what she thought about it.

Rowan and Blair returned to school after Thanksgiving break amid much whispering and rumors. No one knew for sure what had happened on Black Friday, but everyone knew that Tibbets was gone. Some of the girls thought that she had a nervous breakdown; others said that Rowan drove her to it. Rowan and Blair stopped speaking. Blair became friends with Brandy, melting into her clique and becoming, for all intents and purposes, invisible. Rowan remained a lone wolf until the end of the term.

It was for her that Frances had stayed. As she was packing her suitcases the Sunday after Thanksgiving, she heard a knock at her door. She'd grown accustomed to Jane-as-Anna pestering her frequently for cups of tea and preachy advice about keeping the girls in line, advice she now knew was imparted ironically for Jane's own amusement. But she wasn't expecting any visitors after Jane and Tibbets were taken away, after Haley and Elizabeth left to resume their own lives.

Frances opened the door. It was Rowan. Frances regarded her with open surprise.

"May I come in?" she asked. "I understand completely if you don't want me to."

"Of course." Frances held the door open wider. Rowan came in and sat at Frances's desk. She gazed at the open suitcase on her bed.

"You're leaving?" she said with obvious dismay.

Frances smiled wryly. "I'm afraid I've worn out my welcome here. For the second time." She went over to her suitcase and closed it with a definitive click.

"No, you haven't." The ferocity of Rowan's tone surprised her, and she turned to see the girl regarding her with utmost sincerity. "That's not true, Ms. Teller. Not even a bit. You're the only reason I made it through last term. If I hadn't been able to talk to you, I think I might have gone crazy. I know I couldn't tell you what was really going on—or I chose not to, anyway; I wish that I had. Maybe it wouldn't have gotten so out of hand. But what we did talk about—in class, in your office—it was the only thing that made me feel better."

"Really?" Frances said. She was genuinely surprised. She hadn't thought of herself as impacting the girls, one way or another. She just tried to be honest and do her job. Maybe to make up for all the years of living a lie.

"You were the only one who told us the truth," said Rowan imploringly. "Please come back next term. You're the one support system I have here. I don't know how I'll make it through my final term without you. And I'm not the only one." Rowan recited the various girls Frances had seen who had meltdowns about grades, parents. Pressure. "You've gotten us through some difficult things. And it's only going to get even harder. Without Tibbets here..." She looked at the ground. "I'm so sorry for what happened in the library, for the part that I played. I didn't know what Ms. Raines planned to do truly until it happened, but I'll never forgive myself. I know Tibbets is unstable, dangerous even. But she was my best friend." Rowan looked up, beseeching. "You know?"

Frances was filled with a sadness beyond words. "I know just what you mean," she said.

MARGARET MCBRIDE RESIGNED SHORTLY AFTERWARD. The scandal of having an alumna return from the dead and terrorize three students, then attempt to murder a teacher, was more than either her reputation or her constitution could withstand.

Her final day at Thackeray was the day of graduation. It was a beautiful spring day and proud parents had descended upon Thackeray in droves. They filled the local bed and breakfast, overtook the parking lot, and occupied every corridor and foyer. And they weren't the only ones who were here.

Haley was the commencement speaker. The role was always bestowed upon a Thackeray alumna who'd achieved great success. "I never thought it would be me," she confided to Frances at the front entrance as she smoothed down her cap and gown. "I was afraid I'd come to all the reunions homeless and unemployed."

"Look at you now." Frances smiled and straightened her tassel. "You're on top of the world."

Elizabeth clicked up to them in her red-bottomed heels. She wore a snow-white suit, her hair slicked back in a stylish chignon. "What did I just say about never coming back here?" she asked them.

"Something about there being a reason for it," said Frances mildly. "Right after you shot Jane."

Elizabeth rolled her eyes. "God, I hope she never gets out of the nuthouse. I cannot fathom the prospect of having to testify at a trial."

"I'd kind of rather she was behind bars than in some sanitarium somewhere," said Haley. "I feel like she could get out."

"Don't even say that," said Frances. "Especially not on your big day."

"She's not the only one having a big day." Elizabeth surveyed her, pleased. "I can't believe you finally decided to join the legions of us complacent homeowners, tethered forever to our own piece of land."

Frances had just brought the last of her suitcases down to what had formerly been the headmistress's house. She planned to retire on a farm upstate, and Frances promptly bought the property from her. The spring term and Rowan's words had an effect on her she could have never foreseen. She was pretty good at it, teaching. She thought she might keep at it for a while.

"Just don't tell us you're marrying Rutherford or

anything like that," said Haley. "There's a limit to what's considered happily ever after."

"I'm not going to marry *Rutherford*." Frances rolled her eyes. "Besides, he's still bald."

"AS WE LEAVE childish things behind, let us look to the future: to the brave and ambitious adults we will become, and the accomplishments that lie before us." Rowan smiled and stepped back from the podium. As distant as her classmates had been, no one held back in their tumultuous applause. Frances smiled.

"She kind of reminds me of you," said Elizabeth.

"Really?" asked Frances. "I thought I was more of a Tibbets."

"No, you were driven," said Elizabeth. "Quiet, but driven."

Haley stepped up to the microphone. Frances and Elizabeth cheered.

"I never thought I'd be up here, standing before you today," she began. "When I was at Thackeray, I always felt in danger of becoming invisible—if I didn't win on the field, if I didn't get the best grades. It becomes easy in a highly competitive, elite environment to lose yourself. But I've been in the world for a while now, and I can state this for a fact: it truly is your heart that you lead with in this world, not letters or trophies, nor any other accolade the world can ever bestow. It's the lives that you touch that makes a difference. That's what truly leaves your mark on this world. As you go forth in the world today, my greatest wish for you is that you always remain the honest, earnest young women of Thackeray you are today. Never forget the Thackeray motto: loyalty and honor, above all else. Keep these words in your heart and they'll steer you through many a storm. There will be clouds, but there will also be sun. It can't rain forever."

The boys' school had long been in the habit of discouraging the students from throwing their caps in the air: it was unruly, raucous, and undignified; the tassels were an important memento of this day in their lives, someone might lose an eye, etc. When she had graduated, Frances thought they did it at the girls' school just to thumb their nose at them. But now, watching the sky fill with a hundred satin caps, she experienced it for what it was: an expression of pure and unfettered joy.

Today she experienced it in a way she'd never had as a student here. Elizabeth reached down and took her hand. Frances knew she felt it, too. Their graduation, with two of the seats empty and two of their number lost forever more, had been a somber affair. But today was a day of celebration. For Frances, Elizabeth, and Haley, it was also a day of redemption.

Haley joined their side a few minutes later, still clutching her cap. "Would you guys mind if we walked down to the lake?" she asked. "There's something I want to do."

"Sure," said Elizabeth.

"Of course," said Frances.

They linked arms and walked down to the lake. When they reached the edge, Haley crouched near the water. Frances and Elizabeth looked on curiously. Haley carefully moved the tassel over from one side to the other, to signify commencement. "For Bethany," she explained. Tears sprang unbidden to Frances's eyes. Elizabeth swiped at her own with the back of her hand, before her mascara could run.

Haley set the cap on the lake and gave it a little nudge, then stood next to Frances and Elizabeth. The three of them watched as it drifted off into the lake.

"I wish you were here," said Frances. She reached down and took the hands of the other two. It was the opposite of the feeling in the chapel that night, as if a weight had been lifted from their shoulders. She squeezed their hands once, hard. They turned away from the water and walked back up the hill towards Thackeray.

Made in the USA
Coppell, TX
05 January 2024